M000085190

Small Town Secrets

Ruthie & Ron

Thank you for
the memories and
for your observations
and fortitude

Happy trails

Boo

Horse Doctor Adventures

Small Town Secrets

by Elizabeth Woolsey

Horse Doctor Adventures
Small Town Secrets

Small Town Secrets is a work of fiction. Any similarities to places,
or persons living or dead is coincidental.

Cover Design by David Blake
Cover Illustration by Kathy Baldock

Edited by Marilyn Anderson

Published 2021 in the United States

Horse Doctor Press

ewoolseydvm@gmail.com
www.elizabethwoolsey.com
www.facebook.com/elizabeth.w.herbert

Acknowledgments

Thank you to my primary readers, Jodee O'Leary, Julie Laughton, Sharon Spier, DVM, Jane Gropp and Jeanie Olson. Thank you also to my editors, Marilyn Anderson, Kay Boon, Denise Piggott and Shelley Herbert. A special thanks to my staff at Adelaide Plains Equine Clinic, Robert Moller, my clients and friends in South Australia for giving me time to write and stories to tell.

Dedicated to
my daughter
Shelley

Chapter 1

All the signs were there. It was the end of a long, punishing drought. The rain signaled a change for many of us who relied on the land. It also coincided with an event that would change my life forever. It was the beginning of the end.

As I drove my vet truck in torrential rain toward the last call of the day, I phoned my friend to request an extension of her babysitting duties. "Hey, Jules, is this crazy or what? I've got one call to go. Can you stay any longer?"

"Two inches and counting, Carly." I heard Julie walking down the hall in our house. "I can stay, but it'll cost you."

"Inches and not millimeters. That's old school, isn't it? I'm sorry to do this to you. I called the hospital, and Dan's on a home visit. The receptionist didn't know when he'd be back."

"When's the last time you talked to your neighbor? An ambulance pulled up a few minutes ago."

"Oh, no. She has a cold. I hope she didn't fall."

"They don't call ambulances for colds."

"Dan saw her this morning. He never said anything."

Dan and I are living the dream. I'm a veterinarian, and Dan's an emergency-room physician. I come from a farming community and migrated from the United States to a small, rural town north of Adelaide. At the same time, Dan's a city boy from Sydney. I followed the accent. We met at the university's emergency room, where Dan was doing his residency in the States.

I was finishing my internship in equine medicine at the university veterinary school. I sprained my ankle. It would be spectacular to say I'd been injured while wrestling a stallion. Sadly, in fact, I twisted my ankle while sliding in my socks

1

on the freshly waxed linoleum in the corridor of the veterinary hospital. It was a regular competition between the large and small animal interns. Who could slide the farthest? The customary, late-night match followed the semiannual floor waxing on the old linoleum hallway.

I was transported over to the university hospital, where a young, redheaded doctor with an Australian accent was attending emergencies. "Hi, I'm Dr. Langley," was all I needed to hear. Forget his kind manner, above-average looks, and warm hands on my ankle. I was smitten by the accent.

Several days after the encounter, I saw him running in the local park. He acknowledged me with a wave as he and a few other men ran by me while I sat on a bench, throwing a ball for my dog, Buster. My heart didn't skip a beat. That's a ridiculous idea. My heart did increase in rate, and I'm reasonably sure there was a ventricular ectopic beat, which made me catch my breath. I waved, but soon he was gone. Buster replaced the ball in my lap, reminding me that my sole reason for living was throwing the ball for him.

I saw the accent again in the grocery store a week after that. We were both wearing green scrub tops, and I smiled as we passed in the aisle. I instinctively examined my right shoulder to check for any residual manure left from a recent rectal palpation I'd performed earlier on a colicky pony. I couldn't see any, but I smelled my scrub top and checked for the "Eau de Manure." It passed the smell test. *Phew*.

"How's the ankle? Any other sliding competitions this week?"

I didn't hear the question at first. I simply caught the accent. "Pardon? Oh, no, all good, and the floor's too worn for sliding now. We have one or two nights after it's waxed before it becomes too abrasive. Thanks for asking."

"I try to follow up on all my patients."

"Really?" I was confident that it was a lie. I wasn't a total beauty, but I wasn't bad, either. I was above average on the social scale of the contemporary ideal looks for the times. The long blonde hair and slim build didn't hurt, but what woman thought she was anything more than average, considering the one flaw that obsessed her? In my case, it was a small scar on my chin that was a gift from my brother. When we were fighting, he knocked me into the kitchen table, which resulted in a hospital trip and a poor stitch job by the local doctor.

"Oh, yes, all my patients." His face reddened, and he turned away and appeared to intently study the selection of baked beans. He glanced back and smiled. I suggested and handed him the cheapest brand.

"They all taste the same. If money's the criteria, four out of five interns will choose this one." I handed him the generic brand and pushed my cart on down the aisle with no further interaction. He was way out of my league—no sense in torturing myself. Rip the bandage off quickly. Short and sharp. Two months to go, I'm gone and moving back home to work with Dr. Tuttle, my mentor, and family veterinarian.

At the checkout counter, I encountered the "accent" again. He was in line ahead of me. He turned and smiled. I tried to appear blasé as I returned the smile and pretended to be busy with a magazine I'd picked up at the counter. As I emerged from the store, he was standing by the door and appeared to be waiting for someone.

"So, do you have children, or just want them?"

"Huh?" *Why did he ask that?*

"You were reading *Parent's Magazine*."

Now it was my turn to blush, and I did. I hadn't even noticed the magazine or contents which I had pretended to read. "Oh, a friend's having a baby, and I want ideas for a present." A ridiculous reply, and I guessed he realized I was lying too.

"Your name's Carly, right? I don't remember your last name. I know it's probably unprofessional of me, but would you like to meet for coffee or something?"

Replace that bandage and queue the wedding bells. Yes, sir, the game was on. "Well, I suppose I could. Now or another time?" *Appear calm, relaxed, and casual. Don't let him feel your pulse because the tachycardia is a dead giveaway.*

That was then, and now is now—several years and two redheaded children since those first giddy days of infatuation. I currently work as a vet and negotiate child care in rural South Australia.

"Carly? You there?" Julie sensed I'd lost my train of thought.

This jolted me back to reality. "Of course. Could you stay? I won't be any longer than six o'clock. If it's a problem, I can pick up the kiddos and take them with me?"

Dan and I hadn't wasted any time starting a family. The girls were three and five, and both total gingers. I was reasonably sure another one was in the oven, but I was merely a few days late. I hadn't told Dan yet. Of course, he would want a boy, but he would never say it out loud. I didn't care. I knew I'd reproduced myself with Casey, the firstborn. Unlike her younger sister, Faythe, Casey was a total tomboy. She loved all animals and accompanying Mum on veterinary calls.

The word "mum" made me cringe. I wanted to be called mom, but that went out the window when Casey heard the other children at playgroup call their mothers by the colloquial term. Casey was a switched-on little girl. When she wanted something, she called me, mom. This ploy came from coaching by her father, who frequently suggested the children call me "Mom," but secretly was pleased they addressed me as "mum."

The plan was for Dan and me to raise the children in rural Australia. When the girls were old enough to go to high school, we intend to move to a bigger town where their education would not suffer. We might even relocate back to the States. I didn't care as long as the "accent" was by my side.

"Earth to Carly, earth to Carly." Julie was trying to attract my attention, and recognized she was failing. "Stay out all night. My rates double after five, you know."

Julie was my bestie. She was a nurse, who worked in the local community hospital with Dan, and was also an ovarian cancer survivor. The regular babysitter was Mildred Miller, an older neighbor, who was at home sick with a respiratory infection. Julie was only filling in. I met Julie when Dan started attending at the hospital and asked her and her husband, Mick, to join us for dinner. Julie had fifteen or more years on me, but we bonded quickly. Julie's children were finishing school, and it was only in a pinch that I'd called her to ask if one of her daughters could babysit the girls for me today. Julie volunteered herself as her kids were sick, too.

"One hour, pinkie promise." I kicked up the windshield wipers. "Be glad you aren't out in this. It's really coming down. To hell with the drought. The rain gods must be feeling generous."

"Hey, Carly. That ambulance is still parked up across the road. Looks as though your babysitter might be headed to the hospital. Let me go suss it out, and I'll tell you what's going on when you get back."

"Oh, no. I hope she's going to be okay. I'll hurry. I hate for her to deal with this on her own." I felt responsible for Mrs. Miller's safety. I knew she depended on Dan and me both for physical as well as financial support. This was returned in spades with her care of our daughters. I worried that she was alone and ill. If something happened, I would never forgive myself.

Julie made sure I heard her addressing the girls. "Hey, girls. Want some sweets before dinner? We can watch some reality television while we eat ice cream and lollies." Julie laughed. She knew I was strict about snacks before dinner. They didn't watch television, except on special occasions. Our house had poor reception, anyway. However, I was going to hurry home before they were utterly corrupted. I would learn about Mrs. Miller when I returned.

I drove to the property, where three ranch horses were standing in the mud. One horse was holding his leg off the ground while pivoting on the sound limb. The owner was standing under the shelter, waiting for me. Jimmy Medika was a local Aboriginal station hand who lived in the town with his family. He worked on a remote station and was gone for weeks at a time. His wife worked at the bank, and the children were grown and in the process of moving out. Their youngest daughter was in her last year of high school.

"Hello, miss. Thank you for coming." Mr. Medika was particularly formal. "I think it's a hoof abscess. However, since I need to get back up to the station next week, I thought it was best to have you out."

The "station bred," bay gelding is a mixture of quarter horse and brumby. He was a kind horse, but his leg hurt. The pressure of an expanding, infected fluid pocket under the hoof is like a blood blister under a fingernail. Froggy's digital pulse throbbed, and he jumped when hoof testers were applied to the inside quarter of his foot. When he jumped, he knocked me sideways. "Seems like we found it. I'll get a poultice and a sharper hoof knife, and we'll see if we can't get it open and draining. If we can release the pressure, you should be good to go in a day or two. How's his tetanus status?"

"All good, miss. Remember, he cut himself a few months ago. I still have leftover antibiotics."

6

"Don't use any yet, Mr. Medika. Wait until the abscess bursts. You might not require antibiotics, anyway."

"You can call me Jimmy."

"You say that every time, but you call me "miss" or "doctor." It goes both ways, you know." I smiled at him, and he grinned back.

"Maybe someday, miss." Most people called me by my first name, but he and a few others were still formal. I loved my clients, and they could address me as they chose.

I located the tract from the sole of the hoof to the probable abscess. However, because I didn't hit "pay dirt" or frank pus, I finished applying a poultice to Froggy's foot and left for home. I was soaked from the rain and cold. Feeling cold was entirely foreign. I was in heaven. I turned off the car air conditioner and opened the window. The steam was fogging up the windshield, so I had to turn on the defroster.

As I turned into the driveway, I noticed an ambulance and several emergency vehicles still parked at Mrs. Miller's house. I was alarmed. I raced up to my front door to avoid a new rain shower. Julie was inside, watching from the window.

"Dinner's finished. As a bonus, the girls are bathed and dressed in their nightgowns."

"Oh, consider yourself kissed. But, more to the point, what's going on across the street?"

The girls, who emerged from their rooms, ran over to me, which put a crimp in our conversation. Julie shrugged. "I've been waiting for you. Don't know. I didn't want to leave the kids. The ambulance has been there for an hour. It doesn't look good."

"Is that Kendall's car?" Kendall was our friend too. Kendall Bidwell was one of the four local cops. She was a legend in the area and was responsible for initiating several programs for our town's children. Her after-school programs appeared to be working to decrease crime. Rural towns had their share of crime partially due to a lack of kids' activities as they grew up. Alcohol and even drugs were a problem for young and old. Domestic violence was sadly prevalent in our town, as well. Dan often witnessed the resulting injuries with his work as an emergency doctor at the hospital.

Dan and I loved the rural life and the friends we'd met, but challenges still existed. The lack of support for our professional endeavors was one of many. Finding friends with similar interests was another. Dan played footy, and he made numerous friends through sports, but we craved intellectual stimulation. The positives outnumbered the negatives. My friends met my social needs. Both Julie and Kendall read books and were up to speed with respect to the current affairs of the world. Both had a wicked sense of humor, and neither was below taking on challenges. We formed a bond when the town mayor wanted to prohibit horses inside the city limits. As if....

The torrential rain continued. While I started to get the girls ready for bed and prepare dinner for Dan and me, Julie walked over to the cars parked out in front of Mrs. Miller's residence. Everyone was inside the house, and I watched Julie enter Mrs. Miller's home and retreat outside with Kendall. They talked briefly, and then Julie ran back to the house. She returned to our residence soaked.

"Kendall's not saying, but I know enough to say Millie's not babysitting anymore. The ambos and police are waiting for detectives to come from Adelaide before they move the body."

"You're joking." I almost said the F word, but I remembered the little ears listening and eyes watching every move. "Where the heck is Dan?" I picked up my phone to call him, but the battery had died. "What is going on over there?"

Julie was shaking from the wet and cold. "Don't know. Kendall isn't talking. She asked me how long I'd been at your house and if I'd observed anyone entering the house."

"Had you?"

"Nope. The girls and I sat at the window, watching the rain all afternoon, and didn't see anything. Hey, I need to get back home. Just got a text from the sick bay, and supplies are required. Heading to the chemist. You want anything?"

"No. Thanks, though, and thank you for today, too. I guess I'll suck it up and start the kids in day care. I'm dreading the tidal wave of colds and viruses from the cesspool of immunologically naïve small children."

Julie laughed. "Welcome to motherhood. Better now than when school starts." She shrugged. "You can't protect them forever. It's a big dark world out there, and acquired immunity is the only way to survive."

"I guess. It's not the kids. It's me. I'll get whatever they bring home, you know."

"Ever the concerned, caring mother…."

"Yeah, I'm a bit of a fraud." I stared out the window and saw Dan's SUV roll into the driveway. "Here, he is."

As Julie walked down the steps and toward her car, Dan ran past and waved to her. I saw Julie point to the Miller house, enter her little red Kia, and pull away. Dan paused, stood in the rain, and gazed toward the Miller home, turned, and ran up the steps to our house.

As he entered, Dan was already soaked, yet he had a smile and tried to playfully hug me. I backed up and stuck my hands up. "Touch me with those wet clothes, and you're dead meat, mister."

Dan held up his hands in the arrested mode and smiled. I knew he was aware of what happened next door. "Terrible news.

9

They're coming over to talk to me. Was I the last person who saw her? Carly, she was sick, but not that sick, and she was only seventy-two. I assume they'll do an autopsy. I know her husband died several years ago, and they didn't have any kids, but are there any other relatives?"

"I think she has a sister in Melbourne or Sydney." I could hear the girls calling their dad. I pointed to the bedroom where they both slept. "You're being summoned."

He stripped off his shirt and pants. I tossed him a towel and went to the laundry to get him a T-shirt and some sweats. "Can you read to them for a minute while I finish cooking our dinner?"

He grinned and went to the girls' bedroom. Our house was small and old. It boasted just two bedrooms and a small office. This was convenient when Dan's overbearing mother, Mira, visited. A night or two was all she could stand. It was exceptionally inconvenient when my mother wanted to come. Mom had traveled from Idaho twice. Our hide-a-bed accommodation didn't make her want to return anytime soon. We'd bought the house from my bosses when we moved to town. We decided it was more important to live near the hospital than in the country.

I wanted to raise the girls with animals. To date, however, we didn't even have a dog. Because bringing Buster to Australia was simply too complicated, he'd remained with my mother until he died last year. Well, if my twitchy uterus and timing were correct, we were going to finally make a move. I figured it was as good a time as any to inform Dan we might need to expand.

Julie's cooking was not as good as a Miller dinner. I purposely explained to Julie that I would cook for Dan and me. Mrs. Miller did it all. She regularly washed our laundry, kid wrangled, prepared our meals, and even grew a beautiful vegetable garden for us. I was sick, thinking of her dying alone in her house without someone holding her hand. It must have been quick. I was hopeful that her death was painless. Maybe she died in her sleep.

I poured a glass of wine for Dan and some juice for me. He noticed immediately and gave me "the look." He cocked his head to the side and raised his eyebrows. I smiled and nodded. Dan wrapped his arms around my waist and kissed me. "Are you sure?"

"Eighty percent. I haven't done a pee test, but I'm pretty confident. You have a lot to answer for, Danny Boy. You know what this means."

"A netball team."

"A new house." I was ready for this conversation.

"A second car." He grinned like a fool.

"Diapers and late nights."

"Nappy's darling, when are you going to start speaking like the natives?"

"A new wardrobe."

"Bigger breasts."

"A vasectomy."

"Tubal ligation. That way, you can meet with the milkman, and I'll never know."

"As long as he looks like Hugh Jackman."

"You win. I'll have the vasectomy." Dan took his glass, and we clinked them together.

"Well, early days, it can wait until he's born." I wanted to throw Dan a bone. I knew he would love a son.

"Or she. A softball team." Dan sipped his wine and grinned like a kid in a candy store.

"Have I told you that I love you lately?" God, I loved that man.

"Show, not tell. Isn't that what you learned in your creative writing class?" Dan smiled as he sipped his wine.

"I like your thinking, Danny Boy." While we both were happy about the possible pregnancy, we kept watching through the window at Mrs. Miller's house.

"What was she like when you were there last night?"

"Sick, but not dying sick. I can't believe she's deceased."

"Did she have any heart problems?"

"None. I was convinced it was merely a bad cold. I prescribed paracetamol, a decongestant, and rest. I thought she'd be fine in a day or two. Do you have anyone to care for Casey and Faythe tomorrow?"

"Not yet."

Someone knocked at the door as we were finishing dinner. Dan was clearing the table, and I answered it. A plainclothes detective showed me his picture and placard that hung on a lanyard from his neck. "Mrs. Langley?"

I never bothered correcting the "Mrs." for the doctor. He probably didn't know I was a vet, anyway. "Yes, how may I help you?"

"I must speak to your husband. Is he home?"

"Yes, of course. I'll get him."

"Before you do, may I ask you some quick questions?"

"Certainly."

"I understand you employ Mrs. Miller, and she didn't come today due to her illness? And did you go to work or stay home today?"

"She's been sick for a few days. My friend Julie Chambers stepped in for me and was here all day. I was at work until six o'clock."

"I understand. Do you have a number for Ms. Chamber's?"

I picked up my phone, which was still charging on the table next to the door.

"What's going on? Mrs. Miller simply died, didn't she? Is there something else? Is there something I need to worry about?"

"Probably nothing." He was scribbling Julie's name and number.

"What did you say your name was?"

"Detective Ronald Billings, ma'am. I need to see your husband."

Dan came around the corner from the kitchen, put his hand around my waist, and smiled at the detective.

"Dr. Langley?" The detective took a long, hard look at Dan, but then he smiled and laughed. "Danno, it is you. How are you? Still playing footy?" He reached out his hand and shook it warmly.

"Ronald McDonald, you dirtball. How the heck are you? How's Marci? How many kids? I see you met my better half. Carly, this is my classmate, Ronny, the guy I told you about when we stole my dad's car. I guess you've given up your life of crime and joined the other team."

The detective was laughing. "Yep, I play with the bad boys now. Hey, Danno, I need to take you down to the cop shop for a statement. It shouldn't take long."

"Just a sec. Let me get on some other clothes. Carly, if I'm not back in an hour, call our solicitor and try to raise some bail." We kissed. He patted my tummy, and he left with his old friend.

Chapter 2

It was after midnight before Dan returned. Despite his pathetic attempt to cover it with toothpaste, I could smell beer on his breath. He stripped down to his jocks and climbed into bed. We assumed our normal position of spooning. Dan's hand draped over my waist, and he began to rub my lower abdomen and sing a lullaby. His hand moved further down, and I swatted it away.

"All good?" I murmured.

"Sweet as, my beautiful, fecund wife, and mother of my children." His hand moved up and cupped my slightly engorged breast. "You are def up the duff, my dear. Don't bother with the pee test." His hand moved down again, and this time I didn't resist.

In the morning, I made breakfast for the girls and dressed them. Since I had no backup plans for day care, I called the office to leave word that I would spend the morning making new child care arrangements and would probably be late to work. The clinic for which I worked was a mixed practice. I treated the large animals, and owners Henry and Jill Gilbert saw to the smallies.

Their daughter, Katie, was a potential babysitter, but she lived at a boarding school in Adelaide. Because it was the summer school holidays, while she might be home, she would only be a temporary solution. Caring for three-year-old and five-year-old children was no small feat, and Casey was particularly challenging. She never seemed to grow out of the inquisitive, "why" stage, and never wanted to play alone.

I peeked out the window toward Mrs. Miller's house and thought about her. Both Dan and I had relatives who had died unexpectedly in their early seventies, but this passing was a shock. I still had to decide how to tell the children the reason Mrs. Miller wasn't returning. The girls loved her, and we depended on her. Her death was a massive loss to us both as a friend and as a member of our family.

I thumbed through my phone list and wondered if Jimmy Medika's daughter was available. I'd met her a couple of times. She seemed to be more responsible than were many of the local teens. She answered right away. Both of her parents were at work. Yes, she could come, and yes, she had experience with small children. Thank God. Today would be a test run. I didn't even have to pay her. She could be at the house in fifteen minutes.

"May I bring my dog, Banjo?" She suggested it would be an excellent way to break the ice with the children. Jedda Medika was over in a flash. She was polite, like her father. She was tall and thin with chiseled features, unlike the traditional indigenous people in our area. "Hello, Dr. Langley, thank you for letting me care for your daughters."

"I should thank you. Let's meet the children." Banjo wagged his tail and sat down next to Jedda. He was a kelpie cross, and I could tell he was well-mannered and had a kind eye. He was black and tan, but he carried more white on his chest and paws than did a full-blooded kelpie.

I decided to wait to tell the girls about Mrs. Miller. They were playing in the backyard when we walked out. Yesterday's rain had created delicious mud, and the girls took full advantage of this by making mud pies. I groaned, thinking of the washing I would do that evening. Casey immediately hugged Banjo, while Faythe stood back, uncertain about a strange person and dog in her house. She clung to me. I explained to the girls they would have a special treat today, and Jedda had come to play with them while I was at work.

Jedda nodded and wanted to see the girls' rooms and maybe play a game of Chutes and Ladders, which attracted Faythe's attention. After a few minutes, Casey told me I should leave because she, Faythe, and Jedda were having a playdate. "Mum, you're too old, so go to work."

By the time I arrived at the clinic, both of my bosses were involved in consults. I received several messages from clients with questions about their animals. I went to the backroom to return the calls. My morning castration had been rescheduled to the following day due to the mud from yesterday's downpour. I wasn't surprised. I talked to the owner of the local boarding stable about a vaccination policy for her agisters. I also spoke to a thoroughbred breeder about his mare that had failed to conceive all breeding season. Finally, I talked to a new client who had moved here from Western Australia about her miniature pony with intermittent diarrhea and possible sand accumulation. Since Western Australia is known for sand colics, that would be my number one diagnostic rule out.

Horses can accumulate huge volumes of sand in their large colon, which might lead to several problems, such as colic, diarrhea, and occasional weight loss. The pony suffered from diarrhea off and on. The owner had performed numerous sand tests on the pony's manure to check for sand. It's kind of like panning for gold. A handful of feces is placed in a baggie, to which water is added to make a slurry. The sand that migrates to the bottom of the bag is easily detected or felt. Some horses don't pass any sand but still have sizable accumulations. I scheduled an appointment to examine the horse in the late morning. Other causes of diarrhea must also be considered.

I entered the kitchen to make a cup of coffee, and both Jill and Henry had finished their consultations. "Sorry about this morning, guys."

"Hey, that's terrible news about Millie. She was such a good stick. Did you know she babysat for us, too?"

"Yeah, she mentioned it. I have a temporary solution if things go well today. Jedda Medika is available until school starts. I figure it will be day care after that. I'll have it sorted ASAP." I didn't mention my possible news regarding the addition to team Langley.

"Jedda Medika? She was in Katie's class until we sent Katie to Adelaide. Are you positive you want her with your girls?" Jill, who was in her forties, was originally from the UK. She was a hardworking, smart vet, but she was a bit toffee. Jill came from a long line of snobs, as she described her family. Jill still had a bit of that in her, as well. Her husband, Henry, was Scottish and cultured in appearance. Although he was losing his hair and had a considerable paunch, he still was considered a fox. The two together were hilarious. They loved each other madly, and no one would dare criticize the other or their children. Katie was the oldest. She wanted to follow in her parents' footsteps. Katie was in an all-girl prep school for which the tuition was twice the cost of university. Katie was away visiting her grandmother in the UK, so she wasn't available, anyway. The two Gilbert boys were not old enough or responsible for even an hour of babysitting. This was the first summer they would be allowed to stay home on their own.

I peered into the staff refrigerator for some orange juice. "If it's chaos or the kids have all gone walkabout when I get home, I'll regret the decision. I'll call the day care place to check for openings."

"Carly, you have tons of time off coming. If you want a few days to sort this out, let us know. We heard a locum agency is starting up, and we can find out if they have anyone on their register who likes to treat large animals."

"Thanks, Jill. Dan was talking about taking the girls to visit his mother. I'll see how that plays out first. I still must tell them about Mrs. Miller's passing. Not looking forward to that."

I drove to the agistment stable, north of town, to perform a few routine dentals. This procedure includes an exam for any decaying or loose teeth, and often rasping or removing the sharp points from the continually growing teeth. When further work, such as an extraction or radiographs are required, I schedule more time on another day.

I examined a paint horse, who'd been lame for several months. I explained it would be necessary for me to return and bring the X-ray machine. The foot blocked out to a low, heel nerve block. Lidocaine was injected into the nerves along the back of the pastern, which deadened the heel. Following the nerve block, the horse's gait was almost normal. I suspected the navicular bone was the lameness source, but radiographs were required to confirm the diagnosis.

Navicular disease, or as it is currently called a syndrome, can be a source of heel pain. However, there are other possible causes. This horse was particularly pinched in the heels, and maybe the shoeing could be changed. I didn't relish blaming the farrier. He was a touchy old bastard who thought that women should be in the kitchen and, well, you know the rest. For the client's sake, I hoped it was the shoeing and not the navicular bone that caused the pain. The actual navicular disease usually doesn't end well. My own horse had it when I was a teenager. He was retired after a short-lived improvement with corrective shoeing and analgesics. Many new options are now available. Still, it's not a diagnosis I relish giving to a client who loves their horse.

When I phoned the house, Jedda answered to report all was going well. I could hear the girls laughing in the background. "I should be home early today. I think we're in for more rain."

"All good here, miss. Take your time." Jedda sounded confident, which made me happy. If things worked out, we could stave off day care for a few more weeks before school began once again. It was difficult to think of summer in January, but we do live in the Southern hemisphere. Dan called my cell phone to find out how I was.

"Same ol', same ol'. How's work? Anything I want to know?" I was driving and pulled over to talk for a minute.

"Mrs. Miller's preliminary autopsy was performed at the hospital. They didn't determine a cause of death. They're conducting a tox study, but that won't come back for a few weeks. I may be late because I have to give them more information from my medical notes this afternoon."

"No prob, but why are they investigating it, anyway? I mean, she was sick, and she was old." I thumbed through the messages on my phone as I spoke to Dan.

"I guess there's nothing to explain her death. I'm certain it was a stroke or something. The brain was removed, but it has yet to be examined."

"Gross. I assume the funeral will be delayed. Anyone heard of any rellies?"

"Just the sister, but she may be dead, too. I'll try to get more information. I'll pick up a pizza, and the girls and I can go to the park when I get home." Dan's pager went off in the background.

"I may beat you home, and I wouldn't mind a few minutes of sleep if you take the kids to the park."

"Consider it done, my beautiful wife."

"Sex on two consecutive nights—not gonna happen, so save your sweet talk."

"Did we have sex last night? I don't remember."

"Dan, I'm so sorry. All today, I thought it was you who came home late. Obviously, it was someone else." I smiled, knowing I got him.

"Must have been. Was the guy any good?"

"Nope, too drunk, and I had to seek other means of satisfaction." Got him again.

"Well, we know it wasn't me. I would never leave my partner unsatisfied."

"You have priors. Don't get too cocky, mister."

"Pun intended?"

I laughed, and I did beat him home. Oh my God, the house was clean, the girls were playing and not watching television, and a wonderful dinner was warming in the oven.

"Jedda, you are the woman of my dreams. Name your price."

"No, Dr. Langley. It's my pleasure. Today was a trial. I've never done this for anyone but family. I don't know how much to charge."

"I paid Mrs. Miller twenty dollars per hour. Would that be okay?"

"No, miss. That's way too much."

"Well, fifteen is the lowest I will pay. I need you Monday through Friday at eight o'clock in the morning to whenever. I understand school starts next month, but we would love to have you if you can work until the term starts." When the girls asked if Jedda could spend the night, I realized they approved. And like that, Mrs. Miller's existence was a faded memory.

Dan arrived home shortly after I did. He took the girls to the park and put them to bed while I slept. My other two pregnancies were draining. I had a tough time with continuous fatigue. Dan came in, rubbed my back, and suggested we had to eat. I reluctantly joined him in the kitchen. He'd brought some wine. I gazed at him and shook my head. I smiled when he showed me it was nonalcoholic.

"I'm taking a vow of abstinence with you this time."

"Dan, I don't deserve you."

"I'll test you on that someday." He appeared to be serious.

"If this pregnancy goes like the last, you'll be running for the hills." I didn't do the first few months well. I may be the vomit queen. I had no indication to date, but the little bugger couldn't be more than a few thousand cells. It wouldn't be asking too much of me this early in the game.

"Any word about Mrs. Miller?"

"Not since you last inquired."

"Were you present at the autopsy?"

"Nope."

"Why don't they think her death was due to natural causes?"

"I don't think they think anything yet. There's nothing to indicate that. The police are simply following protocol. Have you told the girls yet?"

"No, but I will tomorrow."

"What do you think of Jedda?"

"Did you notice the house? I loved Mrs. Miller, but this girl takes cleaning to another level. Unfortunately, it's only for a month before she begins school. I'll call the day care tomorrow to see whether we can book them for this year. Casey could start reception, but I still want her to start midyear." We had agreed it was best to hold off on formal education for as long as possible.

Dan cleaned the plates while I did some medical records. Since we lived on the edge of civilization, we received a signal for only four channels on the television. Happily, we have decent internet, and thankfully, the vet hospital had cloud-based records. I created a list of tasks for the following day. Besides food shopping, I planned to attempt contacting Mrs. Miller's sister. My address book, which is at work, may have her name. I could deal with that in the morning.

The phone rang as I was headed to brush my teeth. Both Dan and I were on call. I prayed it was for him. Sadly, it was for me. It was the owners of a pony that was shaking. With our unusual

21

rain, the temperatures had dropped. I hoped it was a cold, wet pony. Alas, they had a thermometer, and the pony had a high fever. These were top clients who preferred to pay the after-hours fees rather than wait until morning.

Dan kissed me and promised to keep the bed warm as I left for the faraway property. It would be at least two hours before I would return. Well, try four hours. I became a real Australian when I hit a roo. According to my friends, I wasn't an official Australian until I hit a kangaroo. Sadly, it was fatal. Even worse, my truck sustained severe damage. I checked the roo for babies, but it was a male. At least I didn't have to deal with a joey. Many of my clients raised the joeys in their houses. Pillowcases hung from hooks with various sizes of joeys. I was required to learn marsupial medicine when I started working as a vet Down Under.

When I arrived, the little mare was shaking and had a high heart rate. She had no gut sounds, indicating the intestines had no motility, typical with advanced colic. The color of the gums verged on purple. I explained that the prognosis was poor. However, the owners wanted to try to save her, so I administered intravenous fluids and painkillers.

While we were waiting for a response, their young son came out to the barn. He was different, and I suspected autism. He brought out a book about horse diseases and treatments which he had recently been given. He wanted me to look at it with him in case there was something in the book that would help me to save his sister's pony. He and I went through the entire album together. His parents stared in amazement as he was reaching out to a stranger. I stated that the pony's illness would cause her to be in terrible pain and that sometimes the kindest action was to help the pony die. I didn't hide or sugarcoat the circumstances. I conversed with the young boy as if he was an adult. His mother nodded at me. I explained how we were trying to save her. However, within the hour, the pony went down, and I eased her into the afterlife.

"Say hi to Orbit." I said that when I euthanized horses. Orbit was my old horse that had passed many years ago. The young boy handed me his book. He thanked me and asked me to keep it because it might help me save another pony. I took it and thanked him. I said I would purchase my own copy and return his. His book was written thirty years earlier. I was going to see if I could locate a more recent edition and purchase one for us both.

It was after midnight, and the husband did some tweaking to my truck, so I could safely drive home. I didn't envy the pony owners. In the morning, they were going to have to tell their daughter that her pony had died.

"Thank you for being so kind to our son. I can't tell you how special it was to watch him talk with you. He probably hasn't said two words to anyone besides our family and his special-needs teacher."

The boy had returned to the house with his mother. "No, the pleasure was all mine. I am always interested in ideas that increase my knowledge." We both recognized this special moment.

This reminded me that I had to tell the girls about Mrs. Miller. I drove home and was in bed by two o'clock in the morning. True to his word, the human wheat bag kept the bed warm. He welcomed me with a pat and turned over to envelope me in his arms as I joined him. I cried, thinking about the children losing their pony.

"What? No good?"

"No, I'm definitely hormonal. Well, maybe." I wondered how that boy would fare in life.

Chapter 3

While I slept, Dan woke up the girls and fed and dressed them. When I emerged from the bedroom, he reported that my truck needed to go to the crash repairer immediately. My bull bar was strapped to the mainframe of the truck with wire.

Jedda was due in a few minutes. Dan and I disparagingly stared at each other, realizing we had to talk to the girls about Mrs. Miller. Sadly, it went surprisingly well. Casey inquired if Mrs. Miller was going to see Milky. Our cat, Milky, died after being hit by a car a year ago. Faythe didn't remember our cat, but that didn't stop Faythe from mentioning her whenever we observed roadkill.

"Yep, I bet Milky is rubbing up against her leg right now." I combed Faythe's hair and attempted to braid it while she peered at Mrs. Miller's house.

"Mum, why is ribbon all over the trees?" She saw the yellow crime scene tape placed around the front lawn and driveway across the street.

"I don't know. Daddy, do you know?" Maybe Dan's explanation wouldn't frighten the girls.

"Not a clue. As far as I can tell, Mrs. Miller simply died in her...." Dan nearly said sleep, but then I assume he thought about the children being afraid to fall asleep and didn't finish his sentence.

"In her, what, Daddy?"

"Recliner, sweetie. She was sitting in her chair."

"Can we see her?" I was about to respond when the doorbell rang.

"Jedda." Both girls ran to the door and hugged her and Banjo.

Dan and I immediately were made redundant. "Mum, you can go now. Jedda and I are going to clean and fix up our room this morning." I stared at Casey and shook my head.

Faythe jumped into Jedda's arms and began to ask if she had sat in any chairs the previous night, which I guessed was a reference to the place Mrs. Miller died. "You okay, Jedda?" The girls appeared worried.

"You two better get to your room and start making your beds, or I'll...." Jedda didn't complete her sentence. The girls ran down the hall, shrieking with laughter, while Dan and I glanced at each other and shook our heads.

Henry examined the bull bar when I arrived at the clinic, and he ordered one of the nurses to transfer the new truck's vet equipment into the old vehicle. The damaged truck was driven to the crash repairers for evaluation and an insurance quote.

I went into the back room of the office to check messages and to make some coffee. There was a note to call Kendall. I asked Mrs. Tankard, "Do you know why Kendall called?"

"Not a clue."

Mrs. Tanya Tankard, our receptionist, was an institution in our town. She'd served on the city council for years and knew everyone. Mrs. Tankard was fully aware of all the town secrets and everyone who was anyone. She was the unofficial mayor. The actual mayor aspired to be a member of the state parliament. He never made a controversial decision for fear of losing voters.

I called Kendall, and my call went straight to her message bank. I suspected her call regarded releasing Mrs. Miller's body for the funeral. I loaded my personal belongings into the old truck and took it to the servo to fill it with diesel. I had long given up terms like gas station and gas. Even the crash repair shop name made me laugh. The Aussies love their nicknames. Many of Dan's friends called him Danno.

On my way back to the clinic, Kendall called. I pulled over to the curb and prepared to write down anything about Mrs. Miller's sister. Kendall was to the point. "You need to come to the station for an interview. Some issues have to be cleared up before we can release her body."

"You're kidding! What's the hold-up?"

"Carly, when can you come in?"

"You sound serious. Surely this isn't an investigation? She died. She was old and sick."

"Give me a time. Hey, nice job hiring Jedda. You won't regret it, and it could make all the difference in her life."

"Yeah, what a sleeper. I never suspected Jedda was so good with the girls."

"Time, Langley?"

"I had a bit of drama last night. I committed murder and should cover my tracks."

"Huh?"

"I hit a roo—major damage to the truck. It's put me way behind on the calls. Is noon okay?"

Kendall laughed. "Yeah, that's fine. We can get a statement about both murders then." There was a pause. "I didn't say that. You didn't hear me say that, did you?"

"Say what?" I could tell Kendall was upset she had implied that Mrs. Miller had been murdered. The notion was ridiculous. I returned to the clinic and headed out for some appointments. I was off to see a horse that was losing weight and a pony that was scratching himself to the point of mutilation.

The pony was easy because he had lice, as did the other horses in the same paddock, but he was the only one showing signs. A new horse in the same pen had arrived from the interstate sale yards. I found that any quarantine concept or isolation of horses coming from other states was simply not considered. Fortunately, it was lice and not the highly contagious bacterial infection called strangles. I treated all the horses with an ivermectin product, which is a wormer and a topical product that immediately kills the lice. I then suggested they get some insecticide from the fodder store to treat all the horses. I showed the owners the eggs, which were called nits. I cautioned them that nits would hatch and reinfest the pony if they didn't repeat the same process the next week.

The horse with a significant weight loss was more of a challenge. Her teeth were in excellent condition. Since the mare was consuming decent food, and the owner had given her two dewormers, the most common weight loss causes were eliminated. Sand accumulation might be a problem, but so was liver disease and underlying infection. The horse struggled to breathe. While watching her inhale, I noticed she used her abdominal muscles more than is usual. When I listened to the lungs, I heard crackling and popping. I suspected either an advanced asthma-like syndrome or an aggressive infection. The temperature was normal. While an infection had to be considered, it was lower down my list without an accompanying fever. Cancer was rare but not inconceivable.

I discussed the possible causes with the owner, took blood for analysis, and made an appointment to perform further diagnostics once I received the blood work. While I would love to take a radiograph and ultrasound of the chest, our equipment was not as capable as I was accustomed to in my internship. Because I did have an endoscope, I explained I could investigate the pharynx and down into the trachea. From there, I could get a sample of the fluid in the airways. This procedure might confirm the diagnosis of heaves, which is the common term for asthma-like symptoms in horses.

The owner was eager as this horse was used in Pony Club, and her daughter was a good rider. I additionally suggested a referral to a veterinary clinic and university teaching hospital near Adelaide, both of which possessed all the necessary equipment. The owner wasn't keen to have the horse travel for two hours to either facility. She decided that pending the blood-analysis results, I would return and scope the horse.

That was my trade-off for living in a rural community. I sacrificed having the best diagnostic equipment for my rural lifestyle, as did all the people living on the "edge of civilization," as Dan called it. It was a mutual decision. Dan and I wouldn't exchange it for anything, except for the girl's educational opportunities.

I stopped at the local roadhouse on my way back to the clinic. The best-kept secret in town was Angel's barista bar and her carrot cake. I was going to have to watch what I ate if I was genuinely incubating. I never gave up coffee for the other two, and this one was going to have to get used to small jolts of caffeine, as well. I love my kids, but I have my limits of motherly sacrifices, and coffee was one of them. Angel nodded and signaled she was onto it. My preferred brew was already being prepared. "Want the carrots, too, Carly?"

"Yes, ma'am."

A woman was sitting at the table, typing on a small laptop. I thought she must be new in town. She looked up and smiled. I nodded. "The carrot cake is to die for."

"Thanks." She returned to her typing and didn't glance up again.

"Angel, make it to-go, please. I am expected at the police station in fifteen."

"Carly, Carly Carly. What are they doing you for now? Murder?"

"Don't laugh. That may be closer to the truth than we believe. I think it's about Mrs. Miller."

"Oh, yeah. Terribly sad about poor Millie." Was I the only person in town who called her Mrs. Miller? Admittedly, I had to be the closest person to her. She practically lived with us. It never occurred to me to call her anything but "Mrs. Miller." Angel dumped the coffee grinds and handed me a cup and a small bag containing the "carrots." I nodded again to the woman sitting in the booth, paid for the coffee and cake, and left.

I called the house, and Jedda said everything was under control. I could hear laughing and yelling in the background. "If you say so." I was suspicious. I called the clinic, and Mrs. Tankard said it was quiet and to take my time. Mrs. Tankard was a force to be reckoned with. You would not want to cross her. She smoked, and no one dare suggest she quit. She took several breaks to step outside, but she took a phone with her and never missed a call. I could hear her sucking on a "ciggie." I gritted my teeth. I only once commented that smoking would kill her, to which she replied that no one was getting out of here alive and to mind my own business. *Yes, ma'am.*

I drove to the police station, where several cars were parked around the building. Our police station was small compared with the ones near Adelaide. It was regularly staffed, except at night. Reggie Taylor was the officer in charge. He and his wife, Lu-Anne, lived in the house out the back. Their little boy, who was Casey's age, played on the same soccer team. With such a small community, the children were not segregated into boys and girls. Reggie's son, Tim, was going to be a great player someday. Casey was no slouch, but I wanted to get her going in the local Pony Club.

One thing the Australian's have all over American's is their system for educating young riders in equestrian sports. The Pony Club model is great for teaching children to ride and how to care for horses. Most of it is geared to English riding and eventing, but several Western-oriented kids also started in Pony Club. I wanted to wait until Casey begged me to join. I would find her a horse or pony to keep her safe and maintain her enthusiasm for riding.

Reggie greeted me from behind the counter at the station. He was less than friendly. Way less, which sent alarm bells ringing through me. He pointed to a chair in the waiting room. I saluted, and that did bring a smile to his face, which somewhat alleviated my apprehension. Two men dressed in civvies emerged from the back room and eyed Reggie, who nodded in my direction and pointed at me. One was Dan's old classmate, Ron Billings, and the other was new to me. I wondered where Kendall was.

"Dr. Langley, would you like to step into the back? May we get you something to eat or drink?"

"No, thanks. How long will this take? I wish I could help you, but I really don't know anything."

"Well, that depends on you. This is Officer Billings, and I am Officer Jenkins." I had to stifle a laugh. They stared at me, and Officer Jenkins, a short bald man, gave me a hard look. "Is there something funny?"

"No, sir. I was only wondering which of you is the good cop and who is the bad cop. I think you answered my question." I smirked inwardly.

"Dr. Langley, may we call you Carly?" I nodded. "Carly, we need to caution you. This is a murder investigation, and we take these matters quite seriously. You must know that anything you say to us will be subject to further proceedings. We are already recording your interview with us today. Do you understand?"

"I'll help you all I can, but I left my house at eight o'clock in the morning, and I was out working all that day. I had talked to Mrs. Miller the previous night when she informed me that she was too sick to take care of the children."

"How about we ask the questions, and you answer them?" They spoke into the recorder, announced my name, interview date, requested my residential address and my relationship to the deceased.

"Surely she died of natural causes. She was sick and old." I watched Ron Billings open a large envelope.

"Carly, when did you become aware you were the primary beneficiary of her estate?"

Chapter 4

A copy of Mrs. Miller's will was handed to me. I studied it and glanced up. They could see my surprised reaction. "Just now. Are you kidding?" I eyed them both, and they showed no emotion and didn't say a word. Their silence was unnerving. "Apparently not. It's news to me." I shook my head. "I swear. I didn't know."

Officer Jenkins slid a piece of paper toward me. When I picked it up, I recognized it was from the Office of Martin and Brock, the local solicitors. It was addressed to me and dated last month. It was a letter naming me as Mildred Miller's heir. Curiously, my signature was on the bottom of a page attached to her will. The handwritten signature was mine, but I had not signed this document, and I had no idea that this will even existed. Why would my signature even be on the will? I shook my head and looked up at the two men sitting across from the table. I was stunned. I kept staring at my signature and shook my head.

"You understand the reason we have issues here, don't you? This may all be simply a set of unusual circumstances. Mrs. Miller may have died of natural causes, but we have evidence that may suggest otherwise."

I glared at them and requested the obvious. "What evidence?" I knew I didn't have anything to do with her death, and I couldn't imagine who wanted her dead. *For God's sake, she was old and sick.* I knew the autopsy indicated no signs of foul play, and once the toxicology report was in, the case would be closed.

"Her body's been taken to Adelaide for further forensics. We aren't prepared to say anything more."

"I was at work the whole day when she died."

"How do you know when she died?" Both men smiled as though they knew they caught me.

"Do I need a solicitor?"

I observed a distinct groan from both detectives. "Well, that's your right, but we must have some questions answered. It's just a friendly chat."

"I did not kill Mrs. Miller. I loved her. She was a grandmother to my children. She was a member of my family for all purposes. I don't know where that signature came from, but it isn't mine. I don't want anything from her or her estate. She has a sister, and that is where the estate should go. It can't be any more than the value of her house. She had no other income to my knowledge, and her husband's illness wiped out most of their savings. This is all a ridiculous mistake." I started to get up, and the men glared at me as if I had been caught in several lies. "I think I'll leave unless you are charging me with murder, and you can speak to my solicitor if you have any additional questions."

Neither man said anything, and I raced out of the station, where I bumped into Kendall while exiting the building. "Hey, Carly."

"Hey, back. Don't suppose you want to tell me anything?"

"I've been sidelined as our friendship may be a conflict of interest. Don't worry, I know you. They don't."

"I'd better call Dan. Shit. And you know that's the first time I used that word since I was kicked last month."

"Yeah, it's been about an hour since I used it. Totally understandable." Kendall laughed and shook her head. She touched my shoulder. Without speaking, she told me she was on side.

I got in the car and tried to ring Dan, but he didn't answer my call. I left a message and went back to the clinic. I had two more appointments in the afternoon. I called home, and all was good there. Jedda was taking the girls to the park after a nap.

"You persuaded the girls to take a nap?"

"Oh, no. We're all too old for naps, Dr. Langley. We lie down to read. The girls are under strict orders not to sleep. They can be so disobedient, though."

"Remarkable, and thanks." God, I love this girl.

Chapter 5

Dan finally called two hours later. He'd assisted during an appendectomy. I recounted the interview, Mrs. Miller's will, and my forged signature. He was shocked and perplexed. The entire situation was getting out of hand. Dan felt it was time to talk to a solicitor. We'd never required one before, so we were going to have to find one that worked in criminal law. The local solicitor, Hal Brock, played footy with Dan. Besides, Hal's wife nursed at the hospital, but not with Dan. Hal was Mrs. Miller's solicitor and had drawn up her will. Dan said he would call him right away. Hal would know whom we should contact. I was afraid this might mean a trip to Adelaide. I realized this situation was getting serious. The whole notion of either of us committing murder was ridiculous.

When I returned to the office, Mrs. Tankard pulled me aside and informed me the police had come by and asked for my schedule for the previous week. I was relieved. My schedule showed I was working at the time Mrs. Miller died. I quickly updated Jill in between consults. She shook her head and remarked she would help any way she could to facilitate a quick resolution.

Jill gazed up from her computer, where she was entering a report. "I know you're innocent, but why do they even think she was murdered?"

"They won't discuss it. I'm guessing the police have a list of people who had contact with Mrs. Miller during her last twenty-four hours, and I am only one. My work schedule will exonerate me. Even if she was murdered, which we both know isn't the case, at least I will be removed from the suspect list."

"Why would you be on the list anyway?"

"Apparently, she updated her will recently and made me the beneficiary."

"My guess is that you, Dan, and the girls were her 'raison d'être.'"

"I'm getting that impression. I thought Mrs. Miller had a sister. She talked about her as though she was alive."

"She never had any children, and she was probably grateful that you allowed her to play the role of a grandmother."

I still didn't discuss the certain knowledge that I had a bun in the oven. I was now several days late. I checked my schedule and noted I had an appointment at the Walkers. Jen Walker had Standardbred racehorses. She and her never-do-well mining husband, Malcolm, bred, trained their harness horses, and sent them interstate to race. They inseminated their mares with chilled semen. I matched the time of ovulation with the semen procurement and inseminated semen from the selected stallions.

It's pretty simple, except when it's not. We'd bred five mares, and all but one took on the first go and were happily incubating. One mare wasn't pregnant. Despite the end of the traditional spring breeding and foaling season, Jen and Malcolm were anxious to have the mare rebred. The nursing foal at foot sometimes prevents the mare from cycling regularly. Not in this case. This mare was cycling and had been bred twice yet failed to conceive on the first cycle. She conceived on the second cycle but lost the embryo and currently was ready for one last try this season.

I had cultured her uterus to ensure the embryonic loss wasn't from infection. The local laboratory reported no bacterial growth from the uterine swab. I took our portable ultrasound machine and headed out to their property to ascertain if we should order semen for the mare. On the way, I received a call from Jedda. Several policemen wanted to search our house. She wasn't sure what to do.

"Jedda, let me talk to the policeman." I heard some muffled voices when a new voice came on the line.

"Dr. Langley, this is Officer Mark Donaldson of the Major Crimes Unit. I have a court order to search your property."

I was stunned. "Do I have a choice? My children are at home. I don't want to scare them. Can you return in an hour?"

After a pause, the officer came back on the line. "Your nanny has suggested that she take the children to the park while we search the home. We're going to give her a few minutes to get them ready, and then we'll enter."

"Thank you. This is crazy, you realize. You don't even know if Mrs. Miller was murdered. She was old, and she had a virus."

"Dr. Langley, we're simply following orders. We'll notify the nanny when we're done, and she can return."

I immediately called Dan and left a message. He called right back and stated he was heading home. The solicitor he had contacted was out of town and wouldn't be back for two weeks. He acquired the name of another solicitor whom he would call as soon as he was by himself. He told me not to worry. As if.

I drove to the Walkers' farm, where I quickly conducted an ultrasound examination and discovered a large follicle on the left ovary and a smaller one on the right. I attempted to remain calm and not let my client know what was going on.

"Set to jet, Jen. I'll give her the ovulation drug. We can order the semen for tomorrow."

"Fingers crossed, Carly. This will be our last go this season. If she doesn't take, we will have to wait until next season. She's getting a little long in the tooth. We may need to retire her from the breeding shed."

"Okay, the pressure's on. I'll call when I know when to expect the semen later today." I cleaned the ultrasound probe, called the office, and asked Mrs. Tankard to order the semen for the next day. The semen would be collected from the stallion, processed with extender, and shipped to the clinic by courier. We were lucky that the local courier transported the semen from the Adelaide Airport and drove it up at night. I would inseminate her whenever it arrived, even if it was late at night. The drug I administered to induce ovulation would usually induce ovulation thirty-six hours later. We thus timed the insemination to coincide with ovulation, plus or minus a few hours. Actual "live cover" when a stallion and mare are bred naturally was rare these days in the Standardbred industry.

When I called the office to request the semen, I told Mrs. Tankard I needed to run to the house. She was already aware that the house was being searched and had directed the police to the crash repairers, so they could examine my regular work vehicle.

This situation was out of hand and embarrassing. "It's crazy. Carly, we have your back here at the clinic. With Millie gone and no more peach pies, somehow you aren't as valuable an asset to us as you used to be." Mrs. Tankard laughed, and the laugh became a wheezing, coughing fit.

"Be careful, Mrs. Tankard. I'm armed and hormonal. Don't mess with me." I tried to sound casual but failed miserably. "I'll be back within the hour. I should settle the girls and find out what's going on." I drove home via the clinic, and at Jill's request, I left my company phone and tablet, which I used for billing.

When I arrived, the neighbors were all out watching the proceedings. Dan was on the sidewalk, talking to one of the policemen stationed at the front door. I walked up the steps, and Dan stepped back and quietly remarked. "We're screwed."

"What the hell's going on, Dan?"

"They're taking our computers and personal papers."

This was a nightmare. How could this be happening? I turned to look for the girls who were swinging and laughing with Jedda. I walked across the street to the park. We'd chosen our house for the price, but its location near the park was a bonus. Mrs. Miller had lived next to the park. The yellow crime-scene tape on her property was starting to become ragged and break. Still, it was keeping anyone from entering the premises.

I noticed a lady sitting on a bench at the edge of the park. She was typing on her laptop. I realized she was the woman whom I'd seen at Angel's roadhouse. She glanced up and smiled. She reached down into her bag, pulled out a parcel, and held it up. It was Angel's carrot cake. She smiled and gave me the thumbs up. I couldn't hear her, but it was apparent she was mouthing, "Thank you." I nodded as I approached the girls. Faythe ran up to hug me. Casey was glad to see me, but she was trying to kill herself on the swing. "Higher." However, Jedda would not let her go any higher than was safe.

Jedda turned to me with a questioning look. I shook my head, and she recognized that this was not a conversation for small children. I glanced back at Dan, who was arguing with the policemen stationed at the door. I could hear his phone ring, and he stepped away to take a call.

The woman typing on her laptop looked at Dan and back at me. I wondered what she was thinking. *Who was she anyway?* I had more pressing problems. My phone rang, and I retrieved it from my pocket and stepped away from everyone. The call was from my office, informing me the police were impounding my regular and current work vehicles. Henry and Jill wanted to meet with me at my earliest convenience. My life was in a downward spiral. How could anything be worse?

I sat down on the bench near the laptop lady and buried my face in my hands. I was hangry and tired. My pregnancy hormones were starting to play havoc with my mind.

"Bad day?"

"Huh?" The woman, who had stopped typing, smiled at me.

I tried to ignore her and turned to watch the children who were now attempting cartwheels on the grass with Jedda's help. She continued to stare at me. "Well, it isn't one of my better days."

"I don't mean to pry, but it seems as though you could use a friend."

"No, I don't need a friend. I need a solicitor."

"I'm a solicitor."

I did a double-take. The woman looked ten years older than Mrs. Miller. Her gray hair was poorly dyed with an unusual red color, and she was sporting Coke bottles for glasses. Her shirt was torn and thin. She wore jeans that went up to her boobs, which appeared to drape over and down to her waist. "Oh, really? Know any criminal solicitors?"

"I'm a criminal solicitor."

The woman was delusional. She stared in the direction of my house, where I could see that two boxes of God-knew-what were placed in a police van.

"Do they have a warrant?"

"Apparently. Who did you say you were?"

"I'm Della, but you can call me Dolly. My friends call me Dolly. My real name is Della Myler."

I was not in the mood. I felt a severe headache coming on as I watched Dan. He was trying to write down numbers as he spoke on the phone. I observed the old lady who had resumed her typing as if nothing had happened. I walked over to Dan on the hot sidewalk in front of our house.

"Jesus, Carly. The whole legal fraternity is on holiday." Dan was sweating, and he was currently pacing.

"Well, not all of them." I glanced over at the bench, which was now deserted. *Where did she go?*

"Do you know someone?"

I shook my head. "Did you see that lady I was talking to on the bench?"

"No, what lady?" Dan stared over as two policemen came out of the house with two more boxes of our papers. They announced we were free to go back in. Jedda was walking toward us while holding the two girls' hands. I waved her over and noticed she was extremely strict about crossing the street. *God, I really love this girl.*

When Dan's phone rang, he stepped away to answer it. I watched him talking on the phone. He was not happy. He pulled a piece of paper out of his pocket and jotted down another number. My personal phone rang. It was the office, wondering if I could come back now and talk to my bosses. I told Jedda I must go back to work for a few minutes.

Dan closed his phone and looked at the neighbors. Many people witnessed the proceedings while drinking either iced tea or beer. I suspected the latter. Dan turned to me and whispered. "Carly, I hope murdering her was worth it." I kicked him, and he laughed. "Well, it can't get much worse."

My headache had gone up two notches on the Richter scale. "No, it can't. But will you visit me in jail?"

"Hardly." Dan looked at the police who were backing out of the driveway.

"Then I won't visit you, either. I must return to work for a few minutes. The police impounded my regular truck, and this one, too. Jill and Henry want to talk to me. They can't sack me. I scheduled an insemination for later tomorrow, but administrative leave could be on the horizon. Someone at the office can drive me home."

"You go. I'll deal with the kids. It's already time for Jedda to leave. I'll explain to her what's happening."

41

I love that man. I put my arms around him, and he held me while I had a mini cry. I am tough as nails, but this was pushing my limits. He stroked my back. "Ah, my emotional, pregnant wife. You are so up the duff."

"I resemble that remark." I pushed him away. As I turned to the girls, I whispered to Dan, "I'm going to the clinic. If you don't have me off the suspect list by the time I return, I'll look for a new husband."

"That's the problem. Suspect for what? She died. Granted, it was not expected, but it happens. This is so ridiculous. I'm the last one to see her. I should be the number-one suspect." He paused and looked away. "Holy heck, I think I have the answer. I took blood. I forgot to check the results when I heard she died."

"You did? Why?"

"Blood sugar. Since I needed some blood, I thought I might as well get a white cell count. I'll call the lab."

"Run, Forrest, run." I kissed him and walked over to the old clinic truck. My head was throbbing, and I felt nauseous. Was I going to get fired?

The remaining policeman approached me. "We're going to impound your phone."

"May I see the warrant?"

He showed me the warrant and took the phone. Dan's phone was also impounded.

Chapter 6

The clients were at the clinic to pick up their elective surgery dogs and cats. The clinic accepted the spays and neuters early in the morning. As clients finished work, they came by and retrieved their pets in the late afternoon. I knew all the large animal clients, but not all the townsfolk. My scrub shirt and logo were prominent. One woman came out with a large dog pulling her.

"May I help you?" I asked.

She observed me and quickly shook her head without saying anything. Finally, she blurted out, "I'm fine." She stared at me for a moment too long. She shook her head, and that was the first inkling that word had spread. I was a marked woman, and this was going to be the gist of this meeting. I would be stood down until the investigation was completed, and I would be exonerated.

Two people emerged without any animals. I wondered if they would do the same, but they left and didn't show any recognition. Were they plainclothes detectives, too? I walked up the back steps of the clinic. When I entered the coffee room, both Henry and Jill were waiting and working on their laptops. I could see they were upset.

"The police were here to take our main computer. Fortunately, they didn't have warrants for our personal computers. That's the sole reason we can keep going. If we weren't cloud-based, we would be screwed. You're on administrative leave until this is finished. Get the semen into that mare, and that's it until this is sorted. We have a locum coming from the new agency. She'll be here tomorrow." Henry seemed extremely upset. Jill was more empathetic.

"Carly, we know you're innocent, and this must be a terrible burden to you and Dan, but we can't afford to have any bad publicity for the clinic. I'll drive you home."

Well, the hammer had dropped. "I'm sorry. I can't believe this has happened. I completely understand. I'll get the mare done on the q.t." I was enraged and attempted to hide it. It wasn't their fault. If Mrs. Miller was murdered and hadn't died of natural causes, someone was having a good laugh at my expense. "Let me know how I can help. I think the only bill and medical record I haven't done is the Walker mare. I'll follow up on that, but she got the deslorelin at two this afternoon, and she has a forty-millimeter follicle on the right ovary. The police took my computers. I'm sorry to say they took my personal phone, as well. I don't have the logins for the clinic stuff anyway. They were all on the tablet. Again, I am so sorry." I was sorry.

To be honest, it was a bit of a relief. If I couldn't work, then not having a clinic phone wasn't the worst thing. Jill dropped me off at home. Dan and I only had one car, so we could share it. Either I would drive Dan to work, or he would bike there and back.

We had a landline, but Dan's phone was taken, too. Hopefully, he'd checked on the blood results for Mrs. Miller. I entered the house, and Dan sat in the living room with the girls. I shook my head. We wouldn't voice our concerns in front of the girls. Casey was becoming savvy, and she intensely stared at both of us and inquired about what was happening.

Dan was drying Faythe's hair. "Nothing, darling. You and your sister put on your pajamas, and I'll get some dessert. Do you want one scoop of ice cream or no scoops?"

"Daddy, I want two." Casey took her sister's hand. As she led her away, I could hear, "I think they are going to kiss and make a baby. That's why we have to go to bed early." Despite all my troubles, I laughed. *Way too smart for her age.*

After dessert, we both put the children to bed. When we were sure they were asleep, Dan told me that the police had taken Mrs. Miller's blood results. He was not allowed to see them. He'd called his boss, who suggested we accept their refusal to view the blood results. Dan's boss thought if we just let them play their game, we would be more likely to get the investigation over and return to normal.

"The bad news is that the last decent criminal solicitor in Adelaide is too busy to take on the case. He referred us to a good defense advocate in Victoria." He was located twelve hours from here. Dan left a message with the man. Could it get any worse? My head was pounding. I was effectively unemployed. I didn't have my phone or computer. If I didn't do it, and if Mrs. Miller was murdered, possibly the killer was someone Dan and I knew. We were completely in the dark.

"Dennis Denuto." I laughed, thinking of the solicitor in the movie *The Castle*. "We can call Dennis Denuto. I think the other guy is dead." Dan gazed at me as though I was crackers. He shook his head.

"Are you talking about that crazy film where the incompetent solicitor represented the families who were losing their homes?"

"Yeah, it's the vibe." Dan remembered when I said that and almost laughed. "I may have met the female version today. I told you about the old woman whom I saw at the roadhouse and at the park. She said she was a solicitor who knew criminal law."

"Shit creek and no paddles, my fertile wife." Dan took my hand and led me to the bathroom, where he drew a bath and added some salts. "You still smell like a horse. This may be my last night with you. You may be in the slammer by tomorrow."

"So suave and charming. My head is throbbing, so don't get any ideas, mister." I did strip down and eased myself into the warm water. Dan returned and scrubbed me with a luffa.

"Just removing any incriminating DNA. I promise I'm not looking."

"Headache, darling. Nine on the ten scales." He lifted me out of the tub, dried me, slipped my favorite nightgown over my head,

45

and frog-marched me to bed. He handed me two paracetamol and pulled the covers up over my shoulders. We spooned for several minutes. He left our bed as I fell asleep. I woke up several hours later and found him reading a novel I'd given him for Christmas. "Can't sleep?"

"Carly, I think we're in trouble. God knows why they think she was murdered, but at least one of us, and probably both of us, are suspects. How about I worry for both of us? I don't want any hormonal stress on my baby. Do you think you can sleep again?"

"Is the pope an old man? You need to sleep, too. What about work tomorrow?"

"RDO, rostered day off."

"Since when do you get a day off in the middle of the week?"

"I thought we would be heading to Adelaide to see a solicitor. I asked for it when you were being sacked at the clinic. Don't worry. They still love me at work. I get only one day."

Chapter 7

The next morning, Dan called the solicitor, who practiced in Melbourne. He was available, and he could do some preliminary work on the possible case. He needed to have a retainer of ten thousand dollars to even look at it, and he advised us to wait until either of us was charged. If it went further, the solicitor would require a retainer of fifty thousand dollars. If it went to trial, he would expect about three times that.

Dan thanked him and decided it was best to wait and see what happened in the next few days. We owned our house outright, but it wasn't worth more than the legal fees. Dan called a colleague who drove him down to purchase a cheap cell phone and took him to his home to use his friend's personal computer.

Dan's bike was at the hospital, and he was going to ride it home. At least we had our car. After Jedda arrived, I went to Angel's and decided to have my coffee and carrot cake at the roadhouse.

Angel greeted me. She wanted to know if I had seen the paper.

"No. Is there any news about Mrs. Miller?"

"Frontpage, Carly."

The newspaper included a photograph of the front of her property with the crime scene tape. An insert showed Mrs. Miller holding Casey and Faythe. Their faces were blurred. I had taken this picture last year at Christmas time. I had it framed and gave it to Mrs. Miller as a Christmas present. It was displayed on her fireplace mantel. The paper stated her death was being treated as suspicious.

The article read that several suspects were being eliminated, and only one person of interest was now considered as a potential murderer. A possible motive had been established.

I had no telephone to call Dan. My face reddened, and I was close to tears. Angel brought my coffee and cake and sat down across the table from me. We were the only two people in the roadhouse.

"You gonna be okay?" Angel touched my free hand.

"Sure. It's all a mistake, you know. I'm sure it will be cleared up today. I was at work, and Dan was at the hospital when she died. We have iron-clad alibis. They don't even have a cause of death."

When the bell on the door rang, Angel glanced up. It was Kendall and Julie, who were surprised to see me. They smiled and sat down at my table.

"How's crime?" I asked Kendall as my usual greeting.

"You tell me." She sent a hard look my way.

Julie was more sympathetic. "You fought the law, and who won…?" The words made Kendall laugh, but I had to grit my teeth.

"So much for friends."

They ordered their coffees. Kendall reached across the table for the paper. "I can't discuss anything, so let's talk about other things. How's Jedda?"

"A total godsend. Can we keep Jedda out of school this year?"

"Sure, no prob." Kendall swatted me.

"Police abuse." I pretended the swipe was painful. "You guys not working today?"

They both turned to the other. Julie replied, "I start after lunch."

"Me, too. I hate the afternoon shift, but someone has to do it in our crime-ridden town."

"Without discussing the particulars, you have gone from a nobody to the most talked-about woman in town." Julie peeked around to make sure no one was listening.

"I'll bet. Is this the first real crime in the town's history?" I was consuming my cake at a rate that would make me look like a woman possessed.

"Pretty much."

Julie did a double-take and then smiled. "The good news is that they rarely convict pregnant women."

I looked up without giving the game away. "Pardon?"

"Unless I'm mistaken, you're knocked up." She said it with a malicious grin.

"What makes you think that?"

She shook her head, and I glanced down without answering. My silence spoke volumes. Both women stared at me and laughed.

"I'm a few days late. That's all. It's not the first time."

"Yeah, there were two other times I remember." Julie kicked me under the table. "Well, this will be interesting."

After their coffee came, Angel sat down with us once again. "When this is over, may I have a picture of you recommending the carrot cake? Maybe I could supply it to the jail."

Right then, the laptop lady walked in the door. Dolly smiled at me, proceeded to the table at the far end of the room, opened her laptop, glanced toward Angel, and nodded. Angel had already started making the coffee and cutting a new piece of cake.

I pointed to the back of the café and mouthed, "Either of you know her?"

Julie shook her head, but Kendall nodded, and we all leaned in close to hear Kendall whisper. "She's a famous barrister from Sydney. Did you ever hear about the Bondi murders, when the two men were capturing young men and killing them in the seventies?" Julie and I shook our heads. "She was the lead prosecutor. She did several other ones in the early eighties with

49

some underworld figures, and then she retired. She currently writes crime novels. She writes under a pseudonym. She comes up here now and then to hang out. She says she comes to find ideas for books and to return to her roots. Her cousin or some relative is Nigel Thompson, who lives out on Red Rock Road. I think she's a QC."

"A Queens Council? Get out of town." Julie and I were impressed.

"Is she from here?" I had no idea about the town history or famous people who may have come from this area.

"Supposedly, but I don't know where."

"Because Nigel doesn't have internet, she comes into town to load her laptop and to write for a few hours a day. Then she goes back out to Nigel's place and the two of them get lit on homebrew and gin."

I didn't say anything about not having my phone or computer. Since I needed to do some Googling, I decided to walk over to the library to use the public computer. The Walker's semen wouldn't be here until later in the afternoon. By that time, Dan would have bought an inexpensive phone for us to use.

"Can I ask one thing?" I stared at Kendall.

"Shoot. Oh, not in your case. What?"

"How long do the police usually keep a person's phone when they take it?"

"No idea."

I nodded to Dolly, said good-bye to Julie and Kendall, and walked across the street to the library. I logged into the public computer and immediately searched for Della Myler. Yes, she was a QC, and she had worked for the Department of Prosecution in New South Wales and as a defense solicitor. The most fascinating fact was she taught law until a few years earlier. I

50

didn't recognize the law school. I read another news report about Mildred Miller's death, which at least stated the cause of death was yet to be determined and might be from natural causes. *Phew, a beacon of hope and truth.*

I went back over to the roadhouse, and the old lady was gone. The place was getting busy, and I caught Angel at the register. "Does the laptop lady come in every day?"

"Nine o'clock every morning, as regular as the sun. She stays for an hour or two, wanders around the town, and returns in the afternoon for a second data download and a bite to eat. She's onto my carrot cake now. She buys a piece for her and one for her cousin. Thanks for the recommendation, by the way. Want me to put a good word in for you? Sounds like you're gonna need a good solicitor."

"Let me do more investigating first. Dan's looking up some legal eagles in case things go pear-shaped."

"By the sound of things, they are about as pear-shaped as they can be."

"So, will you send me carrot cake when I'm in jail?"

"Not a chance. I ain't supporting no crim."

"Hmm, losing my family and friends is one thing, but no carrot cake. Hang me now."

Chapter 8

Dan and I arrived home simultaneously. He located another solicitor in a nearby town, but the man had no experience with a murder investigation. Progressing to the stage of a trial was the worst thing that could happen. It must be halted sooner. We waited nervously for the toxicology report. I told him what I had learned from Kendall regarding Dolly Myler and her expertise. Dan bought a cell phone and provided the new number to several law firms in hopes that someone would respond to our need for representation.

"Carly, if our lives depend on an old lady who writes crime novels and gets drunk in the afternoon with her country cousin, we're toast."

"Well, when you put it that way. How long do you think it will take for the tox report to come in?"

"At least another week." We had the front-window shades pulled. Dan peered out across the street. "Oh, Jesus."

That was a five-alarm bell since Dan rarely swore. "What?"

"There are news vehicles across the street."

I tripped as I raced across the room. I fell and hit my head on the table next to the couch. Instantly, blood was everywhere. Dan turned and gasped. He immediately retrieved a towel and placed it against my nose, thinking it was a bloody nose. The volume of blood prevented him from seeing that it was a gash next to my eye. When he realized the source of the blood, he paled. "It's a stitch job for sure."

Jedda was out in the backyard with the girls. Dan quietly told her that he was taking me to the hospital. We didn't want to alarm the children. The towel that we used was already saturated by the time he returned. He retrieved another red one, and we got in the car in front of the news crews. The only saving grace was they weren't set up to record any visuals.

I was feeling faint. Dan took off like a shot. The car reversed, and my head jerked forward and back, which made my head throb. I recognized a reporter whom I had watched on the news several years ago. She stared as we drove away. The sole satisfaction was that she was not set up to report, and she had aged. The word parasite came to mind.

After we entered the back door of the hospital, I was placed in a wheelchair. Dan steered me into the minor-surgery room. Julie was in there, dressing a man's hand. She turned and gasped. "Jesus, Carly. What the?" She didn't finish the sentence.

"I fell."

"Should I call Kendall? You know domestic violence has no boundaries."

Dan was not amused. "Julie, get Roger. She needs a few stitches." He helped me onto a gurney and placed some four-by-fours on the laceration on my temple, which was only an inch long. The bleeding hadn't stopped, but it was now manageable. My shirt was soaked. According to Julie, who examined me and my conjunctiva, I appeared pale. She glanced at Dan, and he agreed. I was to receive an intravenous drip to kick up my blood pressure.

"I am inseminating this afternoon, so make it quick."

"You're being investigated for murder and have a laceration, and all you can think of is sex? Isn't it a bit late for that?" She stared at my abdomen.

"A mare, Jules."

Dan gazed at me. I knew what he was thinking. "Apparently, I was a little too ravenous for Angel's carrot cake. It was a guess. It's not for sure, you know," I whispered.

Roger Grimes was the surgical specialist who came up from Adelaide two days a week. We were lucky that today was one of his days. He and Dan got on well. Dan frequently scrubbed in when Roger required a second pair of hands. Roger was a smoker who knew he should quit but smoking and eating were his passions. Sadly, it showed. Despite his lack of self-control, his surgical skills were superb. I knew this scar would be less noticeable than the other one on my chin.

"Carly, do you want me to use anesthetic or not? The anesthesia will double the cost."

"I would get the lidocaine out of my truck, but I am temporarily—ouch, that hurt." Roger injected a local anesthetic. Dan held my hand as I fought back the tears. I realized I would soon feel no pain but, ay chihuahua, that stung. Dan attempted to cure me of the use of the word bloody. This was the perfect time for a "bloody hell." However, I was careful with the girls picking up the expression, which was frowned upon in polite circles in Australia.

"Temporarily, what?" Roger was laughing, and I was concerned this would result in a lousy stitch job.

"Uh, let's say sidelined." He studied the laceration. "You don't know?"

"Know what?" Roger continued to open the suture material and place a surgical drape over my head.

"My wife is being investigated for murder. Rog, old man, do you live under a rock?"

"Whose murder? I guess I do."

"Mildred Miller. You did her gallbladder a few years ago."

"Not the one who makes the cream cakes? She's dead? Bloody hell. No more cream cakes? Is there any end to my downward spiral? This is a travesty."

"I may have inherited the recipe, Roger, and all is not lost. If you can find a barrister to defend me, I might make one for you."

"What about Dolly Myler? Will you hold still?"

Dan and I stared at each other. Since my head was under a surgical drape, all he could see was one eye.

Dan beat me to it. "How do you know this Dolly lady?"

"Appendectomy. I did it about ten years ago. We share dinner when I come up if Dolly's around. She's one smart cookie, and a savage gin player, and a pretty savage gin drinker, too. I'm having dinner with her tonight. Why did you murder Millie?"

Dan was holding my hand, and I felt his grip tighten. "She didn't. I was the last person to see her. I should be the one getting charged. My guess is she died of natural causes. But for some reason, the police believe it's murder. We don't know why, but they think Carly did it because she's the beneficiary of her will."

"Hmmm. Well, I can talk to Dolly. I can't promise anything, but maybe she's bored and wants some legal action."

"Would 'vou haf' her defend you?" My words were somewhat slurred from the anesthetic that migrated under the skin and affected my speech.

"In a heartbeat. If she isn't interested, I'll bet she knows someone who would be. That should do it." He removed the drape. "You are one ugly woman right now."

The anesthetic wasn't the only thing that migrated. I had one heck of a bruise that was going to look like a black eye soon. I surveyed myself in the mirror when I sat up. "Ugly. I hate for the girls to see this." Dan was thinking about the same thing. My clinic called Dan on his new cell phone as we were finishing. They had phoned the house, and Jedda had given the clinic the number. The semen had arrived.

I was woozy and knew I shouldn't drive. Dan drove me to the clinic. He went in to retrieve the box of chilled semen and the instruments required for the insemination. He escorted me out to the Walkers. Much to Dan and Jen's horror, I promptly threw up following the insemination.

"You're an idiot, Carly. I could have done this procedure by myself. I took the insemination course many years ago. You didn't have to come."

"Well, I won't be here for a while until we clear up a small legal matter. The clinic's locum will start tomorrow. I hope to see you in sixteen days for a positive scan." Most mares were scanned for pregnancy fifteen to sixteen days post-ovulation. I performed an ultrasound of her uterus and ovaries after the insemination, and the follicle had become triangular and slightly thickened, indicating ovulation was imminent. Dan packed the ultrasound machine into the car while I cleaned up.

"Yeah, I heard about your troubles. I hope you can sort it out."

"Thanks, Jen. Good luck with the mare. If I'm convicted, send me a picture of the foal when it's born."

Jen laughed. As Dan came back around the corner, Jen advised me, "You should talk to Dolly. She's a real legal eagle."

Dan straightened up and turned to Jen. "You know her, as well?"

"Oh yes, she eats dinner with us regularly when she's out. I could ask her for you."

Dan and I eyed each other. "We have some irons in the fire but hold that thought. Sorry about my wife vomiting in your barn. May I clean it up?"

"Oh, Dan, it's not the first time she's done that. I recollect we had a few sessions with the last one. When's it due?"

"Sheesh, is anything a secret in the community?" Dan shook his head and laughed.

"It's the vomiting. No one had to say a word. Even that shiner wouldn't make Carly puke. She's preggers for sure. Let's hope it's catchy." Jen patted the mare's neck as she led her out of the barn.

Chapter 9

Several news vans were parked around the street and in front of our house. It was difficult negotiating our driveway. Three reporters wanted to speak with us. They were in my personal space, way into that space.

I was ready. I realized if I commented negatively on the reporters' appearances, the recording would be erased. When the first parasite shoved a microphone in my face inquiring if I had anything to say, I glanced at her and spoke in a deadpan voice, "I guess it isn't true. Those ten pounds are real. It's not really the camera. Must be living the high life." When the next one started in, I graciously observed. "Your bosses should be commended for keeping older women on the staff and especially in front of the camera. It's amazing how much that makeup makes you look younger. When I am as old as you, I hope I can hide it as well as you do." I turned and went into the house, confident that those comments would not go to air. Dan was laughing hysterically.

The girls had one glimpse of me and fled to Jedda's arms. "Mummy, you look so bad." Both girls were appalled. Yet, typical of young children, they were still curious.

"Mommy fell, darling. I'll be fine." I knew that Faythe would be horrified, and Casey would be intrigued.

Great, I've already been replaced. As per usual, the girls were fed, washed, and ready for bed. I was too. Dan did the kid honors and spoke to Jedda about how to talk to the reporters. He reminded her not to give our new number to anyone except family and work.

Jedda pointed to a notepad by the landline. There were messages from two of Dan's friends, and one from his mother, who wanted to take the girls for a week. She suggested that Dan could take the girls to the Adelaide airport, and she would fly over, pick them up, and fly them to Sydney. It was not the worst idea. Both of our passports had been taken. We were free to go about our lives so far, though. I called Kendall to find out about the children leaving the state.

"No charges yet. However, since you're innocent— you are innocent, aren't you?"

"Consider yourself kicked, sister."

"Ouch, yeah. I felt that. Well, as a courtesy, call Reggie, and inform him what you're up to."

"I think it'll be only Dan and the girls. He'll take them to see his mom. I'm not fit for the light of day."

"Yeah, I heard Dan bashed you. Julie called."

"Hey, can you guys do anything about the news people?"

"Yes, we can, but I doubt anyone will. You and Millie are the talk of the town, and this is great for business."

"Thanks for the protection. I wonder if Dolly Myler likes to sue the police for false arrest?"

"Ya gotta get arrested first." I could hear Kendall was receiving a page on her walkie-talkie.

"Later, girlfriend. I'm crashing. Big day at the office."

"Carly, for what it's worth, I'm totally on your side until the facts say otherwise. Get some sleep, sister."

I did.

Chapter 10

Dan packed bags for the girls and drove to the airport the following morning. The girls were still a bit upset about looking at my bruised face, which was swollen and turning purple. Dan called Jedda and asked her to come over and possibly run errands and help me for a few hours. I went back to bed and got up at midmorning. It was unthinkable to be so lax. I expected the locum vet to call, and I would recount any cases that needed follow-up or further treatments. I looked forward to talking to a fellow colleague. Locums were usually young and often came from overseas. I missed talking to veterinarians who were of a similar age.

My mom called from Idaho. Thankfully, she was unaware of my dramas. She wanted to come over. The girls were going to be gone a week at most. It would be challenging to have another person in the house with everything going on, even if it was my mom.

"Maybe next month would be better. It's hot as hell right now, Mom. We still don't have any AC, either." That was enough to dissuade her. I did tell her I might be pregnant. She was happy and wanted to notify the rest of the family. "Hold off on that for a bit, Mom. I haven't got confirmation." I didn't tell her about the other issues.

My dad died unexpectedly a few years earlier from a heart attack. She and my brother were my only close family members. My mom was a rock. She was welcome anytime, but this wasn't a good time. It would break her heart to hear about this situation. Despite being on the local and Australian-wide news, the rest of the world didn't know about my alleged evil deeds.

But Mrs. Tankard did. She called to explain she had put a check in my bank at her boss's request. That would see me through the next two weeks. She was wheezing.

"Those things will kill you, Mrs. Tankard."

"Go to hell. From all the goss I'm hearing, it's you I need to be worried about." I have to say that did make me laugh.

"Thanks, though, Mrs. T. Two weeks, wow. I hope it's over sooner than that. Let me know if I can assist the locum with any medical histories or anything. Have her call me."

"It's a guy. The girl decided not to come."

"Get out of town. What's his name?"

"Rich. Richard Hamilton. He's a Yank, like you."

"Have him call me if he needs anything. I only have the landline right now until we get our phones back."

"Will do, and I have a restraining order on you. Until we know you didn't do it, steer clear of me."

"Not funny. Keep smoking. See if I care."

"I love you too, Carly."

As I hung up, Jedda came in and scared the bejesus out of me.

"Sorry, ma'am. Dr. Langley gave me a key. I didn't know you were going to be here. Can I help you or fix you some breakfast?"

I noticed she had new clothes and a more conservative appearance. "How about I make you some breakfast? What was it like out there?"

"There's only one news truck outside. All the reporters are at the police station. They're supposedly releasing some new information about Mrs. Miller's death."

I shot up. It couldn't be the tox report. That was too soon. I called Dan from the landline, who said he was near Adelaide and had stopped to get the girls some food.

"There's some sort of press conference at the police station. Have you had any calls from any of the solicitors? Dan, this is getting to be scary. I need assurance that I can get legal assistance. Now, Dan, I need help now."

"Carly, you're on speaker."

"Oh, got it. I miss you guys." I heard Faythe and Casey laughing. They didn't acknowledge me.

"I'll call you as soon as I've heard from someone. Please, don't worry, darling. You've done nothing wrong. She wasn't murdered. She simply died."

"Okay."

"Try to calm down."

Try to calm down? He wouldn't be saying that if it was him.

He hung up, and I stared at the phone. My head throbbed, and my throat was getting sore. I showered and dressed.

"Jedda, will you take me on a drive?"

"Yes, ma'am." Jedda was folding laundry, and she was eager for a change. I could see she was a bit nervous about being around me. I couldn't blame her. I could be a potential murderer.

"Jedda, I can't thank you enough for coming today. I know what people are saying. It's simply not true. I would never harm anyone."

"That's what my father told me. I believe you."

I doubted that was totally true, but how could I blame her? The phone rang. It was the locum vet. "Hi, Dr. Langley. This is Rich Hamilton here."

"I'm pretty casual. Most people call me Carly. I hear you're from the States. Are you visiting, or are you here for good?"

"Not sure. I've had a slight glitch in my plans. My fiancé up and did a runner on me. I do like it here, but not going to commit right now."

"Ouch. Sorry to hear that." I was already thinking of Kendall. I didn't know what he looked like or even his age. He sounded young enough, but Kendall could be pretty picky. "What can I help you with?"

"I think you performed a preliminary work up on a horse for weight loss. Cricket Williamson? I wanted to touch base before I head out."

"Oh, yeah. What did the blood work show? I'm sorry. I don't think I wrote much up for my exam of the mare."

"Normal CBC and high fibrinogen. Chems are all normal."

"Oh, crap. Well, the mare was breathing hard, and the lungs were a bit harsh, but not out of the park. Her heart rate was elevated—around fifty-six — gums were normal. Lots of abdominal breathing and the rest of the horses were well-fed and fat. She'd been wormed several times. According to the owner, she's treated her numerous times for sand, but that could still be an issue. Welcome to sand city. Where you from?"

"Florida, so I'm quite familiar with sand. The blood work makes me think something more sinister, though."

"What was the fibrinogen? Yeah, it doesn't sound too promising."

"She's in the fibrinogen one-thousand club. Big C until proven otherwise."

"Oh, crap. One aspect that's interesting around here is I find a large number of horses with lymphosarcoma. I've seen at least seven cases. Other vets said the same thing when I went to a vet meeting in Adelaide." I was quite sure this horse was dying.

"Any ventral edema?" This guy was no slouch.

"Nope. Maybe it's a different kind of tumor." I loved talking to another horse vet.

"Yep, CTD for sure. Well, thanks. Sorry about your problems. I'll let you know how it comes out."

"CTD, circling the drain? So nice to have someone who speaks my language. Nice talking to you. Maybe you can come over to tea some night. My husband's on call at the hospital four nights a week. When he's free, maybe we can get together. I'm pretty free right now." I laughed, but it didn't sound genuine. "Well, until they throw me in the slammer."

"Yeah, good luck with that."

He hung up—an American accent—I did miss my countrymen. I loved my life and Dan, but we were raised with different values. I was taught that honesty was paramount, but I would say Dan was raised believing mateship was valued more. I didn't know this new vet, but I guessed he was more like me in ethical values. That might be interesting to Kendall. If I could have him over, I sure as heck was going to invite her, too.

"Dr. Langley, do you mind my asking about the things you were talking about on the phone?" Jedda was in the kitchen and could not help but hear the conversation.

"A normal white blood cell count usually means this horse does not have an infectious process. The high fibrinogen means a significant inflammatory process is going on. A low white blood cell count and high fibrinogen might mean cancer— not always, but it should make one consider the big C. A large cancerous mass might outgrow its blood supply and start to fall apart. The dead cells might cause an inflammatory response, which increases the fibrinogen. The normal chems, or chemistries, probably mean the liver and kidneys aren't the problems. Liver disease is a common problem here due to many toxic plants that target the liver. Do you know about Salvation Jane? It's not simply a pretty, purple, flowering plant. It contains a toxin that causes liver disease. I'm impressed you asked. Are you going into veterinary medicine when you graduate?"

"No, ma'am, human medicine."

"Well, well, well. We should have more conversations like this, shouldn't we?"

"If you don't mind."

"Not at all. Ask anything. Let's get you some food, and then I want to go see someone."

"Just a piece of toast, ma'am. I'm not that hungry."

"If you don't mind my asking, what kind of grades do you make?"

"I do okay."

"What's okay? You must earn good grades to go to medical school. You know, in the United States, you go to college or, as you say, 'Uni.' Then you apply to med after a few years. It's so weird that you can be accepted into medical school right out of high school over here."

"If I keep up my grades, I'll get in."

"Wow. Do you need to be studying right now?"

"No, ma'am. I do a bit when I get home. So, when my dad's horse had an infection in his foot, would his fibrinogen and white cells have been elevated?"

"Probably not as the infection was very small and isolated from the general circulation. I don't suppose you could do me a huge honor and call me Carly?"

"Only when the children and Dad aren't around."

The phone rang. It was from Dan. "Hey, we need a solicitor right now."

"What do you know?"

"There is a report on the ABC radio. They don't know what it is, but an irregularity was detected in Mrs. Miller's tox study."

"Shit. Okay, I'm headed out to find that Dolly woman. Did you hear anything from Roger about his dinner?"

"Yeah. Bad news. Dolly says she's too old, but she'll at least talk to you."

"I guess she's at the roadhouse, charging up her laptop and downloading data. I'll head there now. Dan, if it's true, and Mrs. Miller was given something, a murderer really is around. When are you back? I'm getting a bit scared."

"I'll be back by dinner."

"I want to go before the reporters come back."

"Honey, I love you, but even though you're the mother of my children, I'll come to visit you in jail no more than once a month. Since I have my limits, be certain you get a good solicitor."

"Go to hell, Danno."

Chapter 11

Jedda and I climbed in her car. One television van was parked outside our house, but Jedda and I left without interference. There were several people at the roadhouse. Angel was going to score a financial boom due to the out-of-towners. I asked Jedda to find out if Dolly was in there. I started to describe her, but Jedda laughed and said she was her auntie. Jedda knew who she was. I was perplexed. I could see Jedda probably had some "Caucasian" in her, but Dolly?

I waited in the car around the back of the roadhouse while Jedda surveyed the diner. January's typical weather had returned to its normal "hot-as-hell" range. With my black eye, I would have drawn more attention than I wanted. Jedda returned with carrot cake and a message. Dolly would see me back at her cousin's house in thirty minutes after she finished downloading something to her computer. We drove past the police station, where the remote camera crews were breaking down their satellites.

"Carly?" This was the first time Jedda called me by my first name.

"Yeah?"

"What did you actually say to the reporters?"

"What do you mean?"

"They reported that you responded to them with something that isn't fit to air on daytime television."

"Huh?"

"They remarked when they asked you if you were guilty, your reply was so vile it couldn't be broadcast."

"Bugger."

"That doesn't sound too bad."

I chuckled to myself and told her about what I said. They got the last laugh, and I received an education in the media. *The parasites.*

We drove to Dolly's cousin's house and waited under a gum tree. I was nervous. Dan always told me to be wary of what he called widow-makers. Gum or eucalyptus trees dropped limbs without any warning and sometimes killed people in the process. Dan never allowed us to sleep under native trees when we went camping.

After what seemed like a lifetime, Dolly drove up in her Lexus. She smiled as she got out. "Took you long enough." Dolly was slightly overweight, and she seemed older than her reported seventy-six years. Her hair was now dyed carrot red, and she wore no makeup except lipstick that clashed with her hair. Dolly wore a purple top. This must be the old age lady theme of red and purple. She wore enough jewelry to start her own boutique and dangled a cigarette from her mouth.

She walked toward the house, which was nearly the size of my garage. As we approached the door, Dolly threw out the cigarette and cocked her head. "That damn Nigel won't let me smoke in the house."

Nigel Thompson, a retired architect from Sydney, moved back to his family homestead several years ago. The man had to be in his mid-eighties. He was a bit of a hermit. He came into town for food once a week but otherwise stayed out in this small house.

Jedda related Nigel's story. Nigel had been married but had lost his wife when he was in his middle thirties. She died of cancer, and they had no children. Jedda thought that he never remarried, but she wasn't sure. When he retired, he had some men fix up the old homestead. He was polite and friendly to the locals. He declined most offers of home-cooked meals or invitations of any sort from anyone. Rumors floated around that he had a young mistress. Jedda wouldn't say why, but she was sure that wasn't true. He traveled to Sydney once a year to see his doctor and his former architectural partner until his partner's death two years ago. Dolly showed up sporadically, stayed for a month, and then was gone.

They both welcomed us into the house. Gobsmacked was the only way to describe my reaction to the interior. The exterior hid the internal structure, which went down under the ground—way underground. Lights on, and it was cool. I was given the cook's tour and shown the connections to the solar sources and battery room. The rooms were large and luxurious. Screens that appeared to be windows even changed from light to dark. I was invited to sit at the dining table. Both Dolly and Nigel were seated, but Jedda asked to use the pool room.

"You have a swimming pool?"

"Yes, but Jedda's talking about the billiards room."

"Who in town knows what it's like in here?"

Nigel gazed at me and smiled. "Just our friends."

I returned the smile, but I was convinced they were having me on.

An old dog sat in a bed near the kitchen. With great effort, the dog stood up and walked over to us. This dog was pentosan deficient. Pentosan is a drug used to treat arthritis. It was unfamiliar to me when I moved to Australia. After observing its benefits for old dogs, I began to use it with arthritic horses, as well. I was impressed by how well it worked. I patted the old girl and asked her name.

"Sheba. She's thirteen." Nigel was proud of his dog.

"How does she negotiate the steps to go outside?"

"I carry her."

I cringed as I visualized an old man carrying a forty-pound dog. "I may be able to help her feel a bit better if you're interested?"

"Not if it means a trip to the vet."

I could tell he was serious.

"How about I bring her some medicine the next time I come?" I could call the clinic and ask to buy the medication that I suggest and do the weekly injections when I visit. Nigel was happy with that. I would make sure the clinic didn't lose any money in the transaction. I was never allowed to do freebies at work.

"Coffee?" Nigel stood up and refilled his cup.

"No, thanks." I'd forgotten how bad I appeared until they both stared at me and winced.

"I fell and hit a table last night. Roger stitched me up. He's the reason I'm here."

"Roger got you in the front door. We smokers need to stick together. Since Nigel won't let me smoke here, Rog and I sit out under the gums and try to kill ourselves when he visits. He knows a swift death is a good death."

"Smoking won't make for a swift death, you realize. Well, that's why I'm here."

"Okay, tell me about it." Dolly took out a notepad and wrote notes as I talked.

I proceeded to tell her about myself, my family, and Dan. I explained that Mrs. Miller was our neighbor and babysitter for the two girls and how much we loved and appreciated her. I wasn't a fan of day care and wanted the girls to start reading and hopefully develop a love of nature and learning. Mrs. Miller wasn't the greatest teacher, but she kept the girls from falling into the need for the children's banal television programs that were predominant.

"You don't like *Sesame Street*?"

"No, not really. It's a gateway program to reality television. Do you know the Kardashians?" Nigel shook his head.

"Good. That's a point in your favor." She didn't look up, but Nigel patted my back as he sat down once again. He couldn't hide his smile.

I detailed what happened the day Mrs. Miller died. "I knew she wasn't coming over to babysit on Monday. I called her on Sunday night to find out if she was any better or needed something. She said that she was no better and no worse. Dan decided to see her Sunday night. He drew her blood as she had diabetes, and he submitted it for testing the following morning.

"My friend Julie babysat our girls. Her kids, who were my backup, were sick too. Julie's a nurse at the hospital where Dan works. She stayed with the children the whole day while I worked. I attended clients all day, so I can account for my entire day." I reminded Dolly that it was the day that it rained. I was late getting home, and I called Julie. She mentioned seeing an ambulance and the police in attendance at the Miller residence.

"That night, the police took Dan down to the station and interviewed him. He didn't get home until late. The next day, the police called to interview me, as well. They took our computers, phones and even the computer at the clinic. Our house was searched, and my car was seized."

"Why are they looking at you?"

"She named me in her will as the primary beneficiary, and there's another attached page that has my signature as executor of the will. I swear, I didn't know about it, and I didn't sign it. I didn't know anything about it until the police interviewed me. She can't have had much to give to anyone. She scarcely got by. All this time, we thought she had a sister. There was no reason to kill her."

"You definitely require legal representation." Dolly tapped a pen on the table and took a long sip of her coffee.

I tried to explain my predicament. "My husband called everyone he could, and people are either too busy or still on holidays after Christmas."

Dolly stared at me. I tried to position myself with my bruise away from her line of vision.

"And you really fell? You wouldn't be the first woman in this room who was the recipient of a fist from a disgruntled husband."

"Oh, wow. Sorry, but no, no way. My husband is the most loving, gentle partner, alive."

"Let me think about it. I may know someone who can help you. I'll have to contact my friend."

"I don't think I have much time. I'm going to be arrested. Apparently, the preliminary toxicology report mentions an abnormality."

Dolly went to a small address book near the lounge. She thumbed through it and then looked hard and turned to me.

"It'll cost you plenty, but I'll do it."

"How much?" I wasn't sure she was who I wanted. There were limits to our funds.

"Complete honesty and probably sixty thousand if we go to trial. My fees are nominal, but I will hire a private investigator and maybe buy a copy fax machine. If there's a trial, it'll be in Adelaide. I'll need to have a place to stay as well."

"Well, it can't go to trial. I didn't do anything, and Mrs. Miller must have died of natural causes. The tox screen probably picked up cold medicine. For God's sake, she was sick. Why would I or anyone want to murder her?"

"A million or two. Millie was an extremely wealthy woman. Surely you knew that." I think the look on my face indicated otherwise. "Maybe not?"

Chapter 12

After two hours of planning, Jedda and I left with a "to-do" list and firm instructions on what "not to do." The second was far more critical. I was instructed not to speak to anyone, including my friends, the press, or police, without Dolly's presence. She laughed at how I had responded to the reporters. We would meet the following day, and I was to bring Angel's carrot cake and coffee. Jedda dropped me off at home and left with her list of things that Dolly required.

Dan left a message, saying there was a problem, and he wouldn't be back until late tonight. I attempted to call him, but the calls went to voice mail. Julie phoned and suggested that I come to dinner. Roger and Kendall were also coming. Because I wasn't sure whether it was appropriate, I declined. Since I had no internet and couldn't obtain some of the information that Dolly needed. I began to work on my timelines. One was my life and any "priors." The other was the immediate timeline leading up to the discovery of Mrs. Miller's body.

Dolly found it very curious that I was the target of the inquiry when Dan was the last to see Mrs. Miller. The police must know about another visitor that they aren't divulging. Dolly couldn't be reached by phone at her cousin's home. If anything came up, and I was arrested or retaken into the station for questioning, I was supposed to have Reggie drive out to get her. So, Dolly knew the head of the local police. How had I not heard of her before all of this?

I was hungry and tired, and my reproductive status was no longer in question. This critter was a demanding little blob in my uterus. I would stack on the baby weight once again. Damn, I was such a babe lately. The sacrifices women make to keep the world populated were never-ending. This would be the last for sure.

I would love to give Dan a boy, but he continued to claim that he didn't care either way. He had done more than his fair share of child care after they were born. At night, all I had to do was provide the nourishment. He did the rest.

Australia has a generous financial system to support families after a baby is born. However, I wanted to get out and work. I pumped and stored milk, and Dan stayed home as needed until the girls were a few months old, when Mrs. Miller took over.

She was a natural, despite never having children of her own. Both girls were good, and we knew we had it easy on the kid wrangling. The children never cried when either of us left. Mrs. Miller was another member of our family. We had discussed day care when the girls each hit three years of age, but Mrs. Miller arranged for the girls to attend playgroups. The girls never seemed to care if they had friends or not. Both girls were learning their letters and numbers. Mrs. Miller was worth a million dollars to me alive, not dead.

Dolly admitted she knew Mrs. Miller. While she said they weren't great friends, many years ago, she and Mrs. Miller had played bridge together. This was well before Dan and I moved to the area. Dolly admitted she was annoyed that Mrs. Miller stopped playing cards when she began her babysitting duties.

Dolly also mentioned that she knew about Mrs. Miller's wealth when Mrs. Miller suggested to Dolly that her stocks were being handled by a firm. She was concerned the firm was overcharging her. Dolly admitted that she'd examined the documents and found quite the opposite. The investment firm was doing a great job at a reasonable fee.

Mrs. Miller didn't need an income, so why did she babysit when she could live the high life without touching the principle? Dolly quoted her: "I'm living the high life. I finally get to raise some children without having to deal with them at night. I'm a grandmother."

Now I felt guilty about the times I didn't invite her to family functions or vacations. I should have checked on her that morning. I knew Dan had gone over to see her the previous night, but I also realized that she loved me and would have been pleased to see me, even if she was ill. Being charged with her death was ridiculous. I may have been guilty of neglect that morning, but I had no reason to kill her. I knew I didn't sign the document, and I sure as heck had no idea that she held any significant money or investments. It was all a shock to me.

Jedda called later in the afternoon. She'd run several errands and located Mrs. Miller's sister's obituary, which she sent to Dolly. Dolly would get them tomorrow when she came to town. Jedda found other information that Dolly had wanted. Jedda obtained background information about the other neighbors who might have had an interest in Mrs. Miller. They were good people, but a little 'bogan' and none were close to her. Jedda's auntie had worked with one of the neighbors in the silos during the harvest two years before and cared for the other neighbor when she had postnatal depression many years earlier.

Dan and I were the only people who would benefit from Mrs. Miller's death, except for her a small endowment that was to go to her church. That was the bottom line. We didn't do it. While crime was uncommon around here, a deviant could be lurking in the town. *What am I thinking? She was old and sick. The cold medication probably made the tox analysis suspicious.*

I tried to call Dan, but there was still no answer. I assumed the phone was dead. The charger was next to the bed, and the kids probably had played with the phone on the way down. I lay down for a "baby nap," as I called it. The landline ring woke me up.

The call was from the locum vet.

"Hi, Dr. Langley. It's Rich here."

"Carly," I reminded him.

"Oh, yeah. I wanted to tell you that I euthanized Cricket, and the owner was kind enough to allow me to have a peek inside."

I was impressed. Most locums don't have the time or interest to conduct postmortem examinations. "Awesome. Big C?" I was confident it had to be cancer.

"Nope, way cooler. Equine multinodular pulmonary fibrosis."

"No way?"

"Yep, I saw one in vet school. No doubt. The lungs were rock solid. I'll bet the horse had about twenty percent of her normal lung left. I took pictures. I'll send them to you."

"I've never seen one. Isn't it related to a herpes virus?"

"Well, it's thought to be linked to equine HP-5."

"Damn, I wish I could have seen it. How's everything else going?"

"What's your mobile number, and I'll send it to you."

"Small prob. No phone right now. If you can email it, that would be good. The office has my email address. Thanks so much for getting me up to speed on that. So jealous."

"I'm certain you'll be back on-board next week."

"I sure hope so. Are you at the clinic? Is the terrible Mrs. T still around?"

"Yes, I'm calling from the clinic phone."

"I can't see numbers due to the landline. Can you pass her to me?"

"Of course. Hope to meet you soon and have a proper catch-up."

"It's a bit awkward right at the moment, but yes."

There was a pause, but finally, Mrs. Tankard came on the line. She sang the "Folsom Prison Blues."

"Not funny. Quick question without revealing what we are talking about. On a scale of one to ten, how good-looking is the new guy?"

"Oh, my Lord. Are you adding adultery to your list of crimes?"

"Kendall. I'm thinking of Kendall."

"Eight to nine. Don't you have more important fish to fry? How do you like Dolly?"

"Shit. Is nothing private in this town?"

"Just Millie's murderer."

"Go to hell."

"Yep, that's a foregone conclusion. Save me a seat, though."

"Good news. Dr. Hamilton has agreed to come back when you take maternity leave."

"Let me guess. You talked to Jen Williamson."

"Didn't have to. I could see the glow. I didn't roll off a turnip truck, Carly."

"Is he a match for Kendall?"

"Maybe. I'll do some reconnaissance and decide if he's ready to date again. If you remove yourself from the suspect list, I can withdraw my restraining order."

Chapter 13

I was becoming anxious. It was now after midnight, and Dan hadn't returned. It was difficult to sleep alone. I needed his rhythmic breathing to put me to sleep. I had slept too much in the afternoon, and I was reliving the last few days. I attempted to remember my recent conversation with Mrs. Miller. She'd talked about a July cruise trip that she and her friend were planning. Mrs. Miller was concerned about how we were going to manage child care. Her friend lived in the Barossa Valley, which was south of here. Her friend had returned from a cruise to China. I thought that was a bit extravagant for a woman on a pension, but now I realized that was not the case.

She was sneezing and had a runny nose. She reminded me that I needed to buy tissues for the house. That was Friday. I'd purchased the tissues and called her twice over the weekend. She said it was only a cold. A nurse was coming to the house on Sunday. After the nurse examined her, Mrs. Miller called to say that she was too ill to care for the children, and she was worried that she had already infected them.

I had responded that if it was catchy, they would get it, and we would deal with it when they started to show signs of the cold. Sunday night, when we talked, she mentioned her regular doctor was out of town. Her young and eager doctor was Lydia Johnson, who worked with Dan in the hospital one night a week. She was becoming the most sought-after doctor for women in the town. Even I went to Lydia. She wasn't married, but she had a son she described as the product of her misspent youth, who was a redhead and a promising cricket player, too. He was old enough to go to one of the private boarding schools in the city. She was thinking about moving back to Adelaide so her son, Gavin, could receive more coaching.

Lydia wanted to try to avoid any problems due to prejudice regarding redheads. Lydia also had a friend in Adelaide, whom she saw regularly, and they were considering living together. She never said anything, but I thought it was a woman who had visited once. Anything other than a traditional relationship in a small town was frowned upon. Gavin would be the object of any persecution. I'd met the woman who worked in an accounting firm, and I thought she was rough.

Because Dan was aware Lydia was out of town, he went to see Mrs. Miller on Sunday night. Dan obtained a blood sample and prescribed some medication to be delivered the next day. I'm an idiot. The drugs were delivered sometime in the morning. That person would have seen Mrs. Miller sometime after nine when the pharmacy opened. I made a note. For the first time, I felt I had a lead that might be valuable to the police. I wanted to call them, but I took Dolly's advice and waited until I talked to her.

It was well after midnight when Dan returned. He climbed into bed. Without even saying anything, he spooned me and fell asleep. I was annoyed. It was hot, but we had a ceiling fan that helped. We slept with a single sheet, which was common in the summer. The daytime temperatures reached the nineties and even a hundred degrees regularly. Our house cooled slowly after sunset. I was looking forward to a home with air-conditioning.

After an hour, I woke up to hear Dan on the phone. When he returned to bed, I inquired, "What's going on?" I was trying to make sense of Dan on the phone in the middle of the night.

"The hospital called for permission to give Mrs. McClatchy some pain meds. She had a hysterectomy yesterday, and Roger couldn't be contacted to authorize the medication. Go to bed, darling. After I have a bite to eat, I'll join you."

The next morning Dan rolled over and gave me the signal that he was in the mood. "We haven't been alone in the morning in more than a year. I'm not wasting any time."

"You're gone all day, come home late, wake me up in the middle of the night, and expect me to do the horizontal hokey pokey?"

"Well, yes."

"Do you promise to behave, assist me with my pending arrest, and visit me in jail every day?"

"Maybe. If you're guilty, I might come only every other day."

I kicked him, but he could sense my resistance was wavering. He massaged the back of my neck and tickled my back. All resistance faded.

Later, as we lay together, I remembered his message about being late. "Why were you back so late?"

"It was really nothing. I saw an old patient who had moved down to Adelaide to be closer to the chemo unit. Do you remember Mr. Doudle?"

"Vaguely."

"He's not coping, so I drove him into his chemo appointment and, by chance, saw his oncologist. He appreciated the support. The phone went dead from the girls playing Angry Birds."

"Yeah, I figured that. What did your mom say?"

"She was supportive. She thinks I should leave you as usual, but she is confident you didn't kill Mrs. Miller for a few thousand dollars."

"Uh, well, we need to talk."

"Tonight. I need to get to work."

We showered and were eating breakfast when the phone rang. Dan was called to the hospital and was now urgently needed. Dan left on his bike, but he suggested that we take more advantage of our childless situation and possibly recreate a similar scene tonight. He hugged me and rubbed the back of my neck. Resistance was futile again. I kissed him and told him I was going to see Dolly. He left the mobile phone and car for me.

Jedda wasn't coming in this morning. She and her classmates were going to Adelaide University to tour the campus and facility. She had a meeting with the medical-school personnel. They took a particular interest in her because she would help them with their minority-recruitment requirements in securing government grants. She knew she was getting preferential treatment, but Jedda didn't care. She simply wanted acceptance into med school. Without hesitation, she would use her heritage to its full advantage.

I remember hearing regional students received extra points on their exam scores, which eventually determined their university placement. I was now backing Jedda. My bosses' daughter, Kate, was aiming for veterinary school, so they weren't competing, fortunately. Acceptance in either veterinary or medical school was competitive. These girls were so young to make such important decisions. I wondered about this system and the choices my girls would have to make someday if we were still living in Australia when they finished high school. I was reminded of the little parasite sitting in my uterus playing havoc with my blood sugar, resulting in a natural desire to toss my breakfast.

The news vans had returned to the front of the house. I had to maneuver the car around them to drive to the roadhouse. Dolly wanted carrot cake and coffee. The place was packed. Angel's daughter saw me and rushed out with the required life-saving material. She told me that it was on the house. "Mum said to thank you for all the business."

"Tell her thanks. I'll be expecting home deliveries soon."

"Good luck with that one. Mum doesn't do jail runs." She laughed and turned back to the roadhouse. "Duty calls."

A van followed me from the roadhouse on my way to Nigel's property. I lost it by driving a longer route. When I entered the house, I got the look. "About time."

"Sorry. I was followed."

"By the police?"

"No, reporters."

Dolly eyed Nigel and pointed to a chair. "You can bet the police are following you."

"I haven't seen any. Are you sure?"

"They may be rural, but they aren't hicks. What did you learn yesterday?"

"First things first." I had to estimate Sheba's weight and calculate a dose of Pentosan for the poor arthritic dog. I injected the medication under the skin and demonstrated to Nigel how to follow up if I didn't return. He'd performed injections previously and noted he could do so if needed.

We perused my timelines and discussed the neighbors and other potential suspects. I remarked the chemists must have delivered medicine at some time during the morning. "Dan wrote a script for antibiotics and requested that some cold meds be thrown in, although they didn't require a script."

"I should meet your husband. When can I meet him?"

"Since he's working days right now. He's available any time after five o'clock."

"No good. I don't work after gin o'clock." She paused and glanced up. "Oh, what the hell. How about tonight?"

"Sometimes he's late if he has an emergency. Most of the time, though, he's home about fiveish at the latest. You know, we still don't have our phones, regular cars, and computers back yet. When do you think they'll be returned?"

"God knows. I'll call Reggie when I go into town later." While Reggie wasn't in charge of the investigation, he still was our local contact policeman.

"I feel as if an entire second society exists here in this town that I don't know about. You seem to know everyone, and yet I don't know anything about you."

"Good. Let's go over your timeline for the last two weeks. I called the clinic. Their computer had been returned, and they were printing out your appointments for the last few weeks. Stop in and get that today. I'm going into the police station. I figure it's time they knew who was representing you and your husband. That'll be fun." She rolled her eyes. "Am I representing you both?" She stared at me and paused.

"Yes, please." I hesitated. "Do you want to tell me something?" I was wondering what other interactions she may have had with our local police.

"Tell you about what?"

"Have you dealt with the police here?" I still didn't know much about this woman.

"Just a few times. Reggie and I play poker once a week, and I assisted a client with a drunk-driving charge a few years ago." Dolly glanced over at Nigel, who laughed.

"No, it wasn't me." Nigel was quick to respond when I stared at him.

Dolly took a sip of coffee and commented she couldn't discuss it. I couldn't guess, but I was reasonably sure it must be someone I must know—Roger?

"Okay, let's review this. Do you say you didn't have any physical contact at all with Millie after she went home on Friday, and you worked all day on Monday? Also, as far as you know for sure, the last people to see Millie were your husband and probably a delivery person from the chemist?"

"Julie may have viewed someone from the window when she was babysitting for me that day, but she didn't mention it."

"I'll call her. And I'll call Seth at the chemist. He usually plays poker, as well."

"Is there anyone in the community you don't know?"

"Carly, aside from you and your husband, nope. Remember, I've been coming here for years."

I was ordered to stay out of sight, which was fine with me. I was dismissed. I would be a housewife today, do laundry, and clean. Jedda wouldn't be back until the girls were home late next week. I missed them and decided to call them when I got home. Dan's mom often took them shopping or for a ferry ride to Manly to visit her friends. I thought I might catch up on reading some veterinary journals when the phone rang. It was the locum.

"Carly, Rich Hamilton here. How many Caesars have you done in cattle?"

"A few. You have one?"

"Yep. In truth, I haven't done one, except in vet school."

"Well, whose cow?"

"George Hughes. Do you know him?"

"Oh, Jesus, that'll be interesting."

"Should I bail?"

"No, he's one of our best clients. He's a retired stockman. If he can't get it out, it'll be well and truly dead. Not game to attempt a fetotomy?"

"Not really. What are you up to?"

"Well, not much. It'll be a challenge. George has a crush, but his cows are crazy with a capital C."

"I'll be by in twenty. Don't bother dressing up."

"You can count on it. Remember, I'm only your technical advisor. I'm not working."

"Yep, great. Thanks."

Chapter 14

Ten minutes later, Rich showed up in the old truck. Mine was still getting a new front grille. I had changed into my work clothes, minus the work shirt with the clinic logo in case someone took a photo of me. The reporters were all watching and holding microphones. I smiled and chatted with Rich pretending to be unaware of their presence.

I didn't shake Rich's hand or even suggest we were together in front of the news crews. Rich was of average height with dark brown or black hair and a tan complexion. Mrs. T was correct. Good-looking, but not movie-star good-looking. He was tall enough for Kendall. He appeared to be fit and had a friendly smile. He didn't waste time with small talk. We drove out and away, and an entourage of cars followed us.

"Don't mind my friends. We'll lose them at the gate.

He glanced in the rearview mirror. "We might as well get the formalities out of the way. Are you guilty?"

"Nope. Anything you care to report, Dr. Hamilton? Any run-ins with the law?" I smiled as I turned the tables on my driver.

"A few speeding tickets and a DUI when I was eighteen. Been a good boy for the last six or so years now. Glad to hear you're innocent. We're going pretty far from civilization, and I would be nervous if you said you were actually guilty."

"There's a lot at stake. Have you tried Angel's carrot cake yet?" I gazed seriously at him and tried to hide a smile.

"Nope. Is it to die for? I mean murder for?"

"Was that pun intended? I won't give up her carrot cake for love or money, and Angel insists she won't do deliveries to the slammer."

"Will you present that as evidence at your trial?"

Has a sense of humor. I liked that. "Not gonna be a trial. I have a legal eagle on my side. And there's a bit about evidence. Motive aside, since I didn't do it, any evidence would be deliberately planted." I needed to consider that idea.

We drove up to the gate. Oh, how I wanted to give the news people the one-finger salute, but that would be plain stupid. I resisted and controlled myself. Dolly would be happy. I realized we were safe, as George's property had a gate, and it was a long drive to the corral.

The driveway was along a barbed-wire fence. The cocky gate was complicated. A long pole was placed in a loop on the bottom of the solid fence post. A levered arm secured the top of the gate to the top end of the barbed-wire gate, which, if you had never seen one, would be challenging. It took me several tries to work it out when I first encountered it. Rich stepped out of the truck and had it opened, was through, and then closed it quickly. The man knew his rural gates.

We had a long drive down to the corrals. There was little vegetation, but the dust hid us from the road. When we were out of sight of the paparazzi, we both relaxed. Until we saw the cow…gulp. She was huge, and she was not impressed with life now. No, sir.

Rich took one look, and I knew he was looking for a "get the heck out of Dodge" option. I was, too. She was bawling and running into fences, and she seemed to have no sign of pending birth.

I introduced George to Rich. George had been a stockman for one of the largest pastoral companies in Australia. He was a kindhearted, caring individual when it came to his family and stock. He loved to tease me due to my accent and my lack of knowledge about Australian livestock.

George scrutinized Rich and shook hands. "Carly, you finally got some good help?"

"Well, cows aren't our strong suits, but we're here to serve. I'm really tagging along."

"Yeah, I heard. I hope it's sorted soon. We would hate to lose you. It's tough to get large-animal vets up here."

Rich appeared to be nervous. I could tell George was observing him. George was about seventy and was retired and ran a few cows as a sideline. Furthermore, he was delving into racehorses. George wasn't experiencing much success on the traditional racetracks. George was hitting the bush tracks with his filly and a recently castrated gelding. He'd won a few local races and was having a great time with his granddaughter, who was riding for him. George and his wife, Lynette, were raising their two grandkids. Their daughter and son-in-law had been killed in a plane crash many years ago when flying from one station to the other. The older grandchild was now in Adelaide and had secured a coveted apprenticeship with a plumber. This program required four years, and the lad would have a ticket to wealth and fame in the end.

Karen Birch was the last grandchild to go. Then George and Lynette would be kid-less and free to wander around Australia in their caravan. They wanted to become gray nomads and circumnavigate Australia, along with many other retirees. George would never say anything, but I could tell it had been hard on him. Losing a daughter and son-in-law and taking on two children were not what he and Lynette planned. Karen was a smart kid, but her ambitions were moving to Adelaide and riding racehorses for the city trainers. That is, if he and Rich survived this outback adventure.

George was all-business when he needed to be. "Well, let's get her in the crush and get this calf out."

Rich was hoping for a vaginal delivery. "Do you want me to feel and see if we can do it without surgery?"

George pointed to the calf jack next to the corral. "If that were possible, I would have done it myself and saved a lot of money." He mumbled something I could not hear as he walked into the pen and started to move the cow toward the chute opening. The cow was angry. She charged George and Rich, who had joined him. Rich stepped into the oncoming path and deflected her assault, thereby keeping George from being trampled.

"Thanks, mate." George was a bit embarrassed.

"No prob. You know, as you said, Carly and I will make a lot of money. If you can't sign the check, you're no good to us."

I realized that bastard knew cattle. He'd been having George and me on. He deflected the charging cow as though he'd done it a thousand times.

"This isn't your first rodeo." I think he could tell I was surprised, verging on pissed. He didn't require my presence.

"I was raised on a cattle ranch in Texas before my family moved to Florida." Rich smiled sheepishly. George walked to the other side of the cattle chute, and I gave Rich a look that would have put many men in their graves. "I do know cattle, but I've never done a C-section on my own, honestly," he whispered.

Rich quickly loaded the cow into the small corral leading to the chute where she would be confined. The cow had been in the cattle crush earlier when George and his friend Ron both had a go at extracting the calf. By using chains and the calf jack, which is a lever device to which obstetrical chains are attached, it can be used to leverage a calf out of a cow. This is the way most dystocias are sorted. The cow was reluctant to repeat that experience, but Rich got her into the crush and opened the side panel, and we set to work.

We had cordless clippers, and Rich clipped a large patch on the cow's left flank. He scrubbed it and systematically began to inject the local anesthetic in a line from the top of the flank down toward her ventral abdomen. We tied her left foot back with a loose rope so she could stand and shift her weight but would not be able to kick us. The area was given a second scrub with antiseptics. While Rich was preparing, I set up a table with the instruments, surgical gloves, and suture material.

Rich wasted no time starting an incision in her flank. The cow was surprisingly quiet and tolerated the procedure well. Since George assured us the calf was dead, we weren't in a hurry to get it out. Unlike foals, calves will live for many hours after birthing commences, so a caesarian section is not a rush job. With foals, minutes count because you have a critically short time before the foal dies.

Because the incision seemed a bit small, and George said it was an enormous calf, Rich extended his incision. There was blood, but Rich knew enough not to try to tie off individual bleeders, as the blood loss was insignificant, despite appearances. He bluntly separated the muscles and reached into the abdomen, and I saw him smile. "Got it." He pulled out a leg that was covered by the uterus. I saw what he was smiling about, but George was conveniently standing on the other side of the crush.

Rich made another incision through the uterine wall, reached in, and grabbed the calf's leg. I joined him, and together we pulled out the very alive calf. I quickly rubbed and stimulated the calf. It was especially active and not big at all.

George knew we had it out yet still didn't venture over on the business side of the crush. "I told you it was big."

"Yeah, you did," was all Rich said with a grin on his face. I handed him some suture material. I put on surgical gloves and held out the uterus, which was contracting rapidly, so Rich could close the incision. With that accomplished, I was not needed for the abdominal-wall closure. I peeled off my gloves, handed Rich suture material, returned to work on the calf, and started to clean up.

I had not eaten and felt nauseous from the demands of my own little uterine parasite. Being the vomit queen, I was quite adept at vomiting discreetly. I went around to the far side of the truck and puked while Rich finished the skin layer. I thought George might have seen me, but he was in no position to discuss vomit. George was somewhat green, as well.

Rich finished closing the incision. He informed George that it was safe to come around to the other side, where George saw an extremely active calf attempting to stand.

"Damn, I must be getting old. Ronny's not going to believe this. It's practically a runt."

"Average size to me." Rich retrieved the instruments and headed for the car, where I was busy cleaning up and avoiding anything that might set me up for another bout of nausea.

Watching Rich, who was wiping down the table that George had provided, he inquired, "Are they gonna hire you for a permanent position?" George was impressed and slightly embarrassed.

"Nope. I only have a temporary work visa. I can stay for just two years, and I already blew my first six months in Cairns."

Rich reached into the backseat, rummaged around, and handed me a biscuit. I smiled sheepishly. Rich went back to the corral, gave the cow some penicillin, and handed George the remaining antibiotics to follow up for the next few days. He opened the crush, and the cow jumped out and turned to her calf. The calf was up on its hind legs and rocking on bent knees. He was almost ready to stand.

We got in the truck and dropped George off at the house. He thanked us and asked if we wanted to come in for some tea or coffee. Rich observed me and could see I was barely holding it together. "I want a rain check on that, George. I've got to get back. Carly sets a fast pace, which I must follow. Thanks, though. Hope to see you again before I leave."

"Yep, but I have fifty head to preg-check and ten more cows still to calve in the next few weeks. Your boss won't be happy until you have my last dollar. Highway robbery, you know."

"Maybe you'll let Carly, or I have a try at getting the calf out without surgery next time."

"Count on it." George smiled and shook his head. "I'm getting old."

While we drove down the long dirt road, I dreaded the reception at the gate. "Geez, I hope my fans are gone." I thought about my receding black eye. "You know, I don't always look this good." I rubbed my aching head. I was feeling sick again. "You got any more of those biscuits?"

"Cookies, Langley, cookies. We're among our people, and we can call them the proper name." He reached in the back and handed me his lunch box. "Have as much as you want. I don't want you puking in the truck. How far along are you, anyway?"

"Just a few weeks. This is way worse than the others. The good news is that it doesn't last long. I hope." Rich was a nice guy. I wondered if he had children of his own back in the States. He appeared to be a few years younger than me and hence was a few years younger than Kendall. "Hey, would you be opposed if I set you up with my friend?"

"I'm still in mourning from the last one. I realize I'm a guy, and I should be back on board, but she kind of broke my heart."

"Yeah, you're letting the side down on that one. My friend's name is Kendall, and she's a copper. She's not bad looking."

"Can't ignore looks, but I need a traveling partner. She sounds kind of grounded."

"Yeah. Oh, well. How about you come to dinner next week if I'm not in jail?"

"Will your friend be there?"

"I'll make sure she is. You never know. Kendall may make you want to settle down, or you may make her want to travel. Any food preferences?"

"I'm vegetarian."

"Bullshit. There's a ham sandwich in your lunch box."

"No preferences. I like anything."

As we came around the corner, only one car was waiting. I recognized Kendall and smiled. "You can have a sneak peek right now."

Chapter 15

I jumped out of the car and walked over to the gate. "Howdy, partner." I had my back to the truck as I tried to get Kendall's attention without Rich seeing my face. I raised my eyebrows and smiled.

"I thought you'd been sidelined." Kendall didn't look happy. She waved at the flies that had gathered. "I came to observe a C-section with the new vet. Have you met Rich Hamilton?" I pointed back, so he couldn't see me. "Hubba, hubba."

Kendall stared at me and frowned. "Nope, but nothing like a girl in uniform to attract a guy," she whispered.

Rich, who was sitting in the car with the air conditioner going, could not hear our conversation. Kendall was a fit, good-looking woman. She had dark straight hair and a dark complexion from her distant Aboriginal heritage. The police uniform never made anyone look good. I hoped Rich could overlook the belt and walkie-talkie that hung from her hip.

"I'm supposedly watching a murderess and waiting for the said woman to make a slip. I replaced another copper from the city, who got sick of the flies."

"Well, sadly, you're wasting your time. I don't suppose you have any news about the toxicology report?"

"Carly, Carly, Carly. You know I can't divulge any information about my work."

"Yeah, I forgot. Duty first." I admired her dedication to her work but was annoyed that she took it so far.

"I hear you lawyered up." She didn't sound impressed.

I opened the gate and signaled for Rich to come through. As he drove past us, he opened the window and smiled. "Hello, officer. Did I do anything wrong?"

"Well, that depends. Consorting with the prime subject of an investigation might be considered as something wrong."

"Well, if it helps, I interrogated her, and she says she didn't do it." He smiled again, and I could see he was interested in Kendall. "I have a vested interest in throwing her in jail. If she's in the slammer, I get to keep my job."

"American?" Kendall smiled broadly.

"Through and through."

This was looking promising. "Hey, you two, Take it up later. I have to get home."

Kendall shook her head. "How about I take you home, and Doctor Doolittle heads back to the office?"

"She's a puker. You'll have to chance her chucking in the police car." Rich reached into his lunch box and handed me another cookie. "Another cookie to toss—one for the road."

"Thanks." I took it.

"Simply for medicinal purposes." He laughed as he handed me his last one.

Kendall caught the significance and thanked him. As Rich drove off, Kendall turned to me and asked, "And?"

"And what?"

"Is he single?"

"On the rebound and quite bruised, according to the terrible Mrs. T, but he's recovering."

"I wouldn't mind helping with the recovery process."

"Oh, so you're interested?"

"Maybe. One thing I can tell you is the coroner is releasing Millie's body, and she'll be buried rather than cremated."

"Oh, good. I guess I'll have to arrange for the funeral."

"Not so fast. You're not going to the funeral, are you?"

"Why wouldn't I?"

"I doubt they'll let you near her until you're cleared."

I don't know why this upset me so much, but I would meet and discuss this with Dolly tonight. I wished to honor Mrs. Miller. While funerals weren't my thing, she'd mentioned a funeral she had recently attended. She admitted how disappointed she was that people who didn't know the departed arranged it and failed to mention the woman's accomplishments. I knew that she wanted a religious ceremony. Still, she also wanted humor and lots of flowers to go to the local nursing home after the reception. She'd visited her friend with early Alzheimer's numerous times at the nursing home and found the place dreary. She always brought flowers on her visits.

This made me consider what I knew about the woman with many hidden facets of her life. I would start with Dolly tonight. Kendall dropped me off at home. As per usual, the television crews were waiting. I didn't wave to Kendall as I didn't want them to know we were friends. I suggested we have dinner the next week, but she thought we should wait to socialize until the matter was cleared up. She was going to give Rich a few days, and maybe she'd contact him and invite him over to a home-cooked meal.

When I entered the house, I checked the messages on our landline phone. Julie had called and said she would stop by tomorrow. I suspected the police had interviewed her. I called Dan and left a message asking him to get home as early as possible to go to Dolly's together.

I felt something was different when I entered the house. I was sure I had left the counter clean, and the dishes were on the rack, but a knife was lying in the sink. It was a dull knife, and neither

Dan nor I ever used it. I knew it wasn't Jedda, so I assumed that Dan had come home for lunch. *Weird.* With the throngs of press out on the street, no one could enter the house without being seen. I must be imagining it. "Pregnancy brain" was a term used by the clinic nurses who worked with me during my other pregnancies.

Food and sleep, in that order, and I would be right. I overslept and realized we were due at Dolly's in thirty minutes. Dan hadn't returned and had not answered my call. He may not have received the message. I attempted to call him at the hospital, but the receptionist said he'd left early. I checked, and the car was still parked in the driveway. Where the hell was he? I wouldn't trade my husband for anyone aside from Ryan Reynolds, but he was not perfect, and there were times I could brain him.

I needed our phones to be returned. That subject was on my list for Dolly, too. I tried to think about where he might be. I picked up our phone he had left for me that morning and discovered several missed calls from a number I didn't recognize. It might be one of his colleagues or any of the people he dealt with. I wasn't game to call back and invade his privacy. I could account for every single minute of the seven years we had been married. I ignored the first remote fleeting thought of unaccountability. Many of my friends had husbands who had strayed. I counted myself as lucky.

Twenty minutes later, he rode up on his bike. He had no idea that we were summoned to Dolly's. He'd left the hospital early to visit an elderly patient at the nursing home, who was now close to dying. He wanted to make sure the gentleman was being cared for, and the family was happy with the slow process.

We quickly jumped in the car and headed to Dolly and Nigel's house. Dan knew the way. "Have you been there before?"

"Nope, but everyone knows where it is."

"I didn't."

"That's because they don't have any large animals." Dan patted my thigh, and then his hand went up toward the restricted zone.

"Danger. That area is now under the control of a hormonally crazy pregnant lady. Enter at your own risk."

"Can't wait." Dan smiled wickedly.

We drove up the driveway where Nigel, who appeared to have already started the cocktail hour, greeted us. "She's on the warpath. You're eating into her after-hours period. Charges will apply."

Chapter 16

Even drunk, which she clearly was, Dolly was on top of her game. We entered, and I waited for Dan to whistle, but he glanced around and politely waited for introductions to be made. I couldn't believe how nonchalant Dan was about this amazing place. He sat down at the kitchen table without even asking. I was slightly embarrassed about his familiarity. He'd never been there, but he acted like this home belonged to an old friend.

"So, Daniel? Do you go by Daniel or juss Dan?" Dolly slurred her words, and her pen strayed, leaving lines on her notebook.

"Dan's fine, Mrs. Myler."

"Dolly. Juss call me Dolly."

I nearly laughed when she slurred "juss" instead of "just." I could see Dan's concern, and I didn't blame him. We'd obviously hired a lush. Dan sat quietly and listened, but I could tell that he was sitting up straighter and was getting that edgy look I had witnessed when he was stressed.

"Daniel, will you tell me about your lass visit with my good friend, Millie? What was her demeanor, and how 'wuth' her health?"

Dan recounted his last visit while I sat quietly without contradicting him. A couple of statements weren't entirely accurate, but I didn't see any reason to correct what he said. When he finished, he smiled and looked in my direction, and firmly took my hand.

"This all seems fine. Can you tell me about your last visit with Mrs. Miller?"

What the hell? He just told her his account of his last visit.

"I think I'll juss turn on the tape recorder. Damn, where did I put it?" Dolly glanced around but made no effort to get up.

I responded. "We can use our phone. We can record and send it to you through a message." My confidence was draining quickly. Dan and I looked at each other, and I could tell what we were both thinking.

Dan repeated his version. Once again, it was slightly different from the description he had previously given to Dolly. I didn't say anything about that either, but I did have questions.

"Did you talk to the police about returning our phones and computers?"

"Yep." That was all she said - simply "yep." I tried to be polite and not upset her, but I was ready to bail on this woman. "They said they would get back to me." She paused and reexamined her notes. I could tell she was having difficulty reading them.

"Maybe I should come back in the morning when you've had some time to consider all of this." I was pissed and didn't want to go further. I think Dan was shocked. Neither of us had seen anything that resembled legal expertise.

"Well, yes. I think we've done enough for today." She reached for the gin bottle and pointed toward the door. As we stepped out, we met Nigel coming back into the house.

Nigel saluted us and said good-bye, and I could have sworn he was high. As we walked to the car, I glanced down and saw the unmistakable track of a bicycle. How Nigel could ride a bike at his age was beyond me. It didn't matter. We were moving on. I knew Dan wouldn't put up with this when so much was at stake.

After we got in the car, everything hit me. I started to cry while Dan attempted to comfort me. "Hey, it's going to be okay, Carls. We can find someone else to represent you. I'm sure there's someone somewhere, and my mum will help with the costs."

I could barely speak. We were going to be financially ruined by these circumstances. Even when I was found innocent, we would pay a fortune to clear my name. The disruption to our reputations would destroy any prospects of being accepted back in the community. Finding a job in another state would be ridiculous. The vet board would have a black mark against my name. Dan would be tarnished, by association, as well.

I noticed a television crew was waiting on the road as we drove out of Nigel's property, and I knew I had to pull myself together for public consumption. I dried my eyes, blew my excessively runny nose, and sat up straight. My face was red, but I hoped that I could get into the house without anyone noticing I'd been crying. The black eye was still prominent.

Dan dropped me off and went to pick up a pizza. I reached for the keys and realized that he had them. I had to sit in the backyard until he came home. As I went through the gate, I noticed the latch was broken. The tin on the gate was also scratched. Someone had been in our backyard—*those frigging reporters*. Where was the limit to these intrusive parasites? That started me off again, and I began to cry. It was the pregnancy hormones that made me quite emotional.

Dan finally returned and brought pizza and more bad news. Another solicitor from Adelaide, with criminal defense experience, declined to be involved. Was there no limit to my misery? "Carls, you have my vote to fire Dolly. We have no other options to date, though. It's your call."

"I'll meet her in the morning and see what she has in mind. Maybe she's got a suggestion for someone else. I can't see her doing anything that's going to hurt my case. Oh, shit, what case? This entire thing is ridiculous. For God's sake, Mrs. Miller died. She wasn't murdered. There should be an end to all of this. I wonder when that bloody tox report is coming in, so we can put it to rest."

We ate pizza, and I showered and told Dan about the caesarian I assisted on today with the locum. I mentioned that we might have him and Kendall over, so they could meet.

"Is he in his late twenties, of medium build with dark hair, and I would say a seven out of ten?"

"Eight out of ten, but he's several years younger than you are. Did you already meet him?"

"Kendall was eating at the pizza shop with someone new."

"That little sneak. Well, that cancels any dinner plans. Kendall met him at George's. She was assigned to watch me, and I introduced them where she was waiting next to George's gate. The police are following me. I hope something happens between them. She deserves a nice guy."

"Is he a nice guy?"

I thought about the cookies he gave me when I was experiencing morning sickness. "Yes, he is. Better watch out. I wonder if he would be interested in an older pregnant woman?"

"He's not in your league, baby."

"It's another kid-less night. Are we taking advantage, or are you too old for more than one go a day?"

"Take off your top, and let me see how the pregnancy's progressing, which reminds me. You should schedule a prenatal visit."

"Yep, I'll make an appointment next week. Lydia's in Adelaide this week, isn't she?"

"I think you should go straight to the gyno this time. You aren't as young as you used to be."

"Well, I need to obtain a referral letter, anyway. I may be a doctor's wife, but no one is going to see me without a referral."

"I'll give you one. There's got to be some privileges for being the doctor's wife."

"If you insist. Have you got something against Lydia these days?"

"She's somewhat stressed. She's trying to decide about a significant change in her circumstances and lifestyle."

"Got it. Which gyno?"

"Mr. Lim."

"I don't know the reason they go through school, with all the years it takes them to become a specialist, and next they go from wanting to be called Dr. back to Mr."

"Yeah, I know. Now get over here. I'm not giving you a referral without a proper exam."

"Oooh, are we playing doctor again?"

Hours later, I woke up and heard Dan talking in the kitchen. I tried to listen, and it sounded as though he was arguing with someone. One nurse always fought with him about patient treatments. He returned and enveloped me.

"Bad night at the hospital?"

"You could say that. I'll sort it out in the morning." He stroked my neck.

"As long as there are no unauthorized deaths." I fell asleep immediately. In the morning, we called the girls, and both of us talked to them. They were going to the zoo with the neighbor children. They showed minimal signs of being homesick. The plan was for them to fly home on Monday. I would drive to Adelaide and pick them up from the airport since I wasn't working.

I feared the interrogation with Dan's mother. However, if I could convince her of my innocence, a jury would be a walk in

103

the park. I considered inviting Kendall or Julie to accompany me, so no one got their undies in a wringer.

Dan rode his bike to work again, and this time he took the cell phone in case I needed to call him. I was headed to the roadhouse at ten o'clock to pick up the required carrot cake and drive to Dolly's. I planned to assess her competence. If she failed, I would sack her. I was not looking forward to the encounter.

The landline rang. It was Kendall. "Yep, you're right. Great guy. I'm in."

"In love?" I was laughing. Only God knows why, but some levity was refreshing.

"No, maybe in serious 'like.' But it's a start." She began to sing "Summer Nights" from *Grease.*

"It might be over by fall."

"Maybe, but those summer nights."

"Tell me more, tell me more."

"A pizza date next week."

"Wedding bells, wedding bells?" I sang to the *Grease* tune.

"Enough, Langley. You left a message to call?"

"Any chance you are off from work and can go with me to Adelaide to pick up the kiddos on Monday?"

"In the remote chance, you aren't in jail? Possibly. I'll check with the boss about it. Not losing my job by consorting with the enemy."

A chill went through me. "You know something I don't?"

"You know better than to ask."

"Inquiring is the better part of finding out what the hell's going on. I definitely wish the tox report would come through."

"Hey, got to go. I need to get ready for a blue-light dance for the unruly cretin teens."

"Well, glad something good is coming from this situation."

"Early days on the new guy. But so far, all systems go for launch."

I went down to the basement to do some laundry. Our basement was wet from the recent rain. The musty smell was unusual, as was the recent deluge which had caused some minor flooding. I still had a creepy feeling about a possible intruder. I'd mentioned the knife to Dan, and he said that he'd left it in the sink. He'd used it to get a rock out of his shoe. That didn't explain the marks on the gate leading to the backyard. He had no explanation for that, and he told me to be careful and keep the shades pulled.

There was a door in the basement and steps leading up to the backyard. The door had been jammed for a while now, and we'd never bothered to fix it or even lock it. It would take dynamite to get it open. We usually had the sliding latch in the lock position, but it was broken. Nevertheless, I was glad to start the laundry and returned upstairs. Dan could replace the lock.

I wondered how Jedda was doing. She was due back from her university visit today. I hoped she would be able to make the transition to university and living in the city. I'd met many capable high school students who aspired to go on with their education but were not willing to leave home or our town to pursue their dreams. Australia was different from the States because there was no expectation that university students would live on campus or even in dorms. Most students lived at home and commuted to university. In our town, the commute was two hours each way. She would have to find a place to live in Adelaide.

I'd have killed for a computer, but alas, the police were still examining and holding ours. To hell with it. I drove to the police station. I saw Reggie, who was entering the office. He had two bags and greeted me cautiously.

"Since you have legal representation, I can't really discuss anything. However, while you're here, I can tell you that your solicitor has filed to have all your items returned, and it seems we must comply."

"Everything? Even our computer?"

"What about Mrs. Miller's body?"

"It's over at the morgue. I can't say any more. We'll get everything after you sign the release documents. Well, except for your clinic car. That's down at headquarters in Adelaide. It'll be here this afternoon."

I signed the papers, and one of the deputies helped me load our cell phones, several boxes of documents, and our computers into my car. I returned home and threaded the needle of reporters and vans back into my driveway. A reporter watched me bringing several bags of our possessions back into the house, and she stepped up and offered assistance.

"I know I'm old, but I am well-preserved if you need a hand." It was the older reporter whom I had, let's face it, insulted a few days ago. She smiled and seemed genuine.

"Well, thanks. My counsel has forbidden me to speak to anyone."

"Good advice. I hear you got Dolly Myler. Interesting. We all thought she was finished."

"I'd better do it alone." As I replied, a bag of papers tore, and papers went everywhere. The reporter helped retrieve the scattered documents. She handed me the pages and returned to her van. It made me think about the reporters parked outside my door. Most were young and eager, but this woman was old. I assumed she had passed her use-by date, and she was hanging on to her job by agreeing to sit in the boonies, waiting for a break in a case that might not go anywhere. Knowing I was innocent, and this story sure as hell was a dead end, I nearly felt sad for her. Almost.

It appeared that she may have spent a fortune on plastic surgery to keep herself looking acceptable for the camera. I wondered about her life as I messaged Dan that we had reconnected to the outside world before I drove to Dolly's.

Chapter 17

Dolly was outside, talking on her phone, with a cigarette dangling from her mouth. Nigel was nowhere to be seen. She waved and pointed to the house. I gave her the thumbs up as I entered the house. I could hear Nigel in the kitchen singing opera. He wasn't bad for an old man. Since he didn't hear me approaching, he was singing uninhibited. He had to be in his eighties, but his voice sounded young and in perfect pitch.

I coughed, and he turned and blushed. "You weren't supposed to hear that."

"Sorry, Dolly sent me inside. She's on the phone."

"A perpetual state, I'm afraid."

"May I help you with the dishes?" The place was a mess. I started to clear plates from the table. It seemed to me as if they had other visitors the previous evening.

He realized I figured that a bomb had gone off. "Poker night."

"Oh, are you richer or poorer?"

"I don't play. Dolly lost her shirt last night. I think your seamstress, Roger, was the benefactor of the night's activities." He glanced at my ever-decreasing black eye.

I laughed. That was probably the reason the hospital contacted Dan last night. Roger's surgical cases were often complicated. They frequently required adjustments with postoperative analgesia. "Let me help you anyway."

"I can already see a difference in Sheba."

"Excellent news." That stuff is the bomb. I knew she was going to be even better in a few days.

As we were finishing the dishes, Dolly sat down at the kitchen table and opened a file. "I hear you already retrieved your phones and computers. Their application to the court was flawed, so the investigators had to give them back. Unfortunately, the damage was already done. However, the good news is that anything that would implicate you must now be disregarded. A small win for justice."

Okay, I was reassessing my faith in Dolly. Recalculating route—cancel any intentions to switch teams—I'll take her, even if she's sober for only eight hours per day. I attempted to high five her, but she ignored me. I withdrew my hand, but Nigel came over and high-fived me.

"Back to business. We should clear up several inconsistencies. According to the clinic schedule, you had ample time to go home and kill Millie between your calls in the late morning. Can you account for the time?"

"Huh? I worked all day. I never stopped."

We studied the schedule. While it would have usually taken me merely a few minutes to rasp teeth on one horse, the gelding had a rotten molar that needed to be extracted. I'd stayed for more than an hour. "We can call the owner. She'll confirm I was there until noon."

"She says you were in and out."

"Bullshit." I was incredulous.

"She says it was a two-minute job, and you used your fingers to pull out the tooth, and yet charged her as if you had taken an hour. She disputed the charges, and the clinic agreed to reduce the fee."

"That's total crap." I was enraged. "Let me call the clinic."

"Later, because we have a great deal to get through." And we did. Most of the inconsistencies were resolved, but the dental timing was outstanding. After an hour of reviewing the timeline, we narrowed it down to the disputed period. If I had killed Mrs. Miller, that is when it would have occurred.

"Well, they now have motive and opportunity. We'll get to the means soon."

"Colonel Mustard in the garden with the lead pipe."

"Yes, but instead, it's you in her house with?"

"With nothing. I didn't do it, and I didn't have an opportunity. I have no idea what that horse owner is on about. I was there for more than an hour."

"Was anyone with you? A nurse or a driver?"

"No. It was raining extremely hard. Because our nurse had a cold, I suggested she stay in the clinic where it was dry."

"She claims you didn't even ask her to accompany you, and she would have been happy to go." Dolly gazed at her empty coffee cup, swirled the few remaining sips, and ruefully stared at me.

"I swear I asked her." I thought for a few seconds. "Maybe I didn't. I don't remember, but that was what I was thinking." My heart sank, and I felt ill. The bile rose in my throat. The morning sickness raised its ugly head. I excused myself, went to the bathroom, and tossed my breakfast, or what remained of it. My head throbbed, and the tears were welling. I tried to compose myself and returned to the table.

Nigel pointed to the stairs leading outside. I opened the front door. Dolly was outside smoking and talking to someone. She waved me back into the house. Nigel peered at me and offered me some Scotch Fingers. He might be an old bachelor, but he was savvy enough to recognize a pregnant woman's need for food.

Dolly returned and stared at me hard. She peered down at her notes, tapped her pencil, and glanced up. "What do you know about phenobarbital?"

Chapter 18

I thought I was going to pass out. This couldn't be happening. I was speechless. Nigel patted my arm as I stretched it out on the kitchen table to rest my head. I was headed for a migraine.

"Carly don't confess to me. If you do, I'm duty-bound to report it to the court, and I won't be able to represent you. Am I clear on that?"

Without lifting my head, I nodded.

Nigel continued to rest his hand on mine. "Can I get you some paracetamol?"

"I need something stronger. I'm certain I'm getting a migraine."

Nigel went to another room. He came back with what seemed like a cow bolus. "Try this."

"What is it?"

"Just try it."

He handed me a glass of water. I almost gagged trying to swallow it. The tears were flowing, but I dabbed at them.

"Take your time." Dolly appeared nearly sympathetic. I'd never perceived any emotion from her. It was minimal, but that was the minute I realized she was on my side. I finally had an ally.

I laughed. Dolly and Nigel stared at me as though I was crazy. "You know, I've always thought Australia handed down the most pathetic sentences for murder. I guess I finally think the judges may be fair."

"You'll probably be arrested. I'm confident I can get you out on bail, but you'll spend a day or more behind bars."

"I need to call Dan."

"I already called him. He's coming out right now. Sorry, but the police are on their way, too."

"I need to talk to my girls." I ran up the stairs and out to the tree where the reception was scratchy at best. I dialed my mother-in-law's cell phone. She answered, and I asked to talk to the children. She said they were with the other kids, but I heard Casey laughing. In a stern voice, I demanded, "Now."

There was a pause, and then Casey was on the line. "Hi, Mummy. I can't talk. We're going to get ice cream."

"Casey, I love you and miss you."

"Oh, Mum, don't be sad. I'll be back next week."

"Tell you what. When you get home, we're going to get a puppy."

"Do you promise? Can he sleep with me? Faythe's too rough, and she wets the bed too much."

"We'll see. I love you, bug."

"You too, Mom," and as she handed the phone back to my mother-in-law, I heard her scream to Faythe, "Mom says we're getting a puppy." I distinctly heard her say "Mom" and not "Mum." I also heard Dan's mom correct her and say, "Mum."

Dan drove up in Roger's car, jumped out, hugged me, and told me he loved me. Dan promised I would be released as soon as possible and how sorry he was. He and I both cried. "It's so ridiculous. Everyone knows you didn't do it."

"Phenobarbital, Dan. For God's sake, how would she get that into her system? Who but a vet has much of that on hand? Do you use it for anything?"

"Carls, I used it many years ago in my residency, but it was just for short-term use on a man with seizures."

Dolly watched us. She stepped away and made a phone call. When she returned, I explained that I had phenobarbital tablets in my vet truck to control horses' seizures. I had used the pills a time or two in the last year. I used pentobarbital to euthanize horses. Would the two be confused on a toxicology screen?

"Did you have any in your truck?" Dolly tapped her pen on her notepad.

"Yes, both."

The amounts of either of the drugs would be noted from the impounded vet truck. However, I remembered that the forensic evidence wasn't admissible in court. Dan appeared desperate. He continued to stroke my back and comfort me. "Do you log what you use?"

"No, neither are controlled substances in veterinary medicine here in Australia. It would be on the bill, and the phenobarbital would be in the medical records." Since the phenobarbital comes in tablets, it would be easy to see how much I sold., It would be tough to estimate how much was in the truck, though. I don't know if I could account for it all."

Dolly arranged to drive me into town and visit the police. We all reentered the house. I was regaining my composure. Nigel poured me fresh coffee. He appeared to be genuinely sympathetic and patted my arm. Dan was wild. My headache was still painful, but it had eased somewhat. I had no idea what was in the cow bolus Nigel had given me.

"How the hell could this happen? My wife wouldn't kill anyone." He stood behind me and pressed his head against the wall. "Oh, my God, why did I move to this effing town."

"Hey," shouted Dolly, which brought us all to attention. "We should be calm and rational. I need information, not emotional dithering. I should know about phenobarbital."

I wiped my tears. While regaining my composure, I explained that it is used in animals for seizures. Specifically, I used it in horses and frequently for a condition around here called ryegrass toxicity. It's a toxin that comes from ryegrass that grows wild in the paddocks around here. What is usually a good source of fodder for horses becomes infected with a bacterium that produces the toxin. When horses eat it, they become jittery and shake. Their spasms of shaking can lead to their death.

"If I catch it early, I put them on phenobarbital tablets to calm them until the toxin is gone. It can be weeks, and hence I have many high strength tablets in the truck."

"Do you lock them up?"

"Uh, well, uh." I gazed at Dan, who stared back at me, pleading silently to give an answer, which would explain everything. "No. No, I don't."

"Would there have been any in your home? Could Millie have taken some by mistake when she was at your house?" Dolly tapped her pencil, looking toward the screen that depicted a desert scene, which substituted as a window in the underground bunker. I felt claustrophobic and sick, as well. I excused myself, went into the bathroom, and puked until I almost wet my pants. This has got to stop. My head was pounding, but the actual pain had dulled. I cupped tap water in my hands and splashed my face. The water was sweet tasting. I drank from my hands and returned to the kitchen.

"I need something to eat. I think the morning sickness is taking over."

Dolly sat up straight and looked at me. "Did I know this? Are you pregnant? Are you certain? How far along?"

"Only a few weeks, but 99 percent sure. I was going to make an appointment with the ob-gyn today." I remembered I was expected to meet Julie at the house in an hour.

"Hey, excuse me. I need to make a phone call. I was supposed to meet a friend in an hour."

"Don't say anything," Dan pleaded.

"It's Julie. She'll be okay."

Dolly put her fist down hard on the table. "Dan's right. If your phone isn't tapped, I'd be surprised."

I shook my head and went outside to call Julie. "Hey, Julie, it's me. I can't talk, but I have to cancel our lunch date."

"I got called into work, anyway. I tried to call, but you didn't answer. I heard about the tox report. It's on the news."

"Really? What did they say?"

"A vet drug was found in her system."

"Like hell. It's a human drug, too."

"The police came to the hospital." I cut her off.

"I have to go. I can't talk about it."

"Carly, good luck. I know you didn't do it."

"Well, that makes three. I think the only other person who believes me is Dan." I imagined how devastated Dan had to be. "Will you bring me some carrot cake when I'm in the slammer?"

"I don't know how you can joke. I'd be dying."

"I am dying." I returned to the house. As I descended the steps, I heard murmuring, which ceased as I entered the kitchen. Nigel was gone, and Dan and Dolly were sitting side by side at the table.

"What?" I realized they had to be talking about something important to me.

"Just figuring how to keep you safe." Dan returned to his seat, so I could sit next to Dolly.

"Safe? Is there any chance I won't be arrested?"

"Well, yes, now that I know you're pregnant. We'll try to get you a medical report on the way into the station."

With that, Dan jumped up and went outside. He returned and nodded. "Roger's going to do the honors."

"I don't want Roger. I want Lydia Johnson."

"No, she might not give us the result we want." Dan glared at me, and I knew what he was thinking.

"I'm too ill to be jailed?" I smiled weakly.

I was appalled at every level. I was going to be arrested for something I didn't do. I was going to be questioned, and I wouldn't be allowed to speak to declare my innocence. I was going to jail and would probably be strip-searched. All those things were detestable to me. However, the one aspect that really made me ill was a friend, and fellow professional, would lie for me, so I could get bail. I was going to scam the system. How low would I go? Pretty far, as it turned out.

Chapter 19

Dolly went outside and called Reggie, who explained that the major-case detectives were on their way to interview me. They would probably escort me to Adelaide, where I would be charged with the murder of Mrs. Miller. I would hopefully be presented to a judge who would hopefully release me on bail.

We discussed the bail, and Dolly suggested it would be steep. Dan and I needed to get our assets sorted to be able to post the required bond. Dolly thought a couple hundred thousand might be necessary. The equity in our house might not be enough, and our savings would be required, as well. Dan was convinced his mother would provide the rest. I had my doubts. I realized my mother would not be able to come up with any money. My father's business failed after he died, and my mother struggled to get by on her savings and a small pension. Dan and I paid for her visits to Australia.

Dan went upstairs and outside to call his mother. He said that she was more than happy to help. I doubted this was the gist of the conversation, but I was grateful. She would keep the girls for a few more days until I was free. Then she would fly over and care for the children if needed.

Dolly was reluctant to let us go, but a police car was parked at the end of the long driveway. Escape was futile, so she permitted us each to take our vehicles to drive to the hospital to see Roger. Roger was out in the smoking area when we arrived. He waved and pointed to the hospital, indicating that he would see us inside. "Carly, how about you and I go into the exam room?"

"Dan can come." I was surprised by Dan's exclusion.

"No, it's fine. I'll wait outside." I was shocked that Dan was so agreeable. "I'll call the bank and check on our finances while you and Roger organize a letter."

I followed Roger into a room with a table. He sat down and observed me without saying anything. "What? No blood test or physical?" I could see he was thinking and was extremely uncomfortable with the situation and what he was being asked to do.

Roger scratched his head and glanced at my recent laceration. "I'm really sorry. I know this is all a big mistake, a complete screwup, and a total injustice. Who had access to the phenobarb? Certainly, it's someone else who gave her the drugs. Would it be someone from the vet clinic, someone who got in your truck, or someone who wants you out of the way? Who stood to gain from both Millie's death and your incarceration?"

I was dumbstruck. I was so intent on clearing myself that I hadn't even thought about who actually did kill Mrs. Miller. "I don't know. I suppose it could've been anyone from my work. I locked the truck at night when I took it home. I might leave it unlocked if I was only going to be home for a while during the day. It doesn't make sense that she would kill herself."

Roger shifted and looked at his watch. "Why?"

I explained, "She was excited about her upcoming cruise. She talked about it, incessantly."

Julie came into the room. "Hey, Rog. What's up?"

"What's going on?" I was surprised to see Julie.

"We think you need some outside protection. We know Dan loves you, but he's blind to external forces, and you need some support that Dan might not be able to provide."

"Ridiculous." I was offended on every level.

"Well, of course, it is, but it doesn't hurt to have people in all of your corners, does it?" Julie was preparing to take the blood. She placed a tourniquet on my arm and took several vials. She took my blood pressure and smiled.

"What's going on?"

"It worked. Carly's blood pressure is sky-high."

"We want a backup sample in case of anything unusual. We think some testing of your blood might adversely affect your case."

I thought for a minute and remembered the bolus that Nigel had given me. It helped with the headache, but I didn't feel even remotely affected by it.

"You guys are serious, aren't you?"

Julie talked while she transferred blood into three separate packets. "Have you considered that a killer is out there, who has access to drugs and wants to pin the blame on you?" Julie and Roger had been discussing this situation.

"Why don't you include Dan in this?"

"We know Dan's innocent, but we think it's best at this stage to keep our thoughts to ourselves. Dan might talk to the police and hamper our private enterprise of Medical Sleuths Inc. Just be careful, and don't take anything you aren't sure about."

"Too late. My head was throbbing, so Nigel gave me something, and I'm not sure what it was."

Both Roger and Julie laughed. "Feverfew, an herb. Was it in a large bolus?" Roger was listening to my chest, and Julie was placing the packets containing the vials into two different bags.

"Huge. Not sure even a cow could swallow it. How do you know?"

Roger replied, "He's famous for it."

When Dan burst in, I noticed there was a distinct change in Julie's demeanor. "Preggers for sure. The only question is how many."

"Oh, shit. I hadn't thought of that." Dan smiled and rubbed my back. "Are you two done with my beautiful wife? We have a date with the constabulary, and we don't want to be late."

"Yeah, we do. Have you filled up our getaway car?" I gazed pleadingly at Dan.

"Nope. If you did the crime, you can do the time. I'll wait for you. I want to go home until we're summoned. Dolly said that she would call to let us know when they're ready for us."

"Shouldn't we wait here, so the press doesn't follow us?"

"No, I want to be alone with you for a while. I called the kids. It seems you told them we can get a puppy. Where is the puppy going to live? Who's going to take care of it if you're in jail?" Dan was furious.

I was shocked. "Dan, can't we talk about this later?" Julie and Roger tried to ignore him. We could all tell he was beyond stressed.

"Okay, let's go home." Dan escorted me out of the room.

Getting through the street was like negotiating an obstacle course. Our friendly police guard, who was diligently following our every move, was having the same problem. He got out of his car and directed the press vans to move to a different location as we emerged from our car and ran into the house.

When we were finally alone, we hugged each other and cried. Dan was holding me and rubbing my back. "I swear, this is ridiculous. Anyone who knows you would know you aren't the one who did this. I'm very sorry, darling. Just so sorry."

"Maybe it's time we think about who did do this. Who had access to phenobarbital, and why would someone want to poison Mrs. Miller?" My head was throbbing, and I was nauseous again. Dan told me to lie down, got paracetamol, and made me something to eat. I lay down and closed my eyes, but sleep was elusive, and my perspective began to change. *I was a victim of this tragedy, not the perp. Someone out there killed her, was intelligent enough to blame me, and set me up to take the rap. Who would profit from her death? Who was the real Mrs. Miller? Who killed Mrs. Miller?*

I could see the front room from our bedroom. Dan peered out at the crowd of journalists and shook his head. "Bastards," which was again a rare swear word from my stalwart and loyal husband.

"Dan, I'm getting the soap," which was a reference to his mother's way of dealing with his verbal transgressions when he was a child. It worked for him. "Can you bring me some ice water?"

Dan returned with the water and sat down next to me on the bed. "Anything else?"

"Yes, will you review our timeline? You saw Mrs. Miller the night before she died, and someone else had to deliver her the script you wrote out. Right?" My head still throbbed.

"Right." Dan took the washcloth and added cold water.

"Has anyone interviewed the delivery person? Who's the guy who delivers the drugs for the chemist?"

"Ben Craddock."

"Isn't he in his eighties?" I watched Dan. He kept looking at his phone.

"Or close to that age."

"How's Ben implicated in her death? What would he have to gain? Why would he want to implicate me?"

"Maybe he didn't. It could simply be circumstantial."

"Phenobarbital isn't circumstantial, Dan. And why did Tracey Galt say I wasn't there for an hour when I was?"

"Who's Tracey Galt?"

"Yeah, who is she? Hand me our other phone. The one that we recently bought."

The terrible Mrs. T answered the phone. "I need some info, please." I was not in the mood to be kind.

"I'm not supposed to talk to you. Hold on." Mrs. Tankard put me on hold. The next thing I heard was the lyrics from the song, "I Fought the Law." She then laughed so hard she fell into a wheezing coughing fit.

"Why did you guys change the vet bill and let Tracey Galt say I'd been there only a short time?"

"Yeah, why did we? Long story short, she's a pain in the ass, and she's done this before. You know she used to work here many years ago. The boss instructed us to give her what she wanted and notify her that we won't be doing any more work for her. It was done right after you left. I was supposed to tell you, but I forgot. You gonna kill me?"

"No, I've never killed anyone. You can put that in your pipe. Can you call Reggie and give the cops a statement?"

"Yes, ma'am. Do you want me to call them right now?"

"It would be nice."

"Consider it done." Again, she hummed the tune from "I Fought the Law." She laughed and hung up.

I was interrupted by my regular phone ringing. Dan answered it. "It's Dolly. She says she will meet us at Angel's in fifteen minutes."

I closed my eyes. "Might as well get some carrot cake as my last meal."

Chapter 20

When we arrived, Angel leaned against the counter with two pieces of carrot cake in her hand. "Last dance?"

"Last meal for sure, thanks, Angel." I returned to the parking lot and saw Dolly.

Dan planned to follow us in our car, but Dolly told him to go home and wait to be called. Dan handed us Roger's letter. It indicated that due to my pregnancy complications, which included nausea, high blood pressure, and hypoglycemia, I was at risk if incarcerated. Dolly briefly read the note and smiled.

We made our way to the police station, where the second group of news vans and journalists waited for my arrival. Reggie and two cops came out to shield me from the reporters and from a few of the locals, as well. Some yelled, "killer." Others tried to support me and shouted that I was innocent. The former outnumbered the latter by two to one.

I was escorted into an interrogation room and directed to sit with Dolly. I was told to state my name and address. Dolly made it clear that she would not allow any questions that might relate to the case. I could tell it was frustrating to the detectives, who had driven from Adelaide to interview me. I shared their frustrations as I wasn't permitted to ask any questions either.

To my surprise, Dolly didn't pose any queries. I wanted to inspect the interview transcript with the chemist's deliveryman and any other witnesses who had been questioned. I wanted to see the chain of evidence, the toxicology report, and the necropsy and histopathology findings. Dolly took notes and said very little. Finally, she asked the most crucial question. "Are you charging my client? Otherwise, we're leaving."

"We're going to hold her in custody, more for her protection than anything else," stated the lead detective. He was the same one who had interviewed me earlier. The detective gazed at me with compassion. Was I falling for this approach? Maybe he was a nice guy. I nearly let down my guard.

"Nope, you either charge her, or you let her go." Dolly placed her papers in a folder and stood up.

Go, Dolly. The two detectives looked at each other and stood up. "We can't ensure her safety."

"You bloody well better. My client didn't do it. If she is injured, your false accusations are to blame."

Dolly and I were left alone in the room. "Carly, they'll take all this information to the department of prosecutions in Adelaide. My guess is they will arrest you either tonight or tomorrow. You'll be under surveillance until a decision is made. When they arrest you, you'll be taken to Adelaide and placed in the Watch House next to the court. You'll be processed and taken to court. From there, you'll be seen by a judge, and your bail will be considered." She smiled weakly. She muttered under her breath, "This wasn't supposed to happen."

I almost missed that because I was concentrating on the "most likely" phrase. "Most likely get bail. What are my chances?"

"Oh, probably ninety percent. Your pregnancy's helpful. Most judges are quite sympathetic to that, especially since your trial won't be for months. They won't want your health at risk while you languish in jail waiting for a trial."

"Dolly, I want to discuss a few issues." I thought about the will that I didn't sign and the dental appointment that was not abbreviated, but I was interrupted.

"Now is not the time. These walls may have ears. Go home, and rest. If you're arrested, I want you to look your best. Can you cover those stitches with makeup?"

Was this woman out of her mind? *For God's sake, I could care less about the way I looked. This situation was ridiculous. I didn't know about the will. My signature had been forged, and I was performing a difficult tooth extraction when she reportedly died. I didn't give anyone phenobarbital. How was this happening to me?*

It hit me like a truck. I was being set up. I could hardly wait to get out of here and into Dan's arms, so we could start figuring out who wanted to pin this murder on me. My assumption was that I had only fifteen hours before I would be hauled away and charged. I had to work fast. Before I left the room, I called Jedda. "I need to talk to you. Can you come to the house in an hour?"

Chapter 21

Dolly and I waded through the throng of reporters as we emerged from the police station. Thankfully, the locals had been dispersed, and we could reach the car without any comments. Dolly was going home. It had been several hours since she had a cigarette, and she said that she was desperate. I wanted to ask her not to drink that night, but I didn't want to infuriate her. I was convinced that the request would have enraged her.

When I arrived back at the house, Dan called to say that he would arrange a bank loan. As I came home, I saw the same reporter who watched me as I entered the house. She smiled and waved. I nodded, returning her wave. When I walked into the house, I was sure someone had entered the house while we were gone.

Nothing was out of place, but I smelled body odor mixed with an unfamiliar deodorant. There was a knock at the front door. Jedda had arrived with her auntie. "Hi, Dr. Langley. This is my auntie, Lois. She wants to talk to you."

I extended my hand and greeted the elderly woman, who was clearly of Aboriginal descent. She had to be in her sixties. Her hair was white and curly, while her hands were rough from hard work. I realized that Jedda must straighten her hair, as I spotted a hint of tight curls where she had missed a lock. They didn't appear to be related, and in fact, they weren't.

Jedda explained Lois was her grandmother's friend. By tradition, she was called an auntie. She was born in the Arnhem Land and was a member of the Stolen Generation. She was raised in a group home. She escaped several times, only to be returned and eventually placed with a white family. She was educated and married a white man. However, she was unable to have children. Her husband abandoned her, so she again attempted to return to her Aboriginal family. She was unsuccessful in finding them, but an unrelated family took her in. The family migrated to our town, where she helped raise Jedda's father, Jimmy Medika.

"Jedda, I'm going to jail. I only have a few hours. I'm so sorry, but why did you bring your aunt?" I turned to Lois. "Should I call you Lois?"

"Yes, miss." She glanced around the living room and smiled. "I used to work here."

"Oh, really?" I didn't have time for this visit. "Jedda, I'm sorry, and I don't want to be rude, but I need to ask you to do some things for me."

"Yes, ma'am." She and her aunt politely sat down and stared at me.

I wasn't sure if I could trust Lois, and I hesitated. Lois noted my reticence.

"Dr. Langley," but I cut her off.

"Carly. Please call me, Carly. Jedda knows I like to be called that." Jedda smiled and nodded.

"Carly," she began again. "You are a good woman. Jimmy says you are fair and a good vet. I want to help you. This town has secrets. Things aren't always what they seem."

I looked at her, and she could see I was confused. "Do you know something that I should know?"

"No, not now, but I know there are people whom you can't trust. Lots of people. You think they're your friends, but they aren't."

"Do you have someone in mind?"

Lois shook her head. "I just know."

"How will this help me?"

"I want to take care of your children when they come back. Jedda will begin school soon. If they arrest you, and you can't come back, I will lay down my life to care for them when Jedda returns back to school. She will be a famous doctor, but she must study. We want to help you."

"You don't have any specific information? You only want to assist with the children?"

"You can't trust anyone. That's my advice." She stood to leave.

"No, please. I really need help. Can you be any more specific?"

"There are good and bad people in this town. I know who they are. You should be careful."

I pleaded again. "Can you tell me who I can or can't trust?"

"Your veterinary clinic owners are not your friends. I worked for them when they lived in this house."

I wasn't surprised, but that hardly helped me with my case. "And?"

"I'm not going to say more. Start with the Gilberts."

"Jedda, can you stay?"

"I need to run my auntie home. I'll come back." They left, but Jedda said she would be back soon.

I was alone when Dan rang. He stated that he was delayed and would be home in an hour. There was a drama at the hospital. He asked what I wanted for dinner. He would stop by the market and get us some steaks and veggies. "Might as well make a night of it."

"Dan, be careful." I wasn't going to say anything on the phone.

"I will, darling. Try to get some sleep. Oh, Roger called to tell us your test was positive. He said to think twins. He was kidding, of course."

"Oh, that's all I need. How did Roger get it back so fast?"

"Dunno. He's headed back to Adelaide. I'll go as fast as I can."

I heard a knock at the door. "It must be Jedda. See you soon, Dan."

"Don't open the door if it's not her."

"I love you." I smiled as I said it.

"You too, Carls. I'm sure we can get this sorted."

I hung up and went to the door. I wondered why Jedda hadn't let herself in. It wasn't Jedda. It was the aging reporter. I started to slam the door, but she declared, "Wait. I'm not here to interview you. I'm here to help."

I started to shut the door, but she added, "I want to warn you." That stopped me. I opened the door a crack. "Don't say a word. Just listen. I've been watching. I have information that might help you. Hear me out."

The phone rang. It was Reggie. The police were on their way. I returned to the door. "I'm sorry. I've got to go. Maybe we can talk when I get back." I thought *if I get back.*

I shut the door. I had to work fast. I made a list of things that I wanted Jedda to discreetly investigate. If I couldn't trust my bosses, I might not be able to trust Mrs. Tankard, either. I immediately called Dan, but he didn't answer. He must be in the thick of it with the bank. I left a message.

I called the locum, Rich Hamilton. He answered, and I quickly asked him to quietly do some sleuthing. I was confident I could count on him. I realized that he would have access to the accounts and details for the day Mrs. Miller was found dead. I explained my concerns and what I thought I would require. If the police were listening, at least they might get the idea that the appointment book had been altered.

"I'm onto it."

"Thanks. I really need someone on my side."

"I'm sure the whole clinic is on your side."

"Possibly, but I can't count on anyone or anything. Will you please not discuss this situation with anyone, including Kendall?"

"Call me Columbo." Rich used an accent that mimicked Peter Falk.

"I'll shout you an old overcoat if that helps." I did laugh, but God knew why. I was heading into the hysterical, manic state of anxiety. "I'll talk to you tomorrow or in a few days when I'm back out. If I get lucky, it might only be overnight."

I wanted Jedda to collect information about the chemist, his employees, and inquire if they had phenobarbital in stock. Could they have mixed up the order? I needed a few other individuals checked out. I knew she would be discreet. When she returned, I asked her not to share any of this information with anyone except me. The only people in the entire town I now trusted were her and Dan. Still, I was afraid Dan might inadvertently give this information to the wrong people.

I tried to call Dan again and still received no answer. I decided to have a quick shower. When I emerged from the bathroom, I put on a plain T-shirt and jeans. I needed something to try to subdue my nausea. I put some paracetamol in my pocket, but I couldn't take any more for a few hours. I figured that any drugs would be taken from me before I was brought to the Watch House. *Would I be able to have some before I arrived in Adelaide?* I assumed that Reggie had contacted Dolly, but Reggie and a detective from Adelaide showed up at my house and said Dolly had not responded to their calls.

"Carly, we will make the formal charges when we get to the Watch House and out of view of the press. You aren't being charged until we get there. I know Dolly would advise you not to speak. However, now is the time if you want to say anything or if we can help you with something."

"You've got to be kidding. No, I'll pass on that. Thanks for the opportunity. Not."

"I'm counting on you to be a good girl and not make a scene while we go past the press."

"You have my word." *As if I would give the press any reason to further inflame my detractors. No, sir. As soon as this is over and I'm cleared, we are getting the hell out of dodge. I'm going home to Idaho. I've had it with this entire system.*

I thought about my mom. I didn't have time to call her, and I realized that she would hear about this secondhand when she woke up. It was only midnight over there, and I dreaded hearing her reaction. I prayed she would know that I was innocent. I knew she would feel helpless and want to come care for the girls. This made me think about my beautiful daughters and what would go through their minds. I wondered if Dan would abandon me. Where the hell was he?

I entered a police van, and Kendall was sitting inside where the press could not see her. "Hey" She extended a hand and patted the seat next to her. "I have the afternoon off, and I haven't been to the big smoke for days. Do you mind if I tag along?"

I peered at her as the tears welled in my eyes. There was no stopping them now. No one could see us, and we both cried. She put her finger to her lips, indicating not to talk. She needn't have worried. I was prepared for a very isolated and silent time. She was in her civvies, and she put her arm around me as I leaned into her. I fell asleep right away. It seemed mere minutes before I was in Adelaide, turning into the parking lot between the Watch House and the court. This couldn't be real, but it was.

Chapter 22

I walked down a laneway between two buildings. The cameramen were filming my arrival. Thankfully, no one was yelling at me. I was still not handcuffed, but that was about to change.

The detectives and several prison officials interviewed me. The detectives then interviewed me again. They asked me the same questions over and over. I would respond to just questions that pertained to my health and my desire to see my two children and husband.

Despite several attempts to ask me questions about the days preceding Mrs. Miller's death, I politely asserted that I would answer only with my solicitor present. My head was throbbing now, and I was once again nauseous. They offered me a soft drink, and I declined, but I requested a biscuit. I didn't dare call it a cookie. At least I trained my girls to say cookie.

The humiliation of a strip search was next. I was outfitted with a jumpsuit. The color was hideous, but I had no options. I was escorted back into an interrogation room, where the same questions were repeated yet worded differently. I figured they were assessing my mental health. *Are they crazy?* Of course, I was unbalanced and becoming more so each hour. I was hungry, tired, and profoundly alone. I had tried to call Dan, but he didn't answer. The guard explained that several attempts had been made to reach Dolly, but she hadn't returned any calls.

I finally received a tray with a sandwich and some jello, which they called jelly. I asked for milk, and they laughed. They brought me some coffee-flavored milk, which I would have not drunk if I wasn't desperate. God knew I was desperate. Exceedingly desperate.

The milk coffee was surprisingly delicious, and it calmed my nausea quickly. I had renewed energy, which I needed as it was close to midnight. I was again subjected to a round of mental-health questions. Finally, I was told that due to the upcoming Australia Day public holiday, I wasn't going to be presented to the court for a bail hearing. I was to be taken to the women's prison.

I couldn't control myself, and I cried. Kendall had not been allowed to go any further than the reception at the Watch House. She'd left with a friend to spend the night in Adelaide. After several hours, I was driven in another van to the women's prison. I was strip-searched again and interviewed. I was escorted to a cell with a bed, toilet, and a camera placed strategically, so they could see if I attempted to harm myself. I didn't, but they watched me vomit a time or two.

I didn't hear from Dan or Dolly until the next morning. I was told I had a call from my solicitor. Knowing that the bail hearing had been postponed, she decided to stay home and work on the case. She said that in this judicial system, a murder charge would not usually get bail. Still, she was sure she could arrange for home detention or housing in the local jail in our town. She apologized and assured me that she, Nigel, and Dan were planning strategies to get me out and have the charges removed.

I had my first doubts about my team. I could understand Dan working so diligently to raise the money to get bail to keep us from going under, but a phone call? I was pissed that he had not attempted to call me. I can't remember ever being mad at Dan. I disagreed with a few things, but this was a "sleep on the couch" violation. I was going to spend the weekend incarcerated, and he had not even bothered to call. Realizing she knew I had been taken to Adelaide, I was also disappointed that Dolly hadn't tried to call last night. Was she drunk again? What the hell was going on?

It was midafternoon before I heard from Dan. He said he had tried all night and early in the morning to call me, but he kept getting a busy signal. He said all but one of the news vans were gone and that life in our town was almost back to normal. He was coming to Adelaide to pick up the kids and his mother the following day. I was relieved that the girls were heading home and inquired when he was coming to see me.

"I'm not." There was a long pause. "They said no visitors were allowed on Sunday. Apparently, they only allow visitors on Saturday." He was leaving work that morning to pick up his mother and our children and planned to drive straight back home with them. He didn't want to let the girls see me in prison.

"Why's your mother coming home? We don't have enough room in the house as it is."

"I can't work and take care of the kids. School starts next week, and Jedda won't be available."

"Well, if you'd come home before I left, you would have met Jedda's auntie, Lois, who offered to take care of the kids during the day. I'll be home early next week. Dan, I don't want your mom hanging around the house when I come back. It will be hard enough to do what I have to do."

"What do you have to do? If you're lucky enough to get out and, by the way, Dolly now says snowball's chance in heck."

"Dan, I'm going to get out. You'd better figure out how to send your mother back."

"Carly, we need her right now. She said she'd be happy to help with the bail or even refinance her house to help get you out. Even with all the equity in our house, we'd be lucky to get fifty thousand. The loan officer at the bank was no help at all."

"Okay, you aren't coming, and we have no money. Any more bad news?"

"Darling, I don't think it can get any worse." Dan sounded exasperated.

"Don't you think Dolly should come?" I was beginning to weep.

"She's hired a private investigator, who needs her up here. She's working on getting you a bond. If we can swing it, it will mean my working double shifts for the next few weeks."

"Dan, I'm not going to skip bail. No one's going to lose money."

"The PI wants his money upfront, darling."

"Oh well, okay. Is anyone getting any leads on the source of the phenobarbital?" My feelings of abandonment were increasing, along with my irritation toward my husband and solicitor.

"No, and that's the problem. You, I mean, we are the only ones who'd benefit from Mrs. Miller's death. Are you sure you didn't sign those papers? I thought I saw you reading and signing them."

"Dan, for God's sake. No, and we shouldn't be talking about that on the phone. They tape all the conversations. Didn't they caution you?"

"Oh shit, I forgot." It wasn't like him to do something so foolish. Was he losing it? My concerns were growing.

"I really need to see you soon."

"Maybe I should hang up. I am majorly sleep deprived. I'm so sorry. I miss you so much." He sounded teary, as well. Maybe I was misreading the whole situation.

"Dan, get me out. That's all I ask. I'll figure out how to make them understand I didn't do anything. I didn't want to say anything else. I couldn't rely on Dan's discretion anymore. He was losing it, and he might make things worse. Was he starting to think I was guilty?

"Dan, I love you. I miss you and the girls, and I want you to give them a big hug for me and tell them I'll be home in a few days."

"You too, darling. You too, and I will."

I returned to my cell, which was essentially solitary confinement. I spent the day with a pad and pen writing up what

I thought was important in my defense. I wrote a letter to my mother, who I was sure currently knew my plight. I didn't write any of my thoughts that perhaps my team was less than adequate, and I didn't write anything incriminating.

I slept during the day and stayed up at night. One guard got sick of seeing me vomit from morning sickness and chipped in to buy me some apples, carrots, and crackers. For the most part, the guards were pleasant and professional. I was a model prisoner. I received a visit from Dolly the day before the bail hearing, and she said she would plead my case. "I'm going to give it my best."

"Plead? Don't tell me I'm not going to get bail." I may have said a few bad words under my breath.

"Carly, it's a murder charge. It's not the possession of marijuana or a DUI."

"But I thought my health was an issue?"

"It is, but it's murder. No one ever thought anything like this was going to happen."

There it was again. What a curious statement. It was as though Dolly knew more about this than she was letting on. A red flag shot up once again. Who was this woman? Was she on my side or not? I decided not to say anything and see how she performed tomorrow in front of the judge.

"Do you have a time you need to be in court? No one's told me anything. Do I get to wear my regular clothes when I go before the judge?"

"Um, well, you won't be going. The court will have a video link to the prison. I'll be there in court."

"What the hell. You're kidding. I want to be there."

"Well, you want to go home, too, don't you? So, really leave it to me." I could see Dolly was in withdrawal from either a cigarette or alcohol. She was tapping the table and shuffling papers. I could see her looking through her notes for something.

"What are you looking for?"

"Oh, Roger's statement. I already filed it, but I can't find my copy."

My heart sank. This woman was hopeless. "Any chance you could have an alcohol-free night tonight?" I laughed as if it was a joke. It wasn't.

"Not a chance in hell." At least she was honest.

The next morning, I was escorted to a room with a video-camera link to the court. The monitor was to be turned on when my case came up. Finally, after an hour, the monitor came on. I saw a judge, who was shuffling papers, conferring with an officer, and looking around. He finally asked if anyone was in the room representing the plaintiff in a bond hearing for Carly Langley.

I waited for a second and then turned to the prison guard, who said the microphone was turned on, and I could speak to the judge. He repeated the question. When Dolly didn't appear, I spoke up. My heart was racing, and my palms were sweating.

"Your Honor, it's me here, and I do have representation, but she seems to be missing." He stared up at a wall-mounted monitor where I could see myself in my prison uniform. I could hear a commotion, and I saw the judge look at what was probably the press in the courtroom.

"Ms. Langley, I think we will move ahead with the next case. Your counsel has one more hour, and then this proceeding will need to be continued tomorrow. Who's representing you?"

"Della Myler, sir." I thought my heart would jump out of my chest. I heard him groan.

"If you want a court-appointed council, we can arrange that, and your case can be rescheduled for tomorrow. Is that an option?"

"Do you mind if I wait for the hour, sir?" My voice was quivering, and I was close to tears.

"One hour, Ms. Langley. I would advise you to consider my offer of a court-appointed representative. This is a murder charge and my options, and therefore, your options are limited."

"Yes, sir." The camera went blank. I lost it. I started to cry, and the guard, who was a woman, put her hand on my shoulder and inquired whether I wanted a glass of water. I couldn't even respond to her.

"These things happen. It might be a miscommunication of the court time. Possibly she was caught up in traffic. You have an hour."

I raised my head and requested a tissue. The guard left the room and returned with a box. I attempted to compose myself. When the hour passed, I stood up, and the television came back on. I sat down and watched the judge admonish Dolly, who showed no signs of contrition. They actually sparred, and the judge announced, "Enough, Ms. Myler. What do you have for the court that would make me give Ms. Langley bail with a murder charge?"

Dolly stood and fumbled through her papers. "Your Honor, I have submitted a letter from a doctor who examined Dr. Langley and found several issues with her health, including," but the judge raised his hand.

The judge interrupted her. "Where is the letter, Ms. Myler? I don't see it in her file."

"I sent it in last week, Your Honor. I have a copy here." She rummaged through her briefcase, returned to the table she was using and spilled the contents. She methodically went through her papers and glanced up at the judge. "I don't seem to have it.

I filed it by fax last week. I may have left it in the fax machine." She didn't even appear to be flustered.

"Ms. Myler, this court hasn't used a fax machine to file papers for several years. I will postpone the bail hearing for the day. I suggest you obtain the original copy of the letter by tomorrow. I would also recommend you bring the doctor, and it better be a compelling case. This isn't a traffic infringement, Ms. Myler. This is a murder case. Is there anything else?"

I watched and, with new clarity, I perceived I had the wrong solicitor. It was as though she was against me. For the first time, I realized that probably everyone felt I was guilty. They were going through the motions. I'll bet Dan even believed I was guilty. Obviously, my husband was pretending to go through the motions. I lost all faith in everyone. I wanted my girls, and I wanted to get out of Australia. My dream life died right at that moment. I could trust no one.

I walked back to my cell, and I didn't even cry this time. I was served lunch, but I had no appetite. The prison doctor summoned me. He sat me down and, along with a guard, asked me the same questions. Did I feel depressed? Did I want to harm myself? Again, my answers were no, no, and twenty more nos. No, prison would not break me down. I was on my own. I was escorted back to my cell.

I was told I would eventually be transferred to the general prison. *Was that a good thing or a bad thing?* I didn't feel as if I was in solitary confinement. The guards were always coming by and were kind and respectful. I wasn't excited about using the toilet in front of them. Still, I doubted it would be any more private in the general area.

In the late afternoon, I was taken to the phone. Dolly didn't even apologize. I wasn't going to share any more information with her. I listened politely when she informed me that she'd personally hand-walked the original letter to the magistrate's office and arranged for Roger Grimes to come to court the following day. I thanked her and hung up. I'm reasonably sure she realized I was less than impressed.

An hour later, Dan called. This time, before he even talked, I reminded him that this conversation might be recorded. There was a long silence before he replied. "Do you think I'm an idiot?"

"Not at all," I said coolly. "I'm firing Dolly."

Another long pause ensued. "I don't think sacking her is in your best interest. Wait until you get bail."

"Dan, I'm not getting bail."

"You don't know that. You might."

"How are the girls? Are you at home? I would love to talk to them."

"No. I'm at work, trying to pay for this fucking mess you got yourself into."

I think that might be the second time that I ever heard that word from him. I was no longer tipping my hand to anyone. I thought I heard Casey's voice in the background. Another nail in my marital coffin. "Dan, it's suppertime. I've got to go."

"Oh, I see. You're dismissing me?" He sounded hurt.

"I'll talk to you tomorrow. In case you didn't know, today has not been a good day."

"I love you, and you need to know that I am doing everything I can to get you out."

"Sure." I hung up and walked back to my cell. I didn't care what he or anyone thought this evening. I knew I was innocent. I was feeling nauseous, and I had to get my blood sugar up. It must be a boy. I felt so different than with the other two pregnancies.

I currently had one ally in Australia. I wondered what Jedda had discovered since I was gone. I had given her specific tasks. I wanted to add a few more things. I knew her final year of high school started next week, and she should concentrate on her studies. I asked her not to call me or discuss anything until I was home when we could talk privately. I hoped she was having some success.

Chapter 23

I was taken to the room with the video-camera link to the court the next morning. My stomach was churning, but I brought some crackers to quell my nausea this time. The new guard was not as kind as the one the previous day. He left me alone in the room. Only a few minutes passed before the television turned on, and I could view the magistrate. It was a different one this time. She was whispering to the court reporter and laughing.

She stared up and realized I was linked to the court, and she straightened up and called the session open. Dolly was in attendance this time, and I could hear her talking to someone.

"So, Ms. Myler, you've brought the doctor who examined the plaintiff before she traveled to Adelaide?"

"Yes, Your Honor. This is Dr. Roger Grimes."

I could see the judge perusing the paper, which must have been Roger's report. "Dr. Grimes?" She turned toward Dolly and Roger.

"Yes, Your Honor."

"I have your qualifications. Do you care to be addressed as Dr. Grimes or Mr. Grimes, and are you a specialist surgeon?"

"Yes, Your Honor. Either Dr. or Mr. is fine."

Because there was a new voice, the camera and video switched to a new face. It must be the solicitor representing the department of prosecution.

"If I may interject, Your Honor."

"Yes, Mr. Colhoun."

A tall, lanky, bald man approached the microphone positioned between the prosecution and the defense tables. "Mr. Grimes is a friend of both the defendant and my esteemed colleague, Ms.

Myler. I'm not sure his summation of the health status is not tainted by this relationship."

"Ms. Myler, is he a personal friend?"

"I don't deny that, but the evidence is clear. Dr. Langley's blood sugar is exceedingly low, and her pregnancy test was strongly positive. Her blood pressure is well above the normal range for a woman in her condition."

"Counselor, is the blood pressure high or low?" The magistrate was looking at the report.

"Excuse me, Your Honor, it is high. I think that's correct." There was some noise, and the camera switched and showed Dolly whispering to Roger. He sat, crossing and uncrossing his legs. Roger had an exasperated expression. Was he annoyed or in need of a cigarette? As she turned to the magistrate, I saw Roger shake his head.

The prosecutor then declared, "Well, it is a bit unusual when the doctor knows Ms. Myler and works with the husband of the accused."

Dolly rose, turned to the prosecutor, cleared her throat, and spoke. "Your Honor, we don't deny the relationships." She smiled, pointing to the prosecutor. "Just as I'm sure you don't deny that my esteemed colleague and Your Honor are both members of the Adelaide Club, and you were seen entering the club at the same time yesterday. I have a photo showing the two of you talking to each other as you entered the club. While I assume you were both professional and engaged in no conversations that might prejudice this proceeding, I expect you to have the same consideration for Dr. Grimes."

I was pleasantly surprised. *Go, Dolly.* The prosecutor produced a report from the prison doctor, who confirmed my pregnancy and low blood sugar. However, he claimed my blood pressure had returned to a high normal range.

"High normal?" countered Dolly. "She's in her first trimester, and this is not the time we would anticipate her blood pressure to be an issue. We would expect if this matter was to go to trial, Dr. Langley would be incarcerated for most of the pregnancy before the trial even begins. We recommend she would be safe and in better hands if she is home with her husband and children, who need their mother. We strongly suggest she is innocent, and it is in the court's interest to allow her to be home-monitored with her family."

The prosecutor stood up again. "Your Honor, I have been advised that the major crimes unit has substantial evidence that Ms. Langley did commit this crime and has every reason to flee. She is a dual citizen, and we consider her a flight risk."

The judge affirmed she would take these submissions under advisement to make a ruling the following day. The screen went blank. Dolly called me right after the court proceedings. "I'm sorry about yesterday. Roger wasn't available, or he would have been there. I had to stall proceedings as his presence was our best chance for bail. I realize you were left wondering. I'm headed back up to Nigel's. A hearing will not be held tomorrow, and they'll send me the ruling by email message. The judge has a family commitment, and she told me to go home. I'll call you tomorrow."

"How did you obtain a picture of the prosecutor with the judge? Was it the private investigator?"

She laughed. "I don't have a picture, and they probably realize it. All three of us went into the building together and had a drink. We're an incestuous lot."

I started to ask her about Dan, but her cell phone went dead. I could handle one more day. Since I doubted I was going to make bail, I began to steel myself. I desperately wanted to see the girls. It was so unfair. Whom could I trust?

I received a letter from Jedda in the afternoon. All it said was she had seen the girls in the park, and they ran up to her, hugged her, and seemed happy. She had the information I had requested. That was all: a short and sharp paragraph, but so full of hope.

The next morning, I received a call from Dolly. "Good news and bad news. Which do you want first?"

"You choose." My heart sank.

"Well, if you have access to two hundred and fifty thousand cash and assets to back up another two-fifty, you can go home."

"Oh, my God. I can get bail?" I was elated.

"Dan says it's out of your reach. I'm sorry, Carly. We've asked around. So far, there are no takers."

"What about Dan's mother? She's rolling in it."

"Not in cash assets. Dan says he will try to sell the house, but that would amount to about a tenth of what you require."

"I have to rot in here?" My voice broke, and I desperately wanted to roll up in a ball and return to my cell.

"I can try to expedite the court case, but we need more evidence in your favor. To date, my private investigator hasn't found anything that will help your case. I'll call you tomorrow. I'm thrilled that at least we are in with a chance. I may seek to have the amount reduced."

It killed me to say "thanks," but I did. I returned to my cell, where there was an envelope and a small package. It had been opened and inspected. There were two letters from the girls. One was a handwritten note, and one was a picture. The o in "Mommy" was scratched out, and the letter u replaced it. My guess was Dan's mom had a hand in that. Casey went on to write, "I love you, and please come home, and when are we getting the puppy?" Faythe's picture contained two stick drawings of a mother and a little girl. My heart was broken. A small, framed photograph of the girls was inside the box.

After lunch, I fell asleep. In the middle of the afternoon, I was awakened and instructed to pack my bags. I was going home. My bond had been posted. "By whom?"

"Dunno. Some anonymous fan."

"What?" I was shaking.

"We actually don't know. It was done by courier, and that's all we know. If you want to decline, that's an option."

I stared at my guard and shook my head. "Are you effing kidding me? No, I'll accept anything from anyone."

Chapter 24

Free at last. Well, I could settle for house arrest. The conditions of bail were short. I was to stay home and not drink or do drugs. I could leave my home just for medical appointments after notifying the local police, as I was well out of the close control of the prison. I was required to report to the police station two times a week and had to be available for a spot check at any time. No problem. Happy to comply. I was and will continue to be a model prisoner.

I walked out into the foyer, where both Kendall and Julie greeted me. I was disappointed that it wasn't Dan. Still, since our daughters had returned, he was working double shifts, trying to keep a roof over our head while we headed toward a trial. I understood. At least, that is what I told myself.

I hugged them both and thanked them for coming. I was taking no chances with anyone, and I declined to discuss the case. Until I had more information, I would only discuss the case with Jedda. I wanted to go home and determine how she did with the list of what I needed. I trusted no one. Well, Dan was the exception. Even then, I felt it was best to keep my suspicions to myself. I think he was at the end of his tether. Sadly, he couldn't be relied on for anything.

Kendall drove us home. Julie had worked at the hospital for most of the night and slept most of the way home. She appeared to be losing weight. Kendall peeked at her and shook her head. "Carrot-cake deficient." We both laughed, and Julie smiled.

I was excited to see my girls. They had returned home with their grandmother a few days earlier. I needed to reconsider my relationship with her. She had really stepped up and cared for the girls while I was gone. I wanted to call my own mother, as well. Dan had called to explain what had happened, and now it was time for me to calm her down.

I had to prepare for a trial. Dolly had called me in the jail and had reassured me that she was doing all she could to prepare for the upcoming court trial. Dolly's private investigator had not unearthed any evidence to clear me. He came at a cost, but Dolly promised me he was worth what Dan was paying him. Poor Dan was barely sleeping. We still had no idea who had posted my bail.

I arrived home, sporting a beautiful ankle bracelet and wearing the same clothes in which I'd left. It was hot as per usual, and I was a bit "wiffy," as they like to say here. Interestingly, only one news van was in front of the house. It was the one with the ancient female reporter. I didn't see her as I was engulfed with two sweet little girls when I stepped out of the car. Julie and Kendall walked me into the house and stated they would be in touch the next day. We all hugged. I thanked them, and they left.

I was teary when I sat down and had each girl on my knees. Dan's mother gave me a hug and seemed genuinely happy to see me. Maybe, Dan finally convinced her I was not the murdering whore she thought I was. Possibly.

"Carly, you must be exhausted. Can I make you a sandwich?"

"Oh, yes, please. I would kill for a PB&J." Oops, perhaps that should have been rephrased. "You two munchkins want one, too?"

A chorus of "Yes, please," resulted.

"Tell me about your visit to Grandma's. What did you do?"

Both girls gazed with faces that showed a mixture of anxiety and relief.

"We went to the zoo with the Mc Donald's, we played, we went to the museum, and Faythe wet the bed every night."

"I did not. Casey, you're lying, and you promised you wouldn't tell. I only wet it once." Faythe launched across the bed and started to hit her sister. Dan's mother came in and yelled at the girls, and they immediately stopped. I could see she had their measure. Or was it more?

"Hey, Casey. You need to help your sister, not embarrass her. We've all wet the bed when we were young, including me."

Casey opened her mouth in shock and said, "Is that why you killed Mrs. Miller?" I was stunned. I didn't know what to say. Where did this come from? I was sure Dan's mom had heard her say it, too. She didn't say anything as she called us to the kitchen table. I glared at her, and she shrugged. I started to bite into my sandwich, and the girls appeared to be shocked. "Mum, we need to say grace."

"Oh, really?" I observed Dan's mother, who smiled.

"Okay, how about I say it? 'Dear God, you and I both know our lives have been tested these past few weeks. Please let everyone realize I would never kill anyone, and please make sure my mother-in-law has a swift, safe journey back home. And thank you for inventing peanut butter. I consider that one of your better inventions. Amen.'"

Without looking at Dan's mother, I casually asked, "Are you leaving today or tomorrow. I can't thank you enough, but it's time for me to mother-up, and I'm sure you are anxious to get home."

"Well, I suppose tomorrow would be soon enough. I'll check with Dan about getting me to the airport. I guess we'll have to wait for him to have some time off."

"Oh, I'm sure Jedda could take you tomorrow. Do you want me to book a flight, or have you already done that?"

"I'll still check with Dan. I don't want to upset him."

"I'm sure he wouldn't mind. Where the heck is he, anyway?"

"He's hardly ever here. The poor boy's killing himself working to save you."

I turned away and rolled my eyes. I was having serious doubts about Dan or anyone trying to save me. Who were my friends? I mean, my real friends. I didn't kill Mrs. Miller. Someone with access to the phenobarbital was involved, if the lab reports were to be believed.

I couldn't shake the feeling that both Dolly and Nigel were not actually on my team. I wondered about my bosses and coworkers at the vet clinic. The other pending question was who posted the bail? I must have a friend out there somewhere.

I decided to think about the source of the phenobarbital. I was going to find a toxicologist who could help me with the bioavailability of phenobarbital. How many tablets would it require to kill a sixty-three-kilogram woman? I must look that up on my own. This job was for Jedda. I had to be careful about what I searched for on my computer. I didn't want to alarm anyone, including Dan. I knew he had nothing to do with this, but I had to be cautious about what I disclosed to him.

My pregnancy was taking its toll on my brain. I fell asleep, and I woke sometime later to Dan kissing my forehead. "Hey, sleepyhead. Dinner's ready, and the girls are starving. Want some nonalcoholic wine?" I hugged him and started to weep. I had missed his emotive smell and touch. "Hey, Carls, my beautiful wife. I'm so sorry I didn't come down to the prison. I've been working my butt off at the hospital. I've missed you so much."

"Me, you too," which was a traditional reply we used for one another. We didn't talk about the pending trial or investigation until everyone was in bed, when we were convinced that no one could hear us.

"According to Dolly, the investigator hasn't really come up with anything." Dan rubbed my back as he talked to me.

"What's his name?"

"I don't actually know. I haven't even met the guy. Dolly described him as kind of undercover."

"Is he local? Lower." I asked, directed Dan's hand down my back.

Dan's hand slipped under my pajama bottom. I slapped his hand.

"Not that low. You're under restriction for not coming to see me."

"Are you sure?" he asked while moving his hand up and to the side, aiming for my breast.

As much as my body wanted it, I was determined to punish him for not visiting me. I resisted. That didn't last long when the rubbing turned to back tickling. He again moved his hand down my back, pushed the elastic on my pajama bottom an inch lower, and kissed the back of my neck. God damn my pathetic resolve.

I woke up early in the morning, but Dan was already gone, and so was his mother.

Chapter 25

One by one, the girls came into bed and fell asleep next to me. I got up to make a cup of coffee and sat in the bed with my laptop open. When I perused the state news, I observed pictures of me leaving the jail and arriving at the local police station.

I was amazed as I didn't see any reporters. Who took those? There was a mole, but who? I checked my emails and sent one to my mom and brother. Even a few friends from high school and vet school wrote to say they heard about my problems. Most were encouraging and supportive, but some were scary. Bob Johnson wrote that I was going to rot in hell. I didn't know him, and I wondered how he got my personal email address.

My mom called, which woke the children again. I explained the girls were with me, which she understood to stop any adult or dramatic conversation. I put the kids on and suggested we switch to Skype. The girls were a bit shy at first, but they were able to see some snow. We talked and barely held it together when I said good-bye. I promised to talk to her early the following day when we could discuss more serious issues.

Faythe placed her arm around my neck. "Mom, what's a serious issue?"

I was pleased she was using "Mom" again, but I thought about how they had to play a line with me and no one else on that subject.

"You know, it's okay to call me 'Mum,' Faythe."

"No, I like calling you 'Mom.'"

"Me, too." Casey wasn't going to be left out.

"As long as you can sing "The Star-Spangled Banner," I really don't mind what you call me."

They broke into a rendition of that beautiful and God-awful tune until I begged them to stop. The girls shouted the words more than sang it.

"Enough. Who wants a waffle?"

Jedda arrived an hour later. She was scheduled to start school the next week, and I had merely a few days of her full attention. She smiled and winked. "J. Medika PI is reporting in."

"Got the dope?" I requested in my best James-Cagney voice. She stared at me without any recognition.

"I thought you had to be drug-free?" she inquired while hugging Faythe.

"James Cagney. Dope is info. Sheesh, you kids." I did an exaggerated eye roll.

"Not a clue, Sherlock." She mockingly shook her head. The girls were all over her, and she was having a difficult time standing up.

"Did you attend the funeral?"

"Yes, it was packed. Standing room only. I wonder if she had simply died, instead of …" She observed the girls' "Well, you know—would have been as big." Jedda had a list of attendees from her Aunt Lois, who knew most of the people and made a point of introducing herself to anyone whom she didn't know.

She handed me the list, at which I quickly glanced. Dolly and Nigel were present. Funny, Dolly hadn't mentioned it. Roger Grimes was also in attendance. Nothing else caught my eye. I knew Julie and Kendall were there, but I was surprised by my bosses and even the terrible Mrs. T.

"Do you know who these other people are? Are they from out of town?"

"My auntie said she would come over and fill you in on them."

"Have you reached the locum vet?" The girls were glued to Jedda.

"Yes, ma'am. I told him you wanted to talk to him, and he said to call him when you got home."

I was satisfied that Jedda had done all she could. I needed some food. I asked her to go shopping for me, and the girls wanted to accompany her.

I sent them to the grocery store with my credit card and gave her the pin number. The three of them took off, and I immediately called Rich Hamilton.

He answered on the first ring but replied he was with a client and would call me back later. I did some cleaning and took the sheets off the bed in which Dan's mother had slept. Friend or foe? It had to be his mom, who suggested to the girls I had killed Mrs. Miller. She'd offered to put her house up for security, but she had left without even saying good-bye. I guess I couldn't blame her.

The basement had been cleaned a bit, and some boxes had been rearranged. I speculated that Dan's mom had been snooping. Most of the cartons that had been disturbed were Dan's. She was probably looking for old pictures. She was a scrapbooker. She had taken photos before and had made beautiful books that she gave us for holidays and birthdays. The police had not taken any of the boxes down here when they raided our house.

One of my packs fell open as I repositioned it. As the contents spilled, several papers fell onto the floor, and one slid under the shelving. I had to get down on my hands and knees to retrieve it. I felt a vial stuck under the shelving. With great effort, I was able to tease it out with the tips of my fingers. It was a plastic bottle with my name on the label. It read minocycline, but that was not what it held. I didn't recognize the tablets. The doorbell rang. What if it was the police checking up on me? I placed the vial back far under the shelving, where I had found it, and ran upstairs.

154

Chapter 26

When I peered through the security peephole on the door, I saw the annoying news lady. She was the last person I wanted to talk to. I didn't have much time before Jedda, and the children would be back. I reluctantly opened the door. "It's not a good time right now." Whom was I kidding? It would never be a good time to talk to someone like her.

"I understand. I'm not your enemy, Carly. I may have information that might help you."

I was dubious. "Like what?"

"Photos and timetables."

"Show me." I had to admit I was curious, and I had little to support my innocence.

"Not now. Do you know who posted your bond?"

"No. Do you?" That inquiry attracted my interest.

"Yes."

"Who?" She now had my full attention.

"I need thirty minutes of your time." She looked at me and appeared earnest. Was it a trap? I didn't know.

"I can't right now. Let me think about it."

"We have a mutual friend who is on your side." We heard a car approaching. We both turned as Jedda drove up with the kids. The journalist handed me a card with her phone number. "When you're ready. I'm leaving today. This is how I can be reached."

I nodded. "I must talk to my husband. Don't sit by the phone waiting for me." I was reluctant to say anything more.

"Just you, and no one else, if you decide to talk. I'd keep it to myself if I were you." She turned and walked away.

The kids each had a rainbow-flavored icy pole. Oh, my God, I was even thinking like an Aussie. When did I switch from popsicles? I took the bags at the door, and we all put the shopping away.

"Jedda, did I have ice cream on the list?"

"The girls remarked you were low. They said their grandmother told them that there wasn't enough to have any for dessert last night."

I opened the freezer. There were two full containers. Hmm, my mother-in-law was a bit of a health-food nutter. "Let's make some lunch. Then you three can go to the park after we have a lie-down."

We made peanut butter and jelly sandwiches, and Jedda told me about school and her upcoming schedule. She commented her auntie Lois was keen to care for the girls when I attended the police station or had to go out.

"Thanks. Do I have her number?"

"Give me your phone, and I'll add in her number for you."

I handed her my cell phone, and she examined it and frowned. "Is this even from the twenty-first century? Where are your pictures?"

I took the phone back and retrieved the photographs. I handed it back to Jedda, and she scrolled through and laughed.

"Gross. You take more photos of horse things than you do your kids."

That got Faythe's interest. "Can I see?"

The girls had been exposed to many gross things in their short lives. Jedda observed me, questioningly. She turned the phone to me and showed me a picture of a decaying tooth I had removed at some time. "Sure, they've seen worse. This is what will happen if you don't brush your teeth, girls."

"Gross," replied Casey.

It hit me in a flash. I had a picture of the tooth I removed on the day of Mrs. Miller's death. Why hadn't I thought about it? It was on my clinic phone. That phone was new, and I realized it would have the photo, date, and time it was taken. I could hardly wait for Rich Hamilton to call me back. He would have the phone and the photograph that would clear me. It would prove I was performing the tooth extraction when I was accused of poisoning Mrs. Miller. I smiled but did not discuss this finding.

Jedda gazed at me and cocked her head. "What?" Her smile, with her perfect white teeth, was quite dazzling.

"I have an idea. It might save my donkey."

Faythe covered her mouth. "Mum, you said donkey. Daddy says, that's rude."

"Oh, I think he means 'ass,' darling, and it has two meanings." I was trying not to laugh. Jedda got up from the table and headed to the bathroom before she lost it in front of my opened-mouthed daughters. At the same time, I explained the difference between a donkey and a jerk.

As I was about to finish the explanation, a phone call from Dan interrupted me. He was beginning to remind me of the other definition of an ass.

"Hey," I said cautiously, "Did you deport your mother?"

"What is your problem, Carly? She took the kids when you went to jail, and mum came back here and helped us while you were away. We should be down on our knees, thanking her, not kicking her to the curb."

"There might be another version of that charitable contribution of hers. Little ears." That was the signal that the kids were listening.

Faythe realized it was her father and shouted as loud as she could. "Daddy, Mum is saying bad words."

There was a long pause from Dan. "Are you okay?"

"No, not really, but I might be soon. Are you on your way home?"

"That's what I'm calling about. I'm headed to the hospice center to visit with my old patient, Mr. Doudle. I'll be home late. Don't wait dinner on me."

"Oh, sure. No prob. You are such a kind, giving man. I'm so glad I married you. Take your time." However, I turned away from the girls and silently mouthed the word "not."

"Okay, Daddy's going to be late. What do you want for dinner?"

"Fish sticks, mashed potatoes, and ice cream." Faythe was in heaven.

Casey was no fool. She hugged me. "I love you, Mom. I know you didn't do it. What would you like for dinner?"

"Uh, lobster, or fish sticks, whatever's easier. Hey, Jedda, I'm a bit tired. Do you mind watching the girls while I have a nap?" I was going to sacrifice their nap for an early bedtime.

"Of course, I need to be home by six o'clock. My father's coming home, and we all want to have dinner together. My sister and brother are in town."

"Wake me by five o'clock, and there will be no work while I sleep. I don't want to see a single dish cleaned or towel folded. Am I clear?"

Jedda saluted me. I hugged the girls and headed to our bedroom. I took the phone in case Rich called. I wondered how he was doing and if he liked the rural life. Jedda woke me at five. I felt like a truck had hit me. I almost couldn't wake up, so I drank some juice, which finally revived me. The dishes were done, the laundry was folded, and the girls had been bathed and were in their nightgowns. The dinner was on the table.

"I could kiss you." I hugged Jedda. "Say hello to your father. Ask him how Froggy is for me."

"I definitely will. Thanks for letting me help."

"No, thank you, Jedda." The girls each jumped in Jedda's arms and begged her to stay.

"Can't, ladies. I have a date with the queen."

Casey gasped, "Do you know the queen?"

"We're besties. The real queen is your mother." She waved and left.

I read stories after dinner and prayed Rich would call. As Casey was falling asleep, the cell phone rang. Finally.

"Hi, Carly. Sorry it's taken me so long. I had another calving out at George's. I met his offsider, Ronny. Didn't go too well this time, and I had to do a fetotomy."

"Cool. Spare me the details. I've got morning-sickness issues tonight. I need a favor."

"Oh, sorry. What can I do for you?"

"I'm going to say this out loud, so anyone listening can know. I should talk to you in person. Just in the off chance, this phone isn't bugged. Is there any way you could come over for a minute? It doesn't have to be tonight. Maybe in the next day or two?"

"I'm at Angel's with Kendall, but she's going on duty, so how about a half-hour?"

"Are you on call?"

"Yep, but it's quiet, and I have the clinic phone, anyway."

That was what I wanted. I had to be careful not to tip my hand. I was certain my phone would be tapped. "Great. Any chance of some carrot cake?"

"I'll see what I can do, but it will cost you."

"I'm desperate. Name your price."

"See you in thirty, Doc." Rich hung up.

Chapter 27

When I peered out the front window, no news vans were visible. There was a God. Rich pulled up in my newer vet truck. I missed that truck and its blessed air-conditioning. I opened the front door and signaled for him to come in, so he didn't wake the girls when he arrived. He smelled faintly like a long-dead calf. I waved my hand in mock disdain.

"Sorry, I did shower, but it was pretty rank."

"I think it's your shoes."

"Shall I take them off?"

"Only if you're bothered by vomiting pregnant women."

Rich took them off and set them on the front porch. He returned and handed me a small parcel. I smiled. It was my beloved carrot cake. "Consider yourself kissed, Doc."

"Are we alone? Got anything to drink?"

"Alcohol?" I was a bit surprised.

"Actually, do you have milk?" He looked sheepish.

"Certainly, and I might join you." I poured two glasses. I offered to share the cake. Thankfully, he declined.

"How may I help?"

"I'm a bit nervous about this. Do you have an opinion about me?"

"Yes. You're a good vet, you try hard, and you don't do early pregnancy very well."

I laughed. "I think you know what I mean."

"To be honest, from the little I know about you, I find it difficult to believe you're a cold-blooded killer."

"Gee, that was convincing. Not."

He shrugged. I poured him some more milk. "Trying to ply me with milk? I can be bought."

"All jokes aside, do you know what I was doing when she was supposedly dying?"

"A dental extraction for a client is the story I heard. Is it true?"

"I was at Tracey Galt's barn, and I really was extracting a molar. You know how tough that is and how long it normally takes?"

He nodded.

"Apparently, she called to have the bill reduced. She claimed it was basically a finger job. I reached in to pull it out without anything more than my fingers. That was not the case at all."

"Well, possibly." I could tell he was questioning my story.

"The horse is nine years old, not thirty. If you could see the tooth, you would realize that it was still quite attached, and it took me a whole hour longer than Tracey suggested."

"Where's the tooth?"

"Hopefully, on your clinic phone. I photograph all of my dental extractions."

Rich frowned. My heart sank, and he shook his head.

"No pictures were on the phone when I got it. It was wiped clean."

I took a deep breath and felt my heart sink. "It had been in the camera, along with the time of the photo. Bugger."

"Double bugger, Doc. I'm so sorry."

Okay. Here's a long shot. I made a credit-card transaction when I was finished. I believe the transaction receipt includes the time. Do you ever have access to the banking receipts?"

"Wouldn't the Gilberts give that to you if you requested it?"

"Maybe, and maybe not. How are you getting along with your bosses?"

"Fine, why?"

"I recently heard a rumor that they might not be the happy couple I thought they were. I'm not convinced the Gilberts are out to save me."

He didn't respond. I could tell he was thinking. I figured they had pressured him to stay and were dumping me in the process. Why? I didn't know. It seemed that the entire town was against me. Did I have a single friend in this hamlet?

"Carly, who paid your bail? I heard it wasn't any of your friends, and I know your husband didn't. Do you know?"

"No. Strange, isn't it. I have no idea who sprung me, or why."

"Somebody must like you." Rich stretched out his hands and extended his feet.

"You're tired. You should go to bed. Rich, can I trust you?"

"That isn't the question, my friend. The question is, can I trust you?"

"I feel evil forces may want me in jail, and I need to know you aren't one of them."

We looked at each other, and he smiled and placed his hand on mine. "What can I do? We Yanks need to stick together."

I started to request a favor, but I heard a car pull up and assumed Dan must be home.

"Rich, I do need something, but it can wait. I want you to meet my husband."

Dan opened the front door and came into the kitchen, where Rich and I sat. He pretended to look as though he'd caught me in a compromising situation. He and I both knew it wasn't, but he might be trying to maintain the upper hand.

"Hey, hon. Why is the truck out front?" Dan came in and put his arm around my waist and kissed me. "Oh, hi. Are you the locum vet for my wife?"

"Yes, Rich Hamilton." Rich extended his hand toward Dan, and they shook.

"Welcome to Hicksville. How are you getting on here? Are you meeting the locals? Getting all the goss."

Who the hell was this man? He sure wasn't my husband. My husband would never talk like that, and he wasn't letting go. He was becoming a stranger. I tried to pretend that it was all normal. I didn't know if Dan fooled Rich or not. I explained to Dan, "I invited Rich over to see if he could help with preparation for the trial. Sadly, he couldn't."

Rich probably noticed the tension, and he walked toward the door and reached for his shoes. "Sorry, I wasn't much help, Doc. I'm sure you'll be acquitted. Thanks for the milk. Nice to meet you, Dan."

I attempted to change the subject and make Dan realize nothing was going on. "Hey, when you and Kendall are free, maybe we can all have dinner one night."

Rich gazed at my leg bracelet. "I think we can eliminate any of the 'your place or mine' discussion. Just let us know. I can bring pizza. You and Kendall can work out the date. See you around, Dan."

"Anytime, bro, anytime." Rich left, and Dan let go of me. Without a word, he walked into the bathroom. I heard the shower, and the next thing I heard was him slipping into bed. He was pissed for sure.

I decided to sleep on the couch. I would wait for another time to request that Rich do some sleuthing for me. I needed to be sure he wasn't going to let me down. A few hours later, Dan woke up and came into the living room. He bent over and kissed me. "I'm so sorry, Carls. I'm so sorry. Come to bed. I need you. You are my sunrise and sunset, and no one is more important."

I followed him into the bedroom. We settled into our usual positions. I was falling back asleep when I heard, "I think I'm going to lose my job."

Chapter 28

That admission woke me up. "Are you kidding? Why?"

"The state health department is restructuring. They'll keep this hospital open with a skeleton crew. The government is starting up some super clinics and will reduce the number of doctors who work at all the rural hospitals."

"When did you hear about this?"

"A few days ago. We held a meeting, and I was named the sacrificial lamb because I'm the youngest."

"The other doctors are ancient. They're barely competent. They need you. This is crazy. It's an hour to the next critical-care unit. People will die. Are they nuts?"

"Carly, it isn't definite. They're having a meeting today, and I learn my fate. I realize it couldn't come at a lousier time. I wasn't truthful today when I said I was visiting my dying patient. I interviewed for a new job."

"Where?"

"The Royal Adelaide Hospital."

"So, we move?" I was close to tears.

I pondered while I listened to Dan's very controlled breathing. It wasn't the worst thing. In truth, I was over this town. I had loved it here until Mrs. Miller died. I knew there were plenty of vet jobs in the city. I had a feeling the Gilberts were going to fire me, anyway. When I was cleared of the charges, they would still believe I was tainted. My goal was to move back to the States, but it might be tricky getting Dan to agree. The laws about relocating children without both parents' consent were black-and-white. We both must accept any changes, or the children stay.

My children and I were dual citizens, but Dan wasn't. I was pregnant and had excellent healthcare in Australia at a much-reduced cost. If there was a problem with the baby I was carrying, it might bankrupt us in the States, even with the new universal healthcare. Oh hell, I think we were close to bankruptcy, anyway. We hadn't received a bill from Dolly and her worthless private investigator, but we both recognized it would be substantial. I couldn't work because I had to remain in the house due to my bail conditions. We couldn't afford child care anymore. I would pay Jedda her last babysitting fees the next day. When was this downward spiral going to end?

Dan was gone when I woke up. How had our marriage evolved into this? Faythe was standing and holding her bear, waiting for me to wake up. She smiled when she saw me, and I lifted the sheet as she crawled in next to me. A few minutes later, Casey joined us. We lay without speaking for several minutes.

"Is Daddy ever going to come home?" Casey sounded a little stressed.

"Daddy was here last night. Did you feel him come in to give you both kisses?"

"No," they answered simultaneously.

"He was home. He said to tell you he misses you, and he'll try to come home later this afternoon to take you to the park." I got up, made some breakfast, and showered. We went out back to the garden, did some weeding, cleaned, and refilled the birdbath. One nice feature of living in Australia is the variety of birds and their melodic songs. My favorites are the magpies, although they tend to attack people walking near their territory. The girls frequently wore their bike helmets when walking in the park to prevent attacks. I think their red hair attracted the birds, as they never went for me.

We had reading time after lunch. I didn't dare mention a nap. "You guys promise not to fall asleep?" They nodded, but we all three slept for a bit. I had an appointment to attend the police station at two. Jedda watched the girls while I quickly drove down and saw both Kendall and Reggie. This was my first attendance, and I wasn't sure whether I had to submit to anything as far as drug testing.

"Not this time," advised Reggie, "but you may be required to next time, so be ready."

Kendall followed me out to the car. "Hey, they aren't kidding. Be careful to limit the milk intake on a night before a police check."

"Yes, ma'am." So, Kendall was aware of my meeting with Rich. "He's kind of a bit of a heavyweight in the drinking department. This might not go well if you pull him over for milk intoxication." We both grinned.

"We've got our eye on you, Langley. Don't try anything funny."

"How are things? Want to have dinner one night? Your treat?"

"Mmm, not sure on that one." Kendall seemed sheepish.

"Is it me or him?" I believed that possibly she felt a bit awkward about consorting with known criminals.

"Well, maybe some of both."

I frowned. "No prob, in my case, but I hope you two are having a good time."

"Yeah, he's a nice guy, but it doesn't look good for the long run. I think he's homesick."

"Bugger."

"Well, early days. I think we'll skip the awkward interactions until we get to know each other better."

"Oh, I got it. No problemo. I'd better get home. Is a quick trip to Angel's out of the question?"

Kendall got into her police car. "Follow me." She pulled out, turned on her flashing lights, rounded the corner, and stopped in Angel's parking lot while I ran in to purchase some carrot cake and returned to my car. She waved and followed me home. As I turned into the driveway, she yelled, "And I don't want to see you out on the streets like that again." I smiled and waved as she drove off. Our next-door neighbor was out watering his garden. He grinned at me and shook his head.

"Hi, Baz. How are your roses?" Baz, which was the Australian nickname for most guys named Barry, was in his fifties. He had battled lung cancer, and he was one of the lucky survivors. His wife, Connie, worked as a high-school receptionist. They were good neighbors. I often cooked them meals on the weekends when Baz was undergoing chemo.

"Hey, Carly. Sorry about your troubles. We arrived back from Noosa yesterday. Went to visit our daughter. I'm a grandpa now." Baz beamed. He had a receding hairline and a smile from ear to ear. He used to be overweight, but it was apparent he was currently struggling to maintain his weight. "How are the girls? You know, they're welcome anytime."

"Thanks, Baz. How are you traveling?"

"Oh, we went by plane."

I grimaced. "I meant, how are you feeling?"

"I know. I'm having you on. Not too bad. Say, I'm really sorry about your troubles. If there's something you need, will you let us know? Connie will come over soon. She has a cold. We believe in you, Carly." He gave me a hug, which brought tears to my eyes. As he hugged me, he whispered, "We need to talk."

I pulled back and observed him. He smiled, winked, and said I would be all right. "Connie and I'll be over in a day or two. Stay strong, young lady."

169

Jedda and the girls were making cookies when I went into the house.

"Do you ever stop?" Jedda grinned and shook her head.

"My dad wants to talk to you. Could you call him?"

"Is it about his horse? The new vet is good. Your dad can trust him."

"No, it's something else." Jedda gazed down at the two girls and then swiped her ear.

"Should I call him now?"

"Maybe later. Dad's out doing some work."

"Tonight?" I was reluctant to discuss my case in front of Dan. While I knew Dan was on my side, I was also convinced he had an agenda. He might think I'm genuinely guilty. It was best to keep my cards close to my chest.

I received an empty text message from my clinic phone. It had an icon I couldn't download. My personal phone was ancient, and it often could not receive images or complicated transmissions. I sent back a question mark, but Rich Hamilton didn't reply.

In the late afternoon, Dan came home. The girls ran to him, and he swooped them up and kissed me. He shook his head. Was that good or bad? He couldn't indicate as he had the girls in his hands. I didn't want to discuss this matter in front of the girls. I suggested that they let daddy have a bite to eat, and they could go over to the park after he had a shower.

"We'll talk later."

"Bad day at black rock? May I get you a beer?"

"No, I'll have one when I get back from the park. Any word from Dolly?"

"No, and I haven't even talked to her since I came home." A trial was months away, and I wasn't counting on Dolly for anything. The private investigator guy is a joke - an expensive joke.

"She's in Sydney. She will return in a few weeks." He was walking toward the bathroom and pulling off his scrub top. His physique was still that of a young man. Riding his bike to work helped keep him fit. He went to a small gym in town, as well. I'd been going in late December but decided to give it up when I thought I was pregnant again. It was still a turn-on to see him naked, but something caught my eye. He had distinctive scratch marks on his back. I was a bit shocked.

"What the hell happened to you?" I couldn't imagine a good explanation. My stomach lurched.

"What?" He had no idea what I was talking about.

"Your back."

He went to the mirror and saw the scratches. "Oh, man. We had a patient go berserk this morning, and we had to restrain her. Meth addict. I didn't realize she got me."

"Oh, darling. Are you all right?" The marks seemed a few days old to me.

"No, but it isn't my back. Let's talk later." He brushed his ear.

"I'll order pizzas if that's okay. I'll have them delivered. Can you leave me some cash in case the pizzas come when you're at the park?"

I helped the girls put on their helmets and prepare their bikes for a ride in the park. Casey would ride her own, and Faythe would be up behind Dan on his bike. After Dan emerged, he went to the bedroom and returned with shorts and a T-shirt. He held a business card.

"What's this?" He showed me the card the reporter gave me.

171

"Oh, the reporter from the news left it and wanted to talk to me."

He tossed it into the trash and said, "As if."

I shrugged. "Might be our salvation. An exclusive might make us enough money to pay our bills."

"Maybe." He eyed the trash and shook his head. "Dolly would kill us." Dan and the girls left, and I retrieved the card. I put the contact number in my phone under a false name and placed it back in the trash as he had let it drop.

The pizza arrived as Dan and the girls came home. I was a hero. "Mom, can we have pizza tomorrow too?"

"Nope. Now get your clothes off and be ready for a bath. I'm fairly sure dad wants to do the honors tonight."

When the girls were finally asleep, I sat down on the couch with Dan. "Well?"

"Not good, Carls." He drank his third beer. I could see he was upset. He wasn't a drinker. "My contract won't be renewed. I finish in two weeks."

"Oh, my God, Dan. Could our lives be any worse?"

"I don't think so. Well, you could be convicted." I could tell he was nearly teary.

"How come nothing is reported in the news about this issue?"

"Because elections are coming up, they don't want to rile up the constituents. The super clinics that are opening are good news stories. We're in a safe seat. The government doesn't care about our community. Our votes are in the bag. No one knows, not even the staff."

"Are any of them losing their jobs?"

"I don't know. I doubt it. The board will quietly reduce staff hours."

"And Roger?"

"He'll be fine. Some of his surgeries will shift to town, but he'll still consult up here. I doubt he even knows. I must go to Adelaide to look for an apartment and to sign some papers. I wish you could come. We'll have to put the house on the market. With your bail conditions, though, we may need two places for a while. I'll call Dolly tomorrow. She would be legless by now."

It did make me laugh to hear that term about Dolly's evening activities. I had to admit that when she was sober, she was brilliant. After sunset, however, she was hopeless. "Dan, we can't afford two places. You know that."

"I can possibly rent a room. Anyway, I should go down to see the admin at the hospital and sign a new contract."

We went to bed. Even though we were both awake, we turned from each other and slept. I woke up during the night to an empty bed. Dan was on the phone, and I assumed he was dealing with a patient at the hospital. I tried to listen, but it was so muffled that I couldn't make out the conversation. He eventually returned. Once again, he left early. This time it was to go to the gym. The next day it was to Adelaide, for which he took an overnight bag.

Julie came by to offer to take the girls to her house. Both she and her daughter were home and could watch them. I was relieved. I needed to make calls and didn't want the girls to hear the conversations. Like most kids, they had radar that warned them to be especially alert for calls involving unusual topics. We had a cup of coffee before Julie left with the girls. Julie was different. I couldn't tell if she was annoyed or merely tired. I felt like she was keeping something from me.

"How are you? Any news about your trial?" I felt Julie was on my team, but I was taking no chances with anyone anymore.

"No, it's all on hold. I won't have a date for a while. How are you? You appear to have lost weight."

173

"Great. Five more kilos to go, and I will be where I want to be. Sorry about everything. What the hell is Dan thinking?" I wasn't certain what she meant. Because he described the rest of the staff as unaware, I wasn't going to blow it.

"How about you? Are you losing any hours yet?"

"No, why?" Julie reached for a cookie and spilled the milk in the process.

"Oh, sorry." She jumped up and got a towel. "I'd better go before I do something else."

"Julie, how bad is the drug scene here?"

"Well, we do have a few. However, since Kendall started her program, I must say it isn't as bad as it was. Why?"

"Oh, just wondering. Is meth much of a problem here? I'm trying to think outside the box about why someone might want Mrs. Miller dead."

"Oh, do you mean that woman who attacked the nurse in the emergency ward?"

"Were you there?"

"No, but I heard about it. Took two ambos to get the cretin under control."

"Dan didn't even realize she'd scratched him."

"Was Dan involved? I didn't know that. I thought it was on his day off. Well, I wasn't there. Come on, you two." She turned to the girls. "Let's get your car seats changed over. Who wants vegemite for lunch?"

174

Chapter 29

I wasn't going to waste a minute. I headed down to the basement. I started the laundry and systematically went through every box on each shelf down there. The place gave me the creeps. I hated this basement, and I had begun to hate the house.

There were numerous family keepsakes, including two boxes of Christmas ornaments. Dan's mom had given us hers, and we made hand-painted ones in December with Mrs. Miller. Fake trees were traditional in this climate. When the tree wasn't in use, it was boxed and hung from the ceiling, so the mice didn't get to it. Last year, we had a revolting mouse plague. The place smelled of dead and decaying mice for weeks after we baited the basement, which was yet another reason for a new cat.

Even knowing I'd recently packed them after Christmas, I reexamined them. There was nothing new in those. The next box contained all our tax returns from the previous few years. I perused them all to determine if we had any unusual payments or deposits. Dan oversaw our finances, and I never bothered to ascertain if anything was amiss. Not anymore. I saw nothing. Holy shit, we paid so many taxes.

I paid my Australian taxes and a small amount to the Internal Revenue Service to maintain my American obligations. During the last two years, I worked full time, and I paid taxes in both countries as I exceeded my tax threshold. I couldn't understand how we could be so destitute if we both had above-average wages that I knew we were collecting. How was this possible?

The next box was filled with my pictures and memorabilia from my childhood. This lot included photographs, report cards, letters from my mother and father when I was young, and swimming and tennis awards. My trophies and ribbons from horse shows were still with my mother. It made me think about where I had come from and where I was going. Was my future here in Australia or back home in Idaho?

I had dogs and cats from the time I was born. I had my first horse when I was three. My poor girls didn't have any pets. I promised them a dog, and I needed to follow up on that commitment. I wanted horseback riding lessons for Casey. I felt quite inadequate as a mother. The pressure to be a supermom and an outstanding veterinarian was never-ending. I was currently neither a terrific vet nor a super mom. Any puppy procurement would have to wait until we sorted where we were going to live. I would be certain we had a puppy before a court trial. I knew Dan wouldn't get one for the girls. God forbid that I wasn't around to ensure their childhood was as idyllic as mine was.

The next box was full of Dan's memorabilia. His report cards showed what a good boy he was. The reports showed straight As and frequently included messages that would make any parent proud. "Dan is a pleasure to teach. Dan is the kindest student I've ever taught. Dan could be a prime minister someday."

I didn't find anything that would suggest Dan was anything other than the man I thought I had married. I sorted through two more boxes of papers and mementos the girls had made that I wanted to keep. The following two boxes were filled with old clothes. Most were the girl's toddler-size clothes. I was glad I hadn't thrown them out since another one was on the way. This reminded me that my blood sugar was getting low. I swallowed hard and returned to the kitchen to grab morning tea.

The British or Australian penchant for a midmorning or afternoon tea break was one of the few traditions that I considered acceptable. I took a muffin and headed back downstairs. The laundry was done, and I decided to hang it on the line instead of running the dryer. Because the door leading from the basement to the backyard was locked, I went to unlock it before heading out with the basket of wet laundry. When I went to turn the lock,

I realized the door had not been properly closed. The knob hadn't been pulled tight, and the door moved easily. The wood had contracted in the dry heat.

Until Mrs. Miller died, I'd never been concerned about safety or being robbed or assaulted. I was now aware that there was a killer loose, and it sure as hell wasn't me. I climbed up to the backyard, hung the laundry, and returned to the basement.

The last box contained my old pregnancy wardrobe. Dan and I were ambivalent about a third child. If it happened, we would be glad. We hadn't taken precautions in the last two years, and nothing had resulted, which was perplexing. That was the reason we were both so surprised and happy when this little munchkin was found lurking in the incubator.

After hanging the clothes on the line, I returned to the boxes downstairs. My pants were already getting tight, and I searched through the pile of clothes and took out two pairs of jeans, which were one size bigger. Let's not go crazy here.

When I pushed the plastic bin back into the spot where it had been, I noticed a small envelope that had fallen from one of the boxes on the shelf above the clothes. It appeared to be older but did not include any date. It contained several typed pages from the law office of Myler and Maitland.

That was the moment when my life, as I knew it, ended. I recognized the letterhead from Dolly's old law firm. The landline rang, and I quickly replaced the letter in the box that was Dan's. I jumped up, ran up the stairs to the phone, and tripped. I fell hard, twisted my ankle, and hit my head. My sutures from the last fall had just been removed several days earlier. The phone stopped ringing as I crawled up the rest of the stairs. There was no blood, but my head was spinning, and my ankle was throbbing.

I dialed the last-number-retrieval code for an unlisted number. I immediately dialed the phone number for the police station in case the police were checking on me. It wasn't them. I limped into the kitchen to obtain a bag of frozen peas. I sat down on the couch and wrapped my ankle with a tea towel and the peas. I was in shock from the realization that Dan had some dealing with Dolly before we even met. They knew each other. I thought back to when he first went to Nigel's house with me, and he didn't look surprised about Nigel's extravagant bunker lifestyle. I believed the bicycle track belonged to Nigel.

I was confident I wasn't concussed, but my head throbbed. I didn't even get to read the letter or reexamine the small vial of tablets under the cabinet. What else was there? Who was this guy to whom I was married? Why had he used Dolly's firm many years ago?

The phone rang again. It was Julie. The girls were fine, and she wanted to know whether they could go to the swimming pool. I asked Julie if she had rung earlier, but she had not. She would be over in a few minutes to get their swimming togs. I told her to prepare herself when she got here.

"What the hell?" Julie came in and left the two kids in the car with her daughter, Lacey. "I'll drop the girls off at the pool and return in a minute."

"Will Lacey be all right with the two little ones?"

"Carly, she teaches swimming, in case you've forgotten."

"I suppose. Please thank Lacey for me. Why don't you get some money out of my purse on the table behind you, and they can have a treat on me?"

"Be back in ten." Julie shook her head as she left the house. "We need to cover you in bubble wrap."

Julie came back into the house and sat down on the couch. She removed the towel and pea bag, which was almost warm, and whistled. She lifted my leg and gently manipulated my foot.

"Ouch. Bloody hell, Julie."

"You need an X-ray."

"Nope. Can't leave, and it's not broken. I walked on it."

"Hmm, fooled me." She picked up her phone and dialed Kendall. "Man down, sister. I need a hall pass."

Chapter 30

I had to admit the swelling was daunting. When we arrived at the hospital, both Roger and Kendall met me. I'd taken some paracetamol, and my headache had decreased from a ten out of ten to a six. I passed a neurological exam. The ankle was another issue.

"X-rays don't lie, Langley. Stress fracture. No more ice skating for you today." Roger ordered a moon boot and advised me to keep it elevated and not walk on it for a minimum of two weeks. He performed an ultrasound of the tendons, which were damaged, as well. "That's going to be the bigger problem. My guess is you won't be going to the Easter Parade. However, it is you, so who knows?"

Julie went to get the moon boot, and I looked longingly at the ultrasound and back at Roger, who smiled. "Okay, Langley, drop your pants. I unzipped and pulled the jeans down low enough to get to my pubes. He placed the probe above the no-go line and angled it down. "Isn't it a bit early?" he asked.

"Maybe, but it won't hurt to look." He turned the monitor toward me. "You'd probably be a better judge of this than I am."

I strained to visualize the images. It was difficult to orient myself, but I finally could make out a small sphere and was convinced it was my soon-to-be third–born child. Just for a second, I thought I glimpsed another similarly shaped object right next to it. So did Roger, who immediately leaned forward and attempted to focus on both.

"Huh," he commented without any further explanation.

"Double, huh?" I was in shock.

"You have twins in your family?" Roger took the probe as Julie came into the room.

"Not to my knowledge." I was pulling up my pants as Julie came over.

"Not to my knowledge, what?" She eyed us as she handed Roger the moon boot.

"Twins." Roger was laughing.

"Give me that thing." Julie took the probe, and I pulled my jeans down once more. Two tiny embryos appeared as plain as day on the screen.

"Huh," she said, too.

"I need to puke. Can someone hand me a bucket?" Just in time, I was able to toss my cookies into the kidney dish that Julie handed me.

Roger peered over and requested, "How would you like to sleep over here at the Queen's pleasure?"

"Thanks, but no thanks."

"Carly, that wasn't really a question. Let's get her a bed. He examined my pupils again with a penlight. "Just a precaution."

"Can't. The old man is in Adelaide looking for a job. Bloody government."

Both Julie and Roger looked at me with quizzical looks.

"The kids, you two? Motherhood? Responsible parenting? I should go home. They'll be exhausted."

"Lacey and I can deal with that. Want her on a drip, Rog?"

I was seated in a wheelchair and whisked away to a private room, where I was finally alone. I was given some intravenous fluids and a sandwich. The nurse, whom I had met only once before at a Christmas party, was young and kind. She was expected to monitor my neurological status hourly. She took her job seriously. When I had time to think, I recognized this was the day I officially knew Dan was not honest. I had so much to think about. It was apparent Roger and Julie didn't know about any health-care restructuring. One of them should have known.

I felt alone, unloved, and extremely vulnerable. My family and childhood friends were thousands of miles from me. My husband had a secret past, and even my solicitor was hiding some relationship with my husband. I was accused of murder, and I had no competent legal representation.

My assets were in a joint account, and I didn't know how much money was in the bank. Because I was pregnant with twins, I would have limited time to earn money before I could not work. And that was only if I was acquitted of a murder I did not commit. My head was splitting, and my ankle was killing me. I would never trust anyone again. Never.

I called Dan. He didn't pick up the phone. I left a message that I was in the hospital, and the girls were staying with Julie tonight. Despite the young nurse's best effort, I did sleep. I woke up in the evening. Roger was sitting in a chair near my bed, writing on a clipboard. He glanced up and smiled. "Hey, you want some dinner?"

I nodded. I tried to smile back, but it was difficult to have any reason to be happy. A covered tray with food was most likely cold by now. Roger rolled a table over toward my bed and removed the dish covers. There were watery mashed potatoes, some very dried green beans, and carrots so soft they could have been sucked up with a straw. An inch of gravy covered the thin beef.

"Yum, the hospital's finest." I sifted through the food and decided on a stale roll.

"Nothing but the best for Dr. Langley's wife. I've got to step out for a few minutes. May I get you anything?"

"A cheeseburger and fries?" I almost laughed. "I'm not really that hungry."

"Yeah, it's a little off-putting, isn't it?"

Roger poured me some water before leaving. A new nurse was on duty for the night. Hanna Ormsby was an older, experienced nurse. She said she would let me sleep because I had been neurologically normal for the last few hours. The nurse helped me use the bathroom and get back into bed. I called Julie, who said the girls were fine and were already asleep. She would be there in the morning, and either she or Kendall would pick me up and help settle me at home. When I wanted to know if the girls were upset, she observed they had watched television with Lacey and made get-well cards.

I was thumbing through my phone, looking for missed calls, when Roger reentered the room with a paper bag that smelled like hamburgers and fries. He grinned and set the packet on the side table, where my uneaten dinner remained. "Your wish is my command."

"Next to carrot cake, this might be the best meal I've had in weeks."

"Oh, yeah, the carrot-cake addict. You could switch to fags and join me on the bench in a few minutes."

"How many do you smoke in a day?"

"Not that it's any of your damn business, but a pack a day sounds about right. I plan to quit after my first heart attack."

I ate my burger and fries as he finished writing some more in his medical records. When he set his last clipboard down, he turned to me. "Carly, I can't imagine what life's like for you right now. I wish I could help. I really do."

"Thanks. I know I didn't kill Mrs. Miller. And since I know I didn't kill her, I wonder who did."

He turned away and then back directly toward me. "Do you think it's someone you know?"

"Probably. Do you have any ideas?"

"Only the whole town. Thankfully, I was back home when it happened. I'm one of the few people with a legitimate alibi."

"Has the restructuring affected you, as well? Are you coming up here as much?"

He stared at me. "What are you talking about?"

I probably wasn't supposed to talk about it. "According to Dan, there was a quiet restructuring of the health-care system. The new super clinics will play more of a role."

"News to me."

When Roger witnessed my reaction, he tried to smooth out my misconception. "I probably haven't heard about it. Is that why Dan quit? Maybe he got wind of it before me."

I wasn't confident I hid my surprise, no shock, from Roger. If he realized it, he didn't acknowledge it. "Yeah, maybe." *He quit? He wasn't let go. Dan lied to me about that, too. What else?*

Roger stood up. "Well, I'd better go, so you can get some sleep. Unless I'm blind, you're eating and sleeping for two more."

"Thanks so much for dinner, and thanks for the talk. Maybe keep the twin thing to yourself right now."

"Too late, Carly. The entire hospital knows."

So much for client privacy. So much for my life. So much for everything. I was in a spin, and the trajectory was a downward spiral.

My phone rang. Finally, it would be Dan. I reached for it on the tray next to the bed. I wasn't giving anything away. I was not going to show my cards.

I answered before looking at the screen. "Hey, babe."

184

"Hey to you, too." It wasn't Dan, but the locum vet, Rich Hamilton.

"Oh, sorry. I was expecting my husband. What's going on?"

"I'm so sorry to bother you. I have a case that might be one of those plant toxicities that the Gilberts say you know a great deal about. Can I send you a radiograph, and maybe you can tell me what you think?"

"Uh, I'm not able to get to my computer right now."

"Can I send it to your phone?"

"My phone doesn't receive pictures well."

"Oh, darn. Let me describe what I'm seeing." Rich described an ataxic pony with quite low bone density. "Is that oxalate toxicity?"

"Sounds like it, but it's the wrong time of year."

"The pony came from down near Adelaide, and the new owners have been feeding it a heap of bran. Isn't that kind of a third-world diet?"

"Welcome to my world." I sighed. "If you take a radiograph with a lateral view of the fetlock, you'll see mottling of the sesamoid bone and the front of the first phalanx. It's going to be osteopenia, and the pony will be an irreversible wobbler and will never recover neurological functions. In short, if it can stand, it's a miracle that won't last long. Time to call the funeral director."

"The funeral director?"

"George's friend, Ronny. He picks up the dead animals to bury them. I think you've met him at George's place. Mrs. T can give you the number. Say hi for me. He is a godsend."

"Cool. Thanks, Doc. I sent you some pictures earlier. Did you get them?"

"I think I told you my phone doesn't do much more than text messaging."

"You didn't receive the picture of the tooth, either?"

"What tooth?"

"The tooth you extracted on the day you were supposedly giving the old lady a lethal cocktail of phenobarb?"

"You located the picture?"

"Yep, with a date and time. Maybe it's time you got some twenty-first-century technology."

"I had that. It's in your hand." I used the clinic phone for everything. My personal phone was for contacting only family and friends.

"Finally, something to corroborate what I said." It was the first piece of evidence that conclusively demonstrated my innocence. I was wary. "Hey, Rich, will you keep it to yourself?" Of course, I had to consider that *big brother* might be listening. "Now back to your original problem, the pony is toast if it's from osteopenia. By the time you have neuro signs, the spine is too disintegrated, and it's not going to recover. If they have other horses, they should put them on a calcium supplement. We can talk about it later. The nurse is here, and I have to go?"

"The nurse?"

"Didn't Kendall tell you? I had an accident. I'm in the hospital."

"Oh, Doc, I'm so sorry. I wouldn't have bothered you."

"I'll be home tomorrow. Call me then. Or you can stop by, and maybe we can make a trade."

I hung up and received three missed-call notices from Dan. I turned off the phone and asked the nurse if I could borrow a charger. She took the phone and handed me some more paracetamol. Yeah, baby. Hot time in the old hospital tonight. I told the nurse not to pass on any calls tonight. "If my husband calls, tell him that the girls are at Julie's. I am sleeping and will see him tomorrow or the next day." I was going to take back my life. When she left the room, I began to cry.

The next morning, Roger brought me a sausage muffin and coffee from Angel's. "What? No carrot cake?"

"She didn't have any ready yet. That stuff will kill you. It is a fast track to diabetes."

"But such a pleasant journey." I smiled, and he placed his hand on mine.

"Moon boot comfortable?"

I nodded. "Thanks, Roger."

"Think nothing of it. Wish you could talk your other half into not jumping ship. It's a dog's breakfast down in Adelaide as far as the new hospital is concerned. He would be much better off staying up here."

So, it was his decision. What was the drawing card down there? "Well, you know men. I guess you will see each other down there, anyway."

"And you?"

"There's a small problem with a murder charge, but who knows. I'll have to see. I certainly won't be able to leave here for a while."

Kendall came in with a wheelchair. "Taxi."

"Thanks. Do I need to settle up with the account?"

"Don't think so. It's on the house." Roger patted my hand and left the room.

"Cool. Let's get the heck out of Dodge. Any chance for a side trip to Angel's on the way?"

"It's getting to be a bit of an addiction, Langley. There's a twelve-step program for this."

"Hi, I'm Carly Langley, and I have an addiction to Angel's carrot cake." I paused, pursing my lips. "Nope, I haven't hit rock bottom yet. Not gonna happen."

Julie was at my house, and the girls were already there with flowers and a homemade card. My cell phone was dead. It had not been charged, so I plugged it in and didn't turn it on. Two people could play this game.

Julie went out to the clothesline and brought in the laundry. "Hey, would you do me a favor? I think I left the laundry door unlocked downstairs. Can you lock it?"

She returned and shook her head. "It seems as though a bomb went off down there. The door was open, and boxes were spilled everywhere."

Someone had been down there. "Did you lock the door?"

"Yeah. Do you think someone broke in last night?"

"Dunno. Possibly when I fell, I knocked the shelves over." I knew I hadn't, but I wasn't taking any chances. *Trust no one.*

The landline rang a few minutes after I returned home. It was from Dan, who was furious that I had not returned his call last night. He was headed back and would be home in a few hours. He had the job at the Royal Adelaide but finding a house to rent was tough. He said if it took a while, Lydia Johnson, and her son, Gavin, would let him stay with them.

Without a pause, I responded. "Oh, that would be so kind of Lydia. Did she leave due to the restructuring, as well? I thought it was because of her son. Is she still thick with her friend?" Dan and I had discussed her lover and her alternative-lifestyle choice. He was convinced they were merely friends.

"Somewhat of both. I won't bring the girls down until I have my own house, but it's a beginning anyway. Because they want me to start next week, I'll move down this weekend." He didn't reply about Lydia's love interest.

"How am I going to do this with a cracked tibia, Dan? I can't drive, and I still have to attend the police station every few days."

"Well, that's a bit inconvenient. I'm sure you'll think of something."

He hung up without an "I love you." Was that the first time, or had there been others? I didn't know whether I cared or not. I was in shock mode and had been for twenty-four hours. If I was honest with myself, maybe I had been since the morning after Mrs. Miller died.

Dan returned late in the afternoon. He couldn't have been more helpful. Although it killed me, in a pretense of doing more laundry, I'd already gone down to the basement and replaced all the boxes in order. Dan's box was the one in which the order of the contents had been changed, and I quickly went through it. The envelope with the letters from Dolly Myler's law office was gone. Dan had a friend for certain. Or had he come back and taken the packet himself? It didn't matter. I was suspicious that someone else knew something that I was not supposed to know. The envelope was gone, but I had preempted this situation. Before my misadventure on the stairs, I'd removed the documents from the plain envelope, and I'd replaced them with other papers from his collection. The legal documents went into the box that contained the Christmas tree. I had just a moment to observe the records dated almost ten years ago, and the subject was listed as paternity.

Now I was home from the hospital, and I had but a short time to retrieve the papers before Dan would arrive. Negotiating the stairs was difficult and painful. I changed my mind, brought the documents upstairs, and put them in the girls' room on a high shelf with their books. The girls loved it when Dan read their bedtime stories. They had their favorites and rarely wavered from *The Wonky Donkey* and *Madeleine*.

I had to get through twenty-four hours, and then he would be gone again. Was I going to discover who the real Dan was? Was he going to be sorry and repentant, defiant, or simply stay in this pretend state of denial? I would avoid confrontation at all costs. I especially didn't want a dispute in front of the children. I decided to play the sympathy card: I was accused of murder and currently sporting a cracked tibia. I would ask him to shop for me and leave me enough money to get by for a week or as long as it took.

A car pulled up, and I thought it was Dan. The girls ran to the door, but the familiar engine was my vet truck. Rich Hamilton stopped by with images from the pony with osteopenia on a thumb drive. "I thought you would want to see them. I always encode them with a password. You never know who might get into them." This was not lost on me. An image might be accidentally thrown in.

He handed the thumb drive to me, and I thanked him. Rich said he would send me the password later as his clinic phone had been confiscated this morning. It was complicated, and he had to get it off his computer at home. As he was leaving, Dan pulled in.

"Oh, darling. I'm so sorry about all this. How are you?" Dan made sure Rich saw a concerning display of affection. Like any male dog, he was marking his scent on me. "What did the junior vet want?"

"He brought over some radiographs of a pony with a possible fractured spine. He's never seen oxalate toxicity, and he wanted confirmation."

"On a data stick? Why didn't he email the rads to you?"

"That's what I wondered. Rich believed there were too many.

You want to look?" I held my breath.

"No, we need to talk. How do you feel about moving?"

"Can't happen soon enough." Of course, I was thinking the States, he was thinking Adelaide, and my better guess was Sydney.

"I called Dolly, and she suggested you stay put with the girls for the time being. It's going to kill me, but I will batch it for a while."

"Oh, darling. I hate this. How can I cope on my own?"

Dan almost smiled. "I thought about that. Why don't you have Jedda come and stay? Doesn't her school start on Monday? She could live here and help before and after school. It would be only until you can manage on your own."

"Well, I guess we could ask her." I was delighted with the idea. It reminded me I hadn't seen her father yet. "I've got to sit down. I can stand for only so long."

"Why don't you get in bed? I'll run downstairs and start a load of laundry."

Chapter 31

Oh, please, dear God, do not let him say anything about the basement. Please. Please.

"Carly?" Dan yelled up from the basement.

"Yes?" My heart was pounding.

"Are we out of detergent?"

Phew, was that all he was concerned about? "In the cupboard next to the dryer."

"Okay. Got it."

One month ago, I was the happiest wife in Australia. Now I ranged from scared shitless to furious. My number-one goal was protecting the girls. Even if their father was a cheat and a liar, I never wanted them to witness us in a domestic confrontation. One thing I knew for sure, though, he wasn't a murderer. His alibi was ironclad, and there was no way he could have killed her. Well, my alibi was ironclad, too.

He returned and offered to take the girls to the park and dinner and bring me takeaway. "After that hospital food, I'll bet you could use something with taste tonight."

"Roger brought me dinner last night, but anything is good tonight."

"Oh, did you and Roger talk?"

"Yes, we did. In fact, we had quite a talk."

When Dan scrutinized me, I detected fear. "About what?"

"Oh, just things."

"Like?"

"Such as we're probably having twins." That should diffuse any other discussion.

"Yeah, right." I expected Dan wanted me to say, "Fooled you," but I didn't, and I watched him and smiled. It killed me, but I did. The girls heard it, as well.

"Oh, Mommy, are we having a baby?" I nodded and smiled. Casey hugged me, but Faythe was a little more reticent.

"Do I have to share my toys?" Her lower lip protruded.

"Can I name it? I hope it's a boy, so I have someone to play with." Casey was already staking a claim. She was jealous when Faythe came home, but she seemed a little more eager this time. Faythe was not as excited.

"Can we send her back if she isn't any good?" Faythe had her hands clasped as if praying.

"Nope. And it may be more than one. We're not sure, but we may be having twins."

Dan appeared shocked. "That's somewhat surprising. How did that happen?"

"Do you want me to go through the particulars?" I looked at the girls, who were staring at us both and swiveling their heads from side to side.

"Ah, no. That won't be necessary."

"Time for a nap. You all can carry on." I got up on my crutches and headed to the bedroom. I shut the door, clutching the thumb drive. I tossed it into my top drawer and then fell into a heap. I emerged two hours later, realizing there was a real chance I wasn't going to have that luxury again.

Pizza and flowers were on the table. It was a peace offering. "Oh, that is so nice. I hugged and kissed both girls and hobbled over to Dan. I put my arms around his neck and kissed him. He reciprocated, but something was missing. *Maybe it had been missing all along. I hadn't noticed until now. It was an invisible wall. Did he lose that loving feeling a long time ago? Did he think I did kill Mrs. Miller, and he was trying diligently to hold things together? Did he want to preserve the family? Or had he moved on to someone else? Was he contemplating raising four children as a single father? I was thinking about the same thing as a single mom.*

My next moment of terror was bedtime and a bedtime story. The girls announced they wanted another story. I stood at the doorway when Dan reached up on the top shelf and selected a book right next to the one with the legal documents. He read that one, after which he read the favorites. Finally, he told them it was time to sleep. I was on the couch, reading, or pretending to read a veterinary journal. Both girls came out and gave me one more hug, and Casey wished to feel the baby. I put her hand on my belly. She opened her mouth and, with mock shock, remarked, "Mom, you're getting fat."

I took her over my knee, pretended to spank her, and told her never to say that again. She got up, left the room, ran back, and quickly shouted, "Really fat."

Dan came out to the living room and sat down next to me. "Twins, really?"

"Dan, I still haven't had an official obstetrical exam. Roger and I were playing with the ultrasound after he examined my ligaments. Neither of us is an expert on ultrasonography of the human uterus. If I were a horse, I'd be squeezing one."

"It's not too late to." He made a squeezing motion with his hand. "You know."

"Nope, you know we both wanted another, and this one will be our last. The last thing I want is losing one or both."

"Me, either. I'm thinking of you and the trial and all that will happen this year. The effect on a fetus with you so stressed might not be good for it or the embryos. I can't believe it might be twins." I saw no joy or pride in his face. He looked like a doomed man.

Bullshit, I thought. "It'll be fine, Dan, really. Did Dolly say anything about her preparation for the upcoming hearings?"

"Uh, to be honest, no." She said she's busy with the pending release of her new book. My laundry needs to dry tonight if I'm going to leave in the morning. I will throw it in the dryer. You need anything down there?"

"Julie brought in the last load I was finishing when I fell. She said it was a mess down there. I think I must have hit the shelves and disturbed the boxes. Sorry for the mess."

"What mess?"

"Oh, Julie must have cleaned it up. I don't know. I was simply going by what she said." I hoped it allayed any suspicion on his part. It made me think it wasn't him down there. *Who was it? Maybe I did cause the boxes to scatter when I fell. I doubted it.*

Dan was gone for several minutes. While he was gone, I cleaned myself and got ready for bed. I took some codeine-based tablets that Roger had given me and was asleep before Dan returned. If he was looking for something, he never mentioned it.

The next morning was Sunday. Dan was going to start work on Tuesday, but he said he needed to get down there and get settled. He made pancakes in the morning and brought me breakfast in bed. The girls were so pleased with themselves and spent the entire breakfast suggesting baby names.

We all kissed Dan good-bye. I waited for thirty minutes before I called Jedda. I apologized for not getting back to her and her father sooner. She offered to come over after lunch with her father, and we could talk.

Jimmy Medika and his daughter arrived during another rare summer rainstorm. Jimmy removed his hat and shoes as he entered the house. He appeared nervous. I wanted him to feel comfortable, but the storm was approaching, which made us both jumpy.

Lightning in our area was worrisome because bushfires were becoming more common. Lightning and strong winds were frequently to blame. Fortunately, the storm doused the region, and the threat of a bushfire was small.

I loved thunder and lightning, but they frightened the girls. They both ran to Jedda, who'd brought Banjo. The girls clung to him. He growled when the thunder roared. It was intense, but the road was steaming after a short line of rain. The birds squawked, and the bright light that reflected off the leaves was the kind that made one squint when staring into the direction of the sun.

I made tea for Jimmy. A moment passed when he simply stared down at the ground and then at his cup. He glanced up and then at Jedda. Since she realized this conversation was not for the girls, she suggested that they take Banjo for a walk.

"Miss, I want to give you some information and perhaps some advice. You have been so good to me in the last few years, and I wish to return the favor." He stared up and didn't smile.

"Mr. Medika, I can use all the assistance I can get. Please tell me what advice or information you have that might help."

"This town is not your friend. There are good and bad people in this town, but the good can be bad, and the bad can be good."

I nodded. "I'm getting that idea, but whom can I trust, and who might want to harm me? I think some people are my friends, but they do things that make me wonder. I don't know whom to trust."

"Your private investigator is merely sitting in a bar all day. He's wasting your money. He is an old friend of Mrs. Myler, and she likes to help him, but it comes at an expense that I figure you can't afford."

"I don't even know who he is. I was told he was undercover, and it was best not to know him." This was according to Dan.

"Your solicitor is also not your friend. She's not who you think she is. She's smart but cunning. Mr. Nigel allows her to stay with him. He isn't her cousin. He's her ex-husband. I think they have an off-and-on relationship. He will never say anything, but I think she still loves him."

"Really? I didn't know any of this. Are you certain?"

"Mrs. Myler is an alcoholic. She gave up the grog many years ago, but she falls off the wagon regularly. She is not to be trusted."

"So, why does Jedda know her so well?"

"My sister cleans Nigel's house. When Jedda was little, she accompanied her. Nigel is helping with Jedda's university fees and has tutored her in math. Nigel is a good man. Mrs. Myler is not. Miss, you need to know that people who you think are helping you are using you to cover themselves. That is what I needed to tell you."

"I appreciate your advice and concern. Need a job as an investigator?"

Jimmy smiled and shook his head. "No, miss. I'm heading up to the station tomorrow. I would appreciate it if you would not say anything to Jedda. I want to keep her out of any danger. She needs to concentrate on her studies. Her mother and I are so proud of her."

"Oh, darn. I wanted to ask if she might stay here with me until I can walk better. I'll make other arrangements."

"Miss, I think that will be all right, but I must ask her mother first." Jimmy got up to leave.

"Let's ask Jedda first." I wasn't sure she would be keen to help out. "Obviously, I'll pay her."

"No. If my daughter does it, it will be as a friend. We aren't paid to assist friends. She can walk to school from here, she will save money on petrol, and I guess that will be enough for the short time she might stay with you."

Jedda was thrilled to stay with us. She would start after school the following night. Her family was having a special dinner that night for her auntie Lois's birthday. She wanted to be home for that celebration. They left, and I needed to make more phone calls. I let the girls watch a video, which guaranteed privacy. They would be glued to the living room for hours if I allowed them to watch as much as they wanted. There was no denying that their father's departure had upset them, and I needed to be mindful that they loved him and had no reason to think otherwise.

I called Rich to leave a message, requesting him to stop by at his convenience. I'd already tried the thumb drive. The radiographs of the pony were not password protected. It was apparent the pony suffered from osteopenia. However, a second file, entitled equine dentistry, could not be opened.

I then called the journalist, who said she had information that would be helpful to my case. Again, I reached an answering machine. I left a message that I was considering her generous offer for the exclusive interview. If she could call me the next day, we could arrange a meeting. No sense in pretending I wasn't aware my phone was tapped. I told her that anything she might want to know was handled best face to face.

Dan called to say he was at Lydia's, and he was already missing us. He regretted leaving so soon. He spoke to the girls and said he would call the following day. I didn't discuss anything with him or any of Jimmy Medika's concerns regarding Dolly. Dan was officially off the "need-to-know" list. I put the girls to bed, then conducted an internet search on Dolly Myler.

What you learn on the net can be revealing and informative. Dolly's assertions about her books were the first revelation. She didn't have a publisher. Her books were self-published under her own publishing company. I ordered them all online. She'd been married three times and had a son by the first marriage. Her son, who was in his thirties, was a private investigator. Dolly didn't retire from the bar. She was almost disbarred from the New South Wales registry for misconduct. After several minutes of searching, I found a site called "Rate My Solicitor" with several entries. I found a civil suit against her for misappropriation of funds and failure to provide adequate legal advice to a client. And the list of transgressions went on.

Fired, that was it. End of story. I called her and left a message that her services were no longer required. It was no more than thirty minutes before I received a second call from Dan. "What the hell are you doing?"

"What do you mean?" I knew what he was talking about, but I played dumb.

"You can't fire Dolly. She's our sole hope."

"My hope, Dan. Not yours and she is no hope. She doesn't answer my calls, and she doesn't communicate with me. She calls you, not me. I'm her client, not you."

Dan was silent. Finally, he claimed, "You're making a big mistake, and I'm not happy with this decision. You'll regret it."

"I have lots of things I regret right now, but this decision is not one of them. Enjoy your life down in the city. Don't expect us to join you anytime soon, and don't feel the need to visit us either. The girls and I will be fine on our own."

I hung up and realized that I'd shown too many of my cards. This was entirely too early, and I began to cry.

Chapter 32

The next morning was the first day of school. I had deliberately kept Casey out, even though she was old enough to attend class. There was a midyear intake, and I thought she might benefit from a few more months of maturity before embarking on her educational journey. The school thought otherwise. Only a handful of students were starting in the reception or kindergarten class. Additional students were required for government funding. The school called me that morning. They were phoning around to request that parents reconsider early registration.

I pondered the pros and cons of sending her to school. Would she be bullied if the children knew her mother was indicted for murder? Would the smaller class size mean she would be less likely to be bullied? Would she receive more of the teacher's attention? How would it be for her to start here and then change schools if we had to move down to Adelaide? The pros won. I couldn't go out to buy a uniform. It was strange that public school children wore them as the kids in private schools did. So much for individuality.

I called my neighbors. Connie offered to go to the school uniform shop and pick up two dresses and shoes from the shoe store. She suggested that Casey come with her to ensure they purchased the correct size dress, hat, and footwear.

Connie was at the door in a flash. "Connie, I can't thank you enough." Casey hugged her. She had an envelope with the money that Connie recommended would be needed. I stayed at the door. The crutches were chafing my armpits, and I wanted to spare myself any more pain. Faythe was beside herself. Her world was ending with no father or sister during the day, and the pending introduction of sibling rivalries. It was almost the "terrible twos" again. She needed a playgroup. I considered the options and planned to consult Jedda, who was coming to stay after school.

Casey returned after the shopping trip. She thanked Connie and ran to her room to don her uniform. Casey came out dressed in her blue-plaid dress, navy hat, and black shoes. She was so cute. I took a picture and emailed it to my mother. In a separate email message, I sent it to Dan and his mother, as well. I explained that the school called to ask us to send Casey sooner due to enrollment issues.

An hour later, Dan called again and thanked me for organizing the uniform. He agreed it was for the best that she starts school and even suggested that we consider sending Faythe to a preschool, too. He apologized for the previous night's call and admitted I had every right to choose a new solicitor. Dan planned to ask around Adelaide for one who might take on my case. He deposited money into our joint account and said if I needed anything else, he would be sure I got it.

Jedda returned after school and described the first day as daunting. However, she was confident she was on track to finish the year and attain the scores needed to start university the following year. The girls and I had made a small area for Jedda to sleep in the study. Following a short play in the park, we had dinner, after which Jedda started her homework. Casey decided to make her own study area so she could do homework and emulated her adoptive "older sister."

After the girls went to bed, I received a phone call from the reporter. She apologized for not getting back to me sooner. She agreed that we should talk in person. Since she planned to be up in our area on the weekend, she would stop by on Saturday morning. I thanked her and said anytime that suited her would be fine.

An hour later, Rich knocked on the door. He handed me a bag containing carrot cake with a piece of paper and started to leave.

"What? No milk? Just a note? You do realize, I'm starved for vet news."

He smiled and explained he was on his way to the clinic to treat a seizuring dog.

This made me think. "Hey, could you do me yet another favor? I know the billing program can do this. Will you get me a list of all the clients who were sold phenobarbital say in the last three years?"

He smiled again and gave me the thumbs up. "You got it, Doc."

I took the paper. It contained a hand-written password, "pepper14".

I went to the computer to insert the thumb drive. In the second file, I typed the password and waited for a second. The laptop opened to the data file, which contained approximately five hundred pictures in sequence of the time and date taken. Five photos were taken on the date of the murder. All the images had dates and times embedded in each picture.

In the first image, the camera was reversed. It was a mistake, and it reminded me I had to show Tracey how to change the camera direction. The "reversed" picture showed only part of Tracey Galt's face, but it showed a tattoo on her neck that was unmistakable. The second image was of the horse with the stainless-steel gag employed to hold the mouth open. In the next one, I was holding the long, plier-like instrument clamped onto the tooth. The following photo was inside the mouth, where I had removed the tooth. In the final picture, Tracey cupped the tooth that also showed her wedding band. The tooth was not rotten, but it was fractured, and considerable blood was present inside the oral cavity.

I sat by myself and took in the moment. I was going to be free. There was no mistake about the times and sequence. I felt I'd better research the camera settings and the manipulation of the dates and times. Rich had a set of images, and he could testify that he found them on the phone I had relinquished back to the clinic shortly after the murder. I knew I could have an equine dental-expert prove that I could not have extracted this tooth with my fingers alone.

I was exultant at the moment. How could I get this evidence to the right people? Surely the Gilberts and the police must know this file existed. Several people must know that I was innocent. I sent a text to Rich: "Thanks for the carrot cake." He replied. "No prob. There is more where that came from."

I couldn't sleep. I wanted to tell the world and scream it from the rooftop. *I am innocent, and I have the proof, but how do I go about presenting the evidence? The police must have this data. Why are they covering this up? Is the whole force corrupt?* I didn't mind sitting on this for a few days. I would think one of the television networks might be an excellent way to clear my name. I would wait until I met the news lady on Saturday. If not, one honest newsperson had to be out there.

Chapter 33

The week progressed in slow motion. I received my phone calls from the police station, and I was required to visit the station three times during the week. Julie drove me and stayed in the car park with Faythe while I attempted to pee. Having a pregnancy bladder, I was constantly peeing. I forgot that I might have to produce a sample for them, and I'd emptied my bladder before heading to the station. The desired results took several minutes and several glasses of water. Reggie was not amused. He made Kendall supervise the procurement, which added to my inability to perform the necessary bodily function. Kendall wasted no time berating me for my lack of performance as it was eating into her lunchtime. This made me laugh. Finally, after much harassment, I gave Kendall the specimen. She and two other women, who had joined us in the bathroom, applauded.

"Why are you in such a good mood, Langley? If I were in your shoes..." I stopped her.

"If you were in my shoes, you would be hopping for joy." I held up my moon-booted limb.

"Something's going on. Want to talk?"

"Nope. You'll have to wait. Hey, would you like to get a copy of all my files? I need to see all the evidence."

"You'll have to acquire anything we can share from your solicitor."

"Hmm. Okay, be that way." I pretended to pout.

"What the hell are you up to?"

"Oh, just a little emancipation." I could almost enjoy this repartee.

Kendall gazed at me with a screwed-up face, indicating she was attempting to figure out my new game plan. "It must be good."

"Very."

Saturday finally dawned. School had gone well for all concerned. On Monday, Faythe would start in a preschool that was associated with Casey's school. She now had a uniform, and every morning she would get up and inquire if today was her first day of school. She cried when Casey and Jedda left on their walk to their respective schools and rejoiced when they returned.

Dan decided to stay in Adelaide and moonlight for a super clinic to raise additional funds. He kept asking me to find a new solicitor, but I wanted to wait and discern what the reporter suggested. I didn't disclose my upcoming meeting with the reporter. I might not need a solicitor at all with the evidence that I had collected. Curiously, Rich hadn't stopped by with any information about the clinic phenobarbital scripts. I was worried he was avoiding me.

I asked Jedda to take the girls shopping while I talked to the reporter. Jedda already had an assignment that would take most of the weekend to complete. Jedda said she would help me in the morning, but she thought it was best if she went home for the rest of the weekend. At ten in the morning, Kate Kilroy arrived without a crew. The shocker was she came without makeup, either. Surprisingly, Kate appeared to be about the same as she did on the television. She had to be in her late forties to midfifties. We shook hands, and she launched right into it.

"I'm fifty-two. Yes, I dye my hair, but I've had no cosmetic surgery and no Botox. I am confident you're innocent, I may have evidence that will help you, and I know who got you bail. I know you can't trust even your best friends in Adelaide, and my guess is that it goes the same up here. I want to help you get off, but I need you to cooperate and agree to an exclusive. Are you in?"

"I think I have evidence that should clear me, as well. Why should I allow you an exclusive?" I wasn't giving up my hand without an assurance of fair play.

"Honey, you can have all the evidence in the world. If you piss off the wrong guy in the court, though, you might as well go straight to jail without collecting your two hundred dollars. You require public opinion on your side, and you need a media campaign. I can give you that."

"So, a few news reports aside, what do you get out of this? Why shouldn't I start a bidding war?"

Kate Kilroy sighed. She was on the downside of her career. Sadly, television was for the young and beautiful. She was still beautiful but in a mature way. Youth was a sought-after commodity for the front of the camera. The few women who had been able to continue their television career had made smart choices early and had gone for substance.

I wasn't in Australia ten or twenty years earlier when women like Kate Kilroy reigned the airways. I couldn't say if she was more substance than show, but she was seeking meaningful content. In short, we needed each other. I had to determine if she would sink me in the process.

"Tell me something that I don't know. How can I be convinced you aren't going to do a hatchet job on me?" I folded my arms and sat back, waiting.

"I know who paid your bail. That person knows you're innocent, and that individual is willing to risk a fortune to help you."

"And?"

"And I require an assurance that what I tell you stays with us for the short term. I want to do a story on you, but I need all of this to come out on air. In case you aren't aware, you will be tried in court. If you don't stop the process before a court trial, your chances of an innocent finding are not nearly as good without the public behind you. Certainly, you know that, and your solicitor has told you that?"

"I fired my solicitor. I haven't hired a new one yet. How would you know who put up my bail?"

Kate looked at me without comment for several seconds. I could see she was contemplating whether she could trust me. I was considering the same about her.

"My father put up your bail." She clasped her hands between her legs and leaned forward as though a secret should be whispered. "My father is Nigel Thompson."

She noticed my look of disbelief. "I thought Nigel's wife died, and they never had children. I'm somewhat confused."

"That's the story that he wants people to believe, but he had me, and there may be one other."

"Who's your mother?"

"My mother is the nurse who cared for his wife when she was quite ill. They never married, and he never acknowledged me. When DNA testing came in, he ordered a test. Because he'd been told he was infertile, Nigel had a reason to believe he is not my father. It's been a rocky relationship. However, over the years, we've learned to live with each other." She laughed. "He'll never love me as much as he loves that damn dog."

"Sheba? He won't even take her to the vet."

"Well, he used to spend a fortune on her. He had a run-in with the local vets. I think they misdiagnosed Sheba with seizures or something. It turned out Sheba had an ear infection. He still rants about how incompetent they were and the way he almost put her down because of them."

"Why did he post my bail?"

"He knows you're innocent, and he's so thankful for the arthritis drug you prescribed. Sheba's a new dog. She even plays again. He thinks you hung the moon."

"He hardly ever uttered two words to me."

"Nigel and Dolly aren't what you think." She looked at the stove, and it occurred to me that I had offered her nothing to eat or drink.

"Can I get you some coffee or a cookie?"

"Yes, but could it be tea?"

I hobbled to the kitchen, and she immediately jumped up. "Let me make this, too." She filled the kettle and saw a cookie jar. "You don't keep any phenobarbital in here?"

"Nope, that's in the jar out of the children's reach. Not a good look when the kids go to school on drugs."

Kate gazed at me and shook her head. "I'm surprised you still have a sense of humor."

"Who says I'm joking?" She appeared anxious. I did laugh. "Got ya."

When we seated ourselves in the kitchen, she told me about Nigel and Dolly. She never called him dad. She said that she had nothing to do with Nigel until a few years earlier when he sought her out after the paternity test concluded that he was her father.

"He asked me to meet him when he was back in Sydney. He maintains an apartment there and occasionally returns to visit his friends and colleagues. We had dinner. After that, he wanted me to visit him here in his hideout. I usually come up about once a month. I try to avoid Dolly."

I felt maybe Kate could explain their relationship. "I was told they were cousins, but I have information that they were actually married at one time."

"It is a love-hate relationship. Nigel hired Dolly when my mother requested child support. Since she was successful in court, he never helped my mother financially while I was growing up. When the DNA test became available, Nigel requested it. By then, I was a reporter and on television frequently. I think he could tell the resemblance and maybe felt a little guilty. My mother had breast cancer, but he paid all her bills and obtained the best treatment possible. This infuriated Dolly. They had split up many years before, but they still got together as neither had moved on to other suitors."

"So, they were married?"

"He never really said, but I think they were. All he says is Dolly's as crooked as a country road."

"Yeah, I think I figured that out, too." I knew the kids would be back, and our conversation would have to come to an end. "What do you want from me?"

"I want to help you. To be honest, though, it will also boost my career. Old broads are not the flavor of the month on television these days. I need to market myself as someone with more substance and a little less fun and glamor." She swished her hair in mock deference.

"I need to consider it." I immediately realized that I had a new close friend. She was smart and funny, and she perceived her place in the world without any pretensions. I didn't want to seem too eager. I was almost destitute. I was relying on Dan for money, and I thought that would dry up as soon as he recognized I was on to him and his cheating ways.

"Do you need to talk to your husband? I understand."

"No, actually. I mean, we must keep this to ourselves. Will your station offer me something for the exclusive?"

"I don't know. My bosses are fairly convinced that you're guilty. The network doesn't like to pay crims very much. We could do a book deal. We could cowrite one after it's over."

The last thing I wanted was to write a book. I wanted to get this over and move on. The girls would have to wear this for years, both in school and with the friends they would make in the next few years. "How long are you up here? May I give you my answer on Monday?"

"You mentioned evidence that will clear you. Is it a witness statement or something more solid?"

"Rock solid." I thought about the picture with Tracey Galt's ring and her tattoo. "Since the girls will both go to school on Monday, I can talk then. I may have more information, and we can plan our assault on the criminal-injustice system then." We shook hands as Jedda and the girls returned.

I hadn't provided Kate with any information, and she had spilled her hand and then some. I was more curious about Nigel's beef with the Gilberts and their diagnosis of seizures than I was about the nature of his relationship with Kate and Dolly. The whole thing was incestuous. How was Dan involved?

210

Chapter 34

Dan called on Sunday. I was sure he had talked to Dolly, but he didn't dare say so. "You're making a big mistake, Carly. She's on our side, and you've cut her off. I've called at least four other solicitors and went straight to two barristers, but they aren't interested in your case. They all say you're going to hang. They don't believe you stand a chance. There's too much circumstantial evidence against you."

"Circumstantial, Dan. It's all simply circumstantial. If even a hint of doubt exists, they can't convict me. The next time you talk to Dolly, will you have her send my files back over here?"

"I'm not talking to Dolly. She's your solicitor."

"Tell that to someone else, Dan. She hasn't answered any of my calls. I need the files if I'm going to prepare the next solicitor."

"How are you going to pay the next one? We already owe Dolly a fortune."

I planned to contest the private-investigator fees after this was all over. Dolly hadn't given us any bills yet. I didn't know if she could hold onto the files until her account was paid. If that was the case, I might have to show some of my cards. I hoped to wait until I had one more piece of evidence. Where the hell was Rich these days?

Trying to get both girls ready for school without being able to drive or leave the house was a pain. When I hobbled out to the front to retrieve a bag from the car, I saw my neighbor Connie. I invited her over for coffee. Neither of us was a churchgoer. However, due to his near-death brush with cancer, Baz went regularly.

"Thank God for Sundays, Carly. Since Baz retired, he's driving me nuts. I don't have any time to myself."

"I can't say that Dan's departure hasn't been a blessing, too. The girls really miss him, though."

Sipping her coffee, Connie leaned forward and whispered, "Especially when you're up the duff."

I laughed. I like pregnancy sex. Well, I use to like it, but somehow it didn't seem very appealing any longer. "More coffee?"

"Yes, thanks. I love your Americana style of coffee. May I have another chocolate chip cookie, too?"

"Cookie, Connie? Am I converting you? Next, you'll be singing 'The Star-Spangled Banner.'"

"Only the second-worst national anthem on earth. Girt by sea." Connie was laughing so hard that she started to cough, sending sprays of cookies onto the table.

I mopped it up and was in fits, as well. "It's a toss-up. I always preferred 'My Country 'Tis of Thee,' until I found out it's in the same tune as 'God Save the Queen.' Is nothing sacred?"

When we finally regained our composure, Connie turned to me and put her hand out to mine. "Carly, I don't know how you're holding up like this. You put on a brave face, but this must be killing you."

"Oh, thanks. You know, it's pretty tough. I'm on my own, with a broken leg and charged with a murder I didn't commit. You know, though, I keep thinking about Mrs. Miller. It's as if her death is an anecdote to all the events this summer. It seems no one even cares that she's gone. No family and merely a handful of friends, and I wasn't even allowed to go to the funeral."

"Dolly was her friend, you know. I hope you don't mind my saying this, but it must have killed Dolly that Millie made you the beneficiary and not her."

That hadn't crossed my mind. I was sure Mrs. Miller's sister was the primary beneficiary. I never thought about who would

212

be next in line. I'd forgotten I'd supposedly signed the will as executor. In fact, I had forgotten all about the money. Someone hadn't. Who was going to inherit the Miller money now that I wasn't in the race?

"How do you know all this? Do you know Dolly?"

"Well, she was always over at Millie's. When she came and went, she'd park her car in front of our house. That car annoyed Baz to no end. She parked right next to our driveway, and it was difficult for Baz to pull in and out. According to Millie, they had some argument about Dolly not being the beneficiary. Dolly rarely came after that."

Huh, that's a curious piece of information. Can I spell "conflict of interest?" You bet I can. I can see those legal fees dropping like flies.

"You're a fount of knowledge. We need to do this more often." And I wasn't kidding. Wow.

"Carly, you realize I love your children, and that husband of yours was so kind and helpful to Baz. If there's anything we can do for you, let us know."

It killed me to say it, but Dan had his good points. How did things go so wrong in our lives?

The question was--how much of this do I share with Kate Kilroy tomorrow?

Chapter 35

My cell phone rang as I was making lunch for the munchkins. Rich finally surfaced. "Howdy, stranger. How's your pony? Ten feet under?"

"And then some. Can you direct me to the journal article about this subject? What's the plant called?"

"Yeah, it was a few years ago. I think I have a copy if you want to stop by. Don't bother unless you make a stop at Angel's, though. I'm suffering withdrawal."

"An hour, okay? I've been slammed the last few days, and I can't count on two minutes to myself."

"That'll be fine. I'll dig up the paper. Perfect trade."

I hoped to have the girls fed and resting in their beds. Faythe was so excited about starting preschool that she was not going to accidentally fall asleep during reading time. No, sir. Therefore, when Rich arrived, the girls were in their room and on their beds, but they could hear everything and ensured I knew they were listening. I believe it was a bit of protecting their father. Any strange man in the house was a three-bell alarm. No doubt, they could feel that something wasn't right. It wasn't, but it had nothing to do with this man.

I took a small bag from him and handed him a copy of the paper that described plant toxicity in ponies. "Coffee?"

Rich swiped his hands and said no. He already had another emergency. It was hot out, and he was treating a lot of colicky horses. "Is this area colic central, or what?"

"Good isn't it." Rich had lost weight. He was looking rather gaunt.

"Only if you like tubing horses and money." Passing a stomach tube through the nasal passage down to the stomach to administer various potions to soften and move ingesta along the gastrointestinal tract was the standard of care for horses with colic.

"It hasn't been as hot as it was during the last few years. Count yourself lucky. The first summer I was here, I treated more than twenty horses and ponies with colic in the first month. It's tough to get the horses to drink the warm water, and most people don't realize it until their horse is dehydrated and colicky."

I didn't ask any obvious questions. If the Gilberts had something to hide, they might have passwords to protect their records. "Do you get a day off once in a while?"

"I'm taking off Tuesday. I'm heading to the ocean and meeting a friend."

"The ocean is an unrealized dream these days. Wave to it for me."

"Pathetic."

"It happens when you have kids."

"I can hardly wait."

"Thanks for all your help and the cake."

"All I can say is that the records are like Fort Knox. Fortunately, I am becoming friends with one of the guards."

"The Terrible Mrs. T?"

"None other."

"Do you think she's on side, or not?"

"Unknown quantity. I should have some answers for you later in the week. Duty calls."

Right then, I heard Faythe yell, "Can I get up yet?"

I turned back to Rich. "We all have our crosses to bear. Be careful, will you?" He saluted and left.

I opened the bag with the carrot cake. Inside was an A4 paper, titled sales report, which contained a list of about thirty names of dog owners to whom phenobarbital was dispensed. I knew most of the people, but three of them were unfamiliar to me. One owner, D. Maitland, had a dog named Sheeba. It was two years ago. *Wasn't that the name of Dolly's old law firm, Myler and Maitland?* Sheeba was spelled differently from Nigel's Sheba. The glaring fact was that, for a small country practice, numerous animals were prescribed phenobarbital.

I searched for D. Maitland in the phone book, in which one might be a legitimate client. I thought about when I had tried to look up data on the computer at work. I could access the animal's records, but I was blocked from conducting any significant searches on the program. Because I thought the number of colics in our region was unusual, I wanted to determine if I could correlate them with the air temperatures. After I'd mentioned this to Henry Gilbert, the next morning I had a list of all the colics I'd treated with dates. The program was a common one that many veterinary clinics implemented. However, the staff must have been locked out from the search and stats area.

Jedda returned after dinner and helped me bathe the kids and put them to bed. She'd completed her class assignment and printed it at home. I asked to proofread the document and found only two minor errors. "This is amazing, Jedda."

She took both girls to their respective schools on Monday. It killed me not to settle them into their classes and talk to the teachers. I hated to delay presenting my evidence to the prosecutors, but I recognized it was best to secure all my proof. I figured I better have an idea about who might have killed Mrs. Miller.

Kate Kilroy would be here in an hour. I had a few more questions before I spilled my guts to her. Kate was late. *Was that her habit, or was there another reason?* She was dressed for the camera, but there was no cameraman. "Coffee or ice water?"

"Phew, it's so hot. Yes, the water would be nice. How are you? How was your weekend?" She fanned herself.

"My weekend was fine. How are Nigel and Sheba?"

"Oh, my God, that drug is a miracle," she exclaimed, sipping the water.

I smiled, remembering how many horse and small-animal owners had said that to me. "It definitely is."

Small talk aside, she stared at me hard. "So?"

"Yeah? What can you do for me? Why should I give you exclusive access? If I show you what I have, will you sit on it until I can acquire additional evidence, and will you help me get more?"

"That depends."

"I don't solely want to prove my innocence. If someone administered phenobarbital to Mrs. Miller, I want to find out who did it and be certain that the person pays for what my family and I have endured. I need to identify who killed Mrs. Miller."

Kate leaned forward. "I talked to my boss. He has the authority to agree to a significant reimbursement for your legal fees up until you are either convicted or acquitted."

"Kate, let me ask you, who do you think might benefit from Mrs. Miller's death and my conviction?"

"I suppose it could be several people. I hate to say this, Carly, but have you considered it might be someone close to you?"

"My husband?"

"Yes, well, he's one. Or maybe someone on the police force?" I just knew Reggie and Kendall, but I couldn't figure out how they would gain from an old lady's death.

Kate finished her water and gazed around for more. "Yep, that's a thought."

"Someone who might be next in line to inherit her money or her estate."

Kate sat up straight and stared at me. "Do you know who that is? Does Mrs. Miller have any relatives?"

"I thought she did. But as far as I can tell, she only had a sister who passed away a few years ago. I wouldn't know for certain if she had any nieces or nephews." I got up to serve Kate more water, but she did it herself because it was difficult for me to maneuver with my crutches.

"How about close friends who thought they might be in line?"

"Okay, I'm going to tell you my side of this situation. If you say the right thing, I might show you what I have that will hopefully clear me.

"The first thing is that unbeknownst to me, Mrs. Miller wrote a will naming me as the only beneficiary of her estate, except for a small donation to her church. First, I didn't know about the will, and I sure as hell had no idea about her assets. I honestly thought I was helping her by paying her to care for the girls. She didn't need the money, but I had no idea. I think she genuinely loved the girls and liked the interaction with our family. I don't know why she left her estate to me, and not Dan and me, but she did what she wanted to do, I guess."

"You had no idea?" Kate was taking notes.

"None. The second aspect is that, until I was brought in for questioning the first time, I had not even seen the will. However, my signature was on the will as an executor. This fact would make it seem as though I knew about the inheritance and the money and would have a reason to poison her."

"And you say it's not your signature."

"No, it's not. It looks exactly like mine, but I never laid my eyes on that document until I was in the police station being interviewed. I swear."

"If it was your husband, and you were convicted, he wouldn't get it anyway, so it's hard to believe it's him."

"Exactly. Whoever wanted Mrs. Miller dead planned to have me charged with the murder if the inheritance was the objective. Am I right?"

"I don't know because it's so complex."

"Tell me about it. Guess who was Mrs. Miller's friend and visited her regularly until shortly before her death?"

Kate shook her head. "Who?"

"Dolly Myler. My neighbor mentioned that Dolly parked her car in front of their house, making it difficult for my neighbors to exit their driveway. So, they noticed when she stopped coming."

"Did your neighbors know Mrs. Miller and Dolly?"

"I know they saw Mrs. Miller almost every day, but I didn't ask about Dolly. I didn't want to tip my hand. They were in Noosa when all this happened."

I wasn't ready to say too much more about Dolly at this stage. She was undoubtedly a suspect. I had to think that she and Dan might have collaborated, also. Dan could have easily gotten the phenobarb from my clinic truck.

I had no idea she existed at all until I required a defense solicitor. So many people in town recommended that I should use her. *Could Roger be involved?* I remembered he was one of her biggest fans.

"Where would she get the phenobarbital?"

I wasn't going to talk about my bosses yet, either. I continued thinking about how many dogs and even cats were receiving phenobarbital. I employed and dispensed it for seizuring horses and for ryegrass toxicity in a few pet sheep. Still, when I thought back, I might have administered only one or two bottles in the last few years. The number of dogs on the list was way out of proportion for a clinic this size.

"Didn't you say Nigel experienced a dispute with the vet clinic about Sheba and seizures? Do you know what that was about?"

"No. It might have been that the vet said she was seizuring, wanted to dispense her meds, or perform more testing. It might have been that he thought she was having seizures. I don't really remember. I can ask him."

"Maybe not at this time. How well do you know your father, anyway?"

The implication was obvious. "I don't know all of the facets of Nigel's life. That's definite. I can't believe he would want anyone dead. He has all the money he could want. He lives a fairly simple existence, and I don't even know if he knew Mrs. Miller at all."

"Why does he let Dolly stay with him? If they were married and divorced, why is she hanging around? Several people in town recommended her. Why? I looked her up. It seems she had almost been disbarred, had several complaints brought against her, and it appears she's botched some pretty high-level cases. I think a judge in Sydney described her as a vexatious litigant."

"Where the hell did you find all this out? I don't know anything about this."

"I'd like to say the dark web, but I found a site that rates solicitors. Three people complained about her on that site. I can show you."

"Did you contact any of them? Can you show me the site? Carly, I don't know how the hell you've survived and discovered what you have, but my hat's off to you. I want to help you, and you need to trust me. I don't know any reason you'd believe me, given everything that's happened to you in the last few weeks. If I can assist you, I will, whether I get the story or not. It's a hell of a story, and I want to tell it. I won't lie to you, but I don't know a way I can get you to feel comfortable by confiding in me. I feel you're right to not clear only yourself. I don't believe the police would put much effort into finding Mrs. Miller's killer if you got off. They've bet the ranch on you. Even if you are exonerated, I think the police will look at you for years to come."

"The dingo took my baby?"

"Exactly. You weren't around when Lindy Chamberlin was convicted, after which her conviction was reversed, were you?"

"I watched the movie."

"More people than not still think she did it."

We observed each other and said nothing for what seemed like forever. I remembered my father instructed me on how to argue. Dad claimed, "*You state your point, and the other person makes his or her point, and the next person to talk loses.*"

I stared at Kate, and she finally conceded, "Okay, all or nothing." I smiled, glanced up, and silently thanked my old man.

There was a great deal to discuss, but I wanted to investigate more before saying too much. I felt it was time to show Kate the pictures. I took her over to my little table that had been moved into the living room, so Jedda could have the study. I opened the computer, turned on the flight mode, in case anyone was tapping in, and inserted the thumb drive.

Kate viewed the radiographs of the pony with bone issues and asked about it. She was fond of horses because she'd ridden as a girl. I entered the second file and typed in the password. The pictures Rich had taken off my phone came up. I explained that the images had supposedly been deleted when the police had the phone. *Did the Gilberts do it, or did the cops delete them?* I had to protect Rich. She didn't ask how I came by them. I showed her the photos taken on the day of Mrs. Miller's death and the five pictures with the times embedded in the photos.

"Holy hell. The police don't have those?"

"They say they don't, but who knows for sure? Who deleted them is the two-million-dollar question?"

"May I take them with me?"

"Let me think about that. Once I show these pictures to the world, I will have my alibi. This is the point at which my bosses and the lady who owns the horse might be complicit. I think it might be even more complicated than even I realize, or anyone knows outside of my work."

I explained to Kate the discrepancy of the appointment, the procedure, and the dispute about the bill and the time it took for me to remove the tooth. Why did my bosses throw me under the bus? What were they trying to cover up?

In the end, I had to trust someone, and I guessed an aging journalist, who needed a good story to thrust herself back into the limelight, might be the person to help. She agreed to show them exclusively to her boss. I made copies and prayed she was a woman of her word.

"Kate, only one other person knows these pictures exist and have not been completely deleted. Even my husband doesn't know about them. Please, I beg of you, don't show them to anyone else."

"Carly, you have my word on it. I'm blown away. Forget the evidence you just showed me. I can see you have integrity. When this is over..." Her phone rang, and she didn't finish the sentence. She didn't answer it. "It's my son. I'll call him back in a minute."

"You have children?" I knew next to nothing about the woman I was going to trust with my life.

"Just a son. He's the best part of my life when he isn't driving me to the madhouse or draining my bank account. Treasure those two girls while they're little."

I didn't tell her more were on the way. If I didn't tuck in my shirt, one would never know. Kate said she would be in touch the next day. As she walked out the door, we saw Kendall sitting in her police car across the street.

I watched Kate climb into her Lexus and drive away. Kendall glared at me and shook her head. I nodded and started to walk back into my house. Kendall started the engine and reversed it into my driveway.

"She's a bottom feeder, you know. She's only good for cooking shows on morning television these days."

"Oh, really?" I kept a straight face. I was maintaining all my friends tightly in separate boxes until I knew who a true friend was and who was less than worthy of my time.

"She stays up at the Thompson place. Rumor has it she's his mistress. You'd better be careful if you share any information."

"Wow, thanks for that. Were you sent to watch me, or were you simply stopping by?"

"A little of both. You need to be careful. We heard you dumped your solicitor, so you need to be cautious about hiring another one. I'm sure you and Dan know what you're doing, but I'd hate for you to get one who might not have your back like the last one."

"Thanks, I'll keep it in mind. Have you got one you like?"

"No, that would be against company policy. I'm certain you'll find one."

"Unless you have carrot cake, I'd best be getting back inside my cell." I turned and hobbled back into the house.

Chapter 36

I'd laid out most of my thoughts to Kate. I trusted no one. I had a "for certain sleaze list," a "might be a sleaze list," and a small list of people I could trust.

Dolly, the Gilberts, and probably Dan were on the sleaze list. Dan may not have killed anyone, but he lied about too many other things. In the trust list were Jedda and her father, Connie, and Baz. All the rest were an unknown quantity. I thought Rich was probably on the trust list, but I didn't know enough about him. Obtaining those pictures and the list of clients getting phenobarbital for their animals was something a trustworthy person would do.

How about Mrs. Tankard, Roger Grimes, Julie, and Kendall? Difficult to say one way or another. What about Nigel? They had all been kind and helped me at times, but were they involved in something more sinister? *My guess was one of them was a mole. It was time to sort the wheat from the chaff.*

Also, for what reason did Dan have dealings with Dolly so many years ago? This was the first time I was alone in a week. It was time to look at those papers. I went to pick up the book in which I put the documents, but it was gone. My heart sank. I stared at the pile of books beside the girls' beds, and it lay there, unopened. With my heart pounding, I began to examine the contents. I knew I would discover something about Dan that he'd hidden from me since we'd met.

The header was titled "privileged correspondence." It appeared to be a settlement for a paternity dispute. Dan had a child. He, or someone, had paid a single considerable compensation to an unnamed person to settle and finalize any further obligations concerning a child's birth. The payment ensured the mother would never again contact or impose any responsibility on Dan.

I had to believe that Dan was down in Adelaide, seeing someone. The apparent person was Lydia Johnson and her redheaded son. Dan must be his father. Were his stays in Adelaide in the last few weeks so he could help her move down, and is that why he didn't want me to see her for my early pregnancy?

I thought about his excuse for not coming home. Dan was supposedly helping an old man receiving chemo. What was his name? I didn't remember. I could get that from Dan when he called. I knew he would call tonight to talk to the girls.

Next, I steeled myself for a trip down to the basement. Jedda had taken all the sheets from the beds down to the basement. I needed to start the washer. The trick to starting it was setting a latch just so to engage the motor. I headed to the stairs and sat on my butt to go down safely.

Once the laundry was begun, I thought I should complete my survey of the basement. I got down on my hands and knees to feel under the lowest shelf. There was barely any room for my hand. I could feel the vial that was jammed at the tip of my fingers. It took considerable effort and a metal bar, which was propped up in the corner, to set it free. The vial with my name on it contained tablets. I was certain they weren't the antibiotic minocycline stated on the label. I took the bottle to search for the name of the pills on the computer.

It struck me that something wasn't quite the same. I couldn't put my finger on it, but I sensed that someone had been in the basement. The room was too fresh. A small window was jammed and had never been opened since we lived here. The door was locked. The floor was concrete and slightly wet from the washer runoff, where lint blocked the drain. There was no sign that anyone had walked on it recently. I decided it must have been Jedda.

The wash was almost done. I replaced all the boxes as I had found them. I could tell that Dan's box had been returned in the opposite position from a few days ago. The box label was facing backward. I knew I had repositioned it, so the name was facing forward. A spool of thread had fallen from the box of Christmas ornaments. I cut several small pieces of the string and placed one under each of the boxes. If a box was disturbed, the thread would be moved. Each piece was less than an inch and wouldn't be noticed. When the washing machine finished its cycle, I filled the dryer with clothes and slowly climbed up the stairs. Jedda could get the sheets, and she and the girls could make the beds when they got home from school.

I opened my computer upstairs to search for images of pills. These pills were brown, with the letters OP on the tablets. It was oxycontin. I had no faith in my husband. However, I would stand on a stack of Bibles to say he never would take, or ever had taken, anything like that since I had known him. Never. The label on the bottle was all wrong. As far as I knew, he never had a reason to take minocycline, either. *Someone planted this in the basement to further ruin my reputation, but who?*

I did some catching up on emails from friends. Most of them knew about my plight. Several well-wishers had written to me in the last few weeks. I replied to everyone, declaring that I was okay, and I was confident the legal system would come to its senses. I reiterated I had not committed the murder. With God's help, I would be free from and over this ordeal in a few months. None of my replies revealed what was happening to me or what I knew.

I saw an email from Arron Spencer, who identified himself as Kate Kilroy's friend. He had received the information and would proceed as Kate directed in the next few days. He required my bank account details. I responded with the account name and numbers and thanked him. Another problem was that my only account was a joint one. If the money went into the account, Dan would realize I was collaborating with a news channel. I quickly wrote back to Mr. Spencer, asking him to put the money aside and not into my account.

I didn't hear from anyone for two days, and my case files were not returned to me. I decided to write to Dolly by email and copied the Law Society of South Australia. That evening, Dan called to say he would be back that weekend, and he would have the files. He did not want me to contact Dolly or the Law Society again.

"Dan, this has got to stop. The woman must send me the files. You should not be running interference for her. Do you have the files?"

"No, but she's coming back this weekend, and she says she'll bring them."

I believed that information was more important than being right. "How are you? I'll bet it's torture not being with our girls." I emphasized the words "our girls." He admitted he was homesick and wanted to come home. He would return Friday after work.

"Well, the girls and I miss you terribly." I half-lied. "How are Lydia and your old patient in the hospice? Is he still alive?"

"She and Gavin are both fine, and no, sadly, Mr. Doudle passed away."

"Oh, I'm so sorry to hear that. I had coffee with Connie on Sunday. She says hi. She mentioned how much she appreciated your assistance and visits when Baz was ill and receiving chemo. You're a good man and doctor."

"Oh, thanks. It's not much fun right now, but we'll get through this. Hopefully, we can make a clean break and maybe even shift over to Melbourne or Sydney. I think I've had enough of the small-town life."

"You and me both." I lied again. I put the girls on the phone. They each told their dad they missed him and described the school and their new friends. They expressed they were looking forward to seeing him at the weekend. When they hung up, Casey was a bit teary. She missed her father and commented I wasn't as good a book reader as he was. I agreed and said I would practice. We discussed names for the baby or babies.

After the girls were in bed, I sought a funeral notice for Mr. Doudle. Oh, surprise, he died a year ago. I had to consider Dan was more than merely a liar. He probably was involved with Lydia or someone else. I was beyond furious and heartbroken simultaneously. If I couldn't trust Dan, whom could I trust? I began to grieve. There was no turning back because my marriage was dead. Later, I lay in bed and tried to remember when I noticed a change in my husband. Was it before or after Mrs. Miller died? How long had he been unfaithful? He surely didn't want another baby. I didn't cry, but my throat and head hurt, and sleep was elusive. When was this downward spiral going to end? I needed to protect the girls and the little ones inside me.

The next morning, I made an appointment with the hospital for a first official checkup. The police gave me their approval, and Julie agreed to drive me back and forth on Wednesday of the next week. An obstetrician was scheduled to come to the hospital on Wednesdays to see us rural women. She was a new doctor, and I would ask Dan if he knew her the next time he called. I let the girls phone him anytime they wanted, but I frequently didn't speak to him anymore. He rarely asked to talk to me.

Jedda was my salvation. Oh, how I loved this young woman! She had spirit and grit. She made the girls laugh and never let them sass me. She would come home, take the girls to the park, or shop for our food. She studied well into the night. She taught the girls to clean and to help me with the dramas of life in a moon boot. She was returning home Friday night, and Dan was coming back. He was going to stay until Monday, and he would take the girls to school before leaving for Adelaide, so he could meet their teachers and see the classrooms.

I went to the police station with Julie the next day. Kendall was not around. She hadn't called or talked to me since she saw me talking to Kate Kilroy. I was prepared to provide a urine sample. I answered the standard questions. Had I consumed alcohol in the last week, had I associated with known criminals, and did I have any firearms in the house currently? I would have liked to say, "I'm not sure," but this was no joking matter. "No, no, and no?"

Julie took me shopping to purchase food and some new underwear. My growing body was making my bras and knickers somewhat tight. When we returned home, a car was parked in front of my house. It was familiar, but I couldn't place it. As I hobbled up the steps to the front door, Mrs. Tankard walked with Connie from next door. Strange.

I gave Mrs. Tankard a hard look. "Look what the cat dragged in. I hope you have protection. I have some nice brownies if you don't mind the bitter taste."

"Well, don't you look," Mrs. Tankard paused and assessed my physique, "definitely twins."

"Is nothing a secret in this town?"

"Nope. Not even your visitor last Saturday. What was the old girl's name? Kate Killjoy?"

"Kilroy. Want some coffee?"

"I like to live dangerously. Why not."

Julie had to get to work, so I hugged and thanked her. She said she would see me the next Wednesday for my doctor's appointment at the hospital. I didn't say anything, but Julie had lost more weight. I would ask about her diet when we were alone.

"Oh, no. Are you okay?" Connie appeared worried.

"In case you didn't get the message from the town crier," I announced while pointing to Mrs. Tankard, "I'm back in the maternity ward."

Connie hugged me. "And on top of everything else. How do you cope?"

"I don't. I'm so bored that I'm ready to break out for some excitement. How are things at the clinic, Mrs. T? I need a vet fix, and I haven't seen the young vet since he had a sick pony. I guess he's self-sufficient."

"He is sure nice. Too bad that the good ones are always gay or taken."

"Oh, has he found someone? I tried to fix him up with Kendall, but it didn't seem like it was going anywhere."

"Are you sure? They've been inseparable."

"Rich Hamilton and Kendall? It's news to me." *Were they collaborating?*

Connie poured the coffee, and I did have brownies. Mrs. Tankard was hesitant, but Connie took one immediately. "I need that recipe, Carly. That is delicious."

"It's Betty's. You know, I'm pretty average in the cooking department." I showed her the empty box of the Betty Crocker brownie mix.

"Tanya and I want to make sure you're okay and safe. You know, this town has been less than hospitable to you. We think we should have dinner together. We could make it, bring it over, and brainstorm about ways to prove your innocence."

"That is if you are innocent." Mrs. Tankard was reaching for her second brownie. "If I'm going to die from poisoning, let it be from these."

"Dinner would be lovely. I've been somewhat reluctant to have anyone over for dinner because I'm on bail, but maybe we could have dinner and a chat. I'd really like that."

We talked a little about the town gossip, of which I was the prime topic. Connie and Tanya, as I was finally allowed to call her, each had a third brownie and left with plans to share dinner the next week. They would bring the main course, and I would bake more brownies.

The day after tomorrow, Dan was coming home. I still hadn't determined how much I was going to divulge about all that had transpired. If I told him all I knew, I assumed he would go berserk, and he would probably attempt to have the girls removed from my custody. That thought stopped any early disclosure of how much I knew.

It was almost time for the girls to return home when I heard my clinic truck. I met Rich at the door. He appeared worried, and he asked to come inside. "I have a huge favor to ask."

"Ask away. I'm totally in your debt."

"Can you leave the house and come to the clinic to assist me with a colic surgery?"

"I doubt it. What's going on?"

"You know how you told me about pony colics and the incidence of small colon impactions?"

"You have one?"

"I'm fairly certain I do. The pony is about twenty and belongs to the Raymonds."

"Tigger?"

"Yep, I think you've dealt with him several times. Anyway, he's suffered from colic for a few days, but the Raymonds were away. The people caring for him weren't horse people and didn't realize how sick he was. I've administered both oral and intravenous fluids, but he's ballooning by the minute. I'm struggling to control the pain. They're desperate to save him. I

231

can't do it by myself. The Gilberts are in Bali. The vet down near Adelaide, whom you mentioned, is away, and she won't return until Monday. He won't last that long."

"Crap. Tigger is one of our better ponies. I borrowed him for Casey's birthday last year. She begs me to see him all the time."

"Any suggestions?"

"Trocarize him. Try it. It is the last resort before surgery or euthanasia. This procedure has saved lives in cases when the impaction refuses to budge, and the owners don't want or can't afford life-saving surgery." I explained how to place a long catheter into the flank of the pony to penetrate the large colon, thereby releasing built-up gas. Rich had performed a few trocarisations, but never on a pony. "Don't light a match around him."

Rich laughed. "Doc, this may be our only hope unless you want to break out of jail. I can do surgery, and I can do anesthesia, but I can't do both."

"Deflating the abdomen will at least buy you some time. I've been using ketamine for pain relief lately, too."

"So, about ten milliliters?"

"Huh? Like, what do you mean?"

"According to the records, you gave Tigger twelve milliliters three times the last time he was here for colic. That seems like a lot."

"No way. A pony that size would receive a maximum of one. I think you read that wrong. Was that on his chart?"

"Yes, and in the truck logbook."

"I have no idea what you're talking about. I know you're in a hurry, but may I check the logbook?"

Rich retrieved the logbook from the truck. Veterinarians are required to enter certain drugs that are on a controlled-substance list, such as ketamine. He returned with the booklet and a small bag.

"I brought a bribe." He handed me some of Angel's carrot cake. "Heroin. Angel should have to record her sales on that stuff. I'm addicted now, as well."

"Eh, I'm on the wagon. My drug of choice is currently Betty Crocker brownies."

"Oh, the hard stuff. Don't get me started."

I perused the logbook, from which two things stood out. The dates and animals were correct if memory serves, but the amounts were three or four times the amounts I used with my initials. But it wasn't in my handwriting. Everything was written with a blue pen. I know my pen color had varied. Clearly, this logbook had been altered.

"Rich, I think a few things are falling into place. When did you say the Gilberts will come back?"

"Next Friday. It's killing me, too. Trying to run a practice with all creatures is not my idea of a fun time."

"Try the trocar trick. If Tigger does not improve, bring him over, and we can do the surgery in the backyard." That wasn't going to happen, but I thought I would throw it out to make him feel like I was helping.

"Okay, Doc. How're you holding up? Any news on the case? Did the pictures help?"

"You didn't look at them? By the way, how did you get them?"

"State secret."

"Oh, really?"

"Googled it. iPhone store deleted pictures for thirty days, and one can get them back. Yours were at twenty-nine days."

"There's something rotten in Denmark."

"Doc, I'm aware. I'm not long for this job."

"Where would you go?"

"Back home."

I thought he and Kendall were hot and heavy. "Is Kendall interested in moving countries?"

"No, but we haven't seen each other for a few weeks."

"Not according to Mrs. Tankard."

"The Terrible Mrs. T and I are an item. We're enjoying evenings together at the clinic. She's amazing. A real safecracker. If she wasn't married." He laughed and winked. "I go for the older women, you know."

"For God's sake, be careful. I think we both know what may be happening at the clinic. Some fairly good reasons exist to keep it all quiet."

Rich officially went into my good-guy list, as did Mrs. Tankard. The Gilberts were now officially on my bad list. I'm fairly certain they were selling drugs out of their clinic. Thinking back, the clients were often those who came from long distances. They were "Gilbert-only" clients. Even if the Gilberts were away or overbooked, they insisted on seeing one of the Gilberts or the other. I was so happy with my job that I never even considered something else was going on.

Chapter 37

Friday morning was T-minus thirteen hours and counting to Dan's arrival. The girls were so excited. How could I blame them? They were clueless about their father's duplicity. I would keep it that way until he died if I could. I just hope the death is slow and painful.

The phone rang as I was negotiating the shower. Because I had the moon boot off, I wasn't going to try to answer it. I was no longer responsible for the lives of animals. I finished the shower, dressed, and rebooted my ankle. I was surprised about how quickly the pain was receding. This beat a cast all to hell and back. I probably wasn't supposed to test the limits so soon, but when did I ever follow the doctor's orders?

I recalled my first meeting with Dan when I had a sprained ankle, more than seven years ago. Up until a few weeks ago, I never had one doubt about my husband's fidelity. Not once. When did it start? The phone rang again.

It was Rich. "Uh, Doc." The next person who speaks loses.

"Yeah?"

"Kendall offered to come and escort you to the clinic if you can assist me with Tigger."

"Does Kendall have the authority?" I wondered how the rest of the legal and policing community would comment.

"She says she'll check with Reggie when he comes in. She'll be at your house in fifteen."

"If I return to prison for this action, you can join me. I'll claim I was abducted."

"Oh, thanks. See you in thirty."

I quickly made lunches for all three girls. I explained to Jedda that I was going to the clinic to perform emergency surgery, and she would need to get the girls to school. The girls were tired from a week of school. When I told Casey that it was Tigger, she burst out crying. She wanted to help and hold Tigger. This could be a pivotal moment in her life. What the heck. What were the chances of an adverse outcome? I had conducted a few over the years, and all had survived. Case selection was the key to success. If I didn't think Tigger had a chance, I would call time.

"All right, you can come, but put on your dress since you're going to school right after the surgery." Faythe was not interested in coming. She loved the social interaction at preschool. She was selected to be the class monitor for the day. Her duties included handing out papers and lunches to the students today. She wouldn't miss that for anything. Jedda was happy to get Faythe ready and take her. I would have loved to show Jedda the surgery and aim to convert Jedda from human medicine to veterinary medicine. Alas, though, her academic success was currently more relevant.

Kendall was at the door and yelling for me to come. Kendall, Casey, and I climbed into the police car. As we backed out of the driveway, I inquired whether Reggie had approved. "Uh, well, um. I'm sure he will when he wakes up."

"Holy, f." I stopped, thinking of Casey. "Phooey, if I go to jail, Kendall."

"Mom?" Casey was no fool. Of course, she addressed me as "Mom" instead of "Mum."

"Yes, darling." I was no fool, either. This near verbal transgression called for a term of endearment.

"I won't tell Dad you almost said the f-word."

"Thanks. I'll owe you one. We girls must stick together."

We pulled into the clinic and went straight to the little barn next to the main building. Poor little Tigger was lying down and wouldn't get up. He occasionally rolled onto his back while Rich was shaving his flank. He had already shaved his ventral belly. "I watched a video on YouTube last night from the clinic that does these. They do them standing. I don't know if I'm that game."

"I think that boat sailed a few hours ago. Tigger looks too far gone to stand that long. I went to the cabinet for the anesthetic drugs. Casey patted Tigger and told him he would be fine. I gulped and prayed Casey's first experience would not be a bad one. If I went to jail, it might be her sole veterinary experience.

Tigger became sleepy when I gave him the premeds. Rich prepped both his flank and ventral abdomen. The plan was to do a flank incision, attempt to reach the impaction, and break it down without entering the intestine itself. The impaction is usually hard and the consistency of modeling clay. With careful massaging, it could be broken down, and the blockage could be resolved. I was going to administer anesthesia, and Rich would be the surgeon. To be on the safe side, we decided to use a local anesthetic on the flank incision and general anesthesia. If we couldn't reach the impaction, we still had the option to make a second incision along his ventral midline.

"Okay, Doc, you ready?"

"Willing and able, Dr. Kildare." Kendall sat in the background. Casey and I knelt by Tigger's head, where I had access to his intravenous catheter. I maintained a slow drip of intravenous fluids to keep him hydrated and to ensure he had a readily available vein for the anesthetic.

When I signaled that Tigger was anesthetized, Rich made an incision into his flank. He deftly separated the muscle layers under the skin. In less than five minutes, he was into the abdomen and feeling around. It seemed like forever. I was getting that sinking feeling. My mantra was all colicky ponies are small colon impactions until proven otherwise. *Was this an "otherwise" case?*

Kendall leaned forward in her chair. "Uh, Rich. Carly turns into a pumpkin in an hour. We need to get her home from the ball."

"Tell me you have some authority to let her be here." Rich glanced up at Kendall, who shook her head.

"Well, Reggie's a good guy. His kids rode Tigger at your party, too. I'm betting on a hall pass, but I don't want to test the waters unless it's necessary."

I rolled my eyes, and Rich looked directly at me. It was difficult to guess the expression behind his mask, but I figured it was one of mounting panic. His eyes were narrowing as if he was concentrating, but there was no mistaking a smile under the mask.

"Got it." It took Rich another minute to bring it to the surface. A grapefruit-sized fecal ball was enveloped in the distended, slightly purple, small colon. Even I was impressed.

"Wow, good find, Dr. Hamilton." I watched Casey as she stood up and walked over behind Rich. She was wearing a surgical cap and mask. She leaned in to get a closer look as Rich began to massage the mass without penetrating the intestines. The distended part of the colon, which had been stretched for days, promptly regained color and even some motility when the mass was broken down. "Hard to kill a pony."

"Oh, not if they eat those plants you told me about." I could tell he was impressed, though.

I took several pictures of the impaction and, more importantly, Casey standing behind Rich, observing the surgery. She was extremely cute in her surgical cap and mask and quite photogenic. Well, I thought so. What mother didn't know her child was adorable? I opened some suture material and announced, "No more anesthesia. A good surgeon is a quick surgeon."

And he was an excellent surgeon. Rich let Casey cut the sutures as he finished the skin. When Rich placed the last two skin sutures, we heard Tigger pass gas. "Mom, did you hear that? Tigger popped off."

"Music to my ears, darling girl."

"That's not what you say when Dad does it."

"It's not polite for people to pop off in front of others. With horses, however, it's perfectly okay. In fact, it's desirable. We need to take you to school and get me back home."

Tigger wasted no time in sitting up, resting on his folded legs. He lunged forward a little as he stood all the way up. Rich and I covered his incision with a sterile bandage, which we wrapped with long sticky tape around his abdomen. He began to pass watery diarrhea.

"He received a tetanus vaccine a few months ago. I guess you already started the antibiotics?"

"Yep, did some earlier. Thanks for your help. It sounds like a few people are coming to the clinic. Glad we got this done early." We all heard multiple cars pulling up.

Kendall peered out through the barn door. "Oh, fuck." She continued to watch and repeated, "Oh fuck, fuck, fuck." Casey stared at me but knew not to correct Kendall.

Rich handed me the lead rope, and he and Kendall headed to the office. My heart sank. I was going to be arrested right in front of my daughter. I returned Tigger to a stall and observed he was rapidly deflating. The belly band that he was sporting was already loose. It would have to be replaced later today or tomorrow. Tigger entered the stall and immediately began scrounging for scraps on the stall floor.

"Mom, Dr. Hamilton is a hero, isn't he?"

"You know, accomplishing these kinds of things is a team effort. Everyone, including you, are heroes today, and I've got the evidence right here." I quickly scanned through Kendall's phone, which I had borrowed to take the photos, and sent a few pictures to Jedda, Kate Kilroy, and-reluctantly-Dan. Using Kendall's phone, I could demonstrate I was under police supervision. I made the decision to secure a proper cell phone as soon as it was feasible. I was going to join the twenty-first century. I had photographs, yet I could only put them on my computer.

Reggie and his entourage of three other policemen entered. He smiled, pretending not to see me. He glanced at Casey. "How's Tigger?" He turned to me and rattled his handcuffs.

The relief I experienced at that moment was beyond anything I could have imagined a minute ago. "He'll live. Am I under arrest?" I already knew the answer.

"Only if you aren't home in thirty minutes. I hear we have a new vet in training." He smiled at Casey, who was beaming. Reggie approached Tigger, who was still passing gas and the occasional, watery diarrhea. "And you need to get to school, young lady."

Kendall gave me the come-on with her arm. "We're on our way." Her relief was evident. She quickly buckled Casey in the backseat and drove us to the school. I hadn't been in her school since she had started.

I accompanied Casey into the front office. The staff was wary and quiet while I explained why Casey was late. Casey was standing next to me, and she pulled my arm and whispered into my ear, "Show them the pictures."

I still had Kendall's phone to show the photographs to the school office personnel. One of the office staff members knew Tigger and his owners. The women, including the principal, all crowded around to view a photo of Casey and Rich Hamilton, suturing Tigger's skin. The principal leaned over the counter. "What a morning for you, Casey, but you better get to your class. Do you want someone to take you?"

Casey was shy and shook her head. We walked out of the office, and Casey kissed me and exclaimed it was the best day of her life. She skipped away. A proud mother moment if there ever was one! I turned to Kendall, who was leaning against the police car with her arms folded and smiling. As I approached, she pointed to the passenger seat. "Enough of this hero stuff, Langley. Back to jail. I almost took a bullet for you."

On the way to the house, I received text messages from Dan and Kate. Dan's message praised Casey for a job well done, and Kate's had only a question mark. Because she wouldn't have recognized the number, I replied to Kate on my own phone, "Talk in twenty if you're available."

She responded, "Always available." I wished to update her about the ketamine disparity, but I couldn't discuss this issue on the phone. We should meet again.

Chapter 38

An hour after arriving home, I received a text from Rich thanking me and apologizing for jeopardizing my freedom. He also joked anytime I needed a break, he would be glad to take the "vet in training" with him. I thanked him and requested any information he could locate on the "analgesia topic" we had discussed the previous evening. I didn't want to divulge anything more to whoever was listening.

I prepared for Dan's arrival. I wanted the weekend to go smoothly. I wasn't about to disclose any of my findings and concerns until I had my ducks in a row. I attempted to identify some logical explanation for his recent behavior. I could forgive him for mistakes in his youth, but he had lied about past events. My suspicions were validated, and I didn't want to sleep with him. In the greater scheme of things, I felt though I could at least pretend to love him. The sex thing was a different matter. It would be interesting to see if he wanted to fool around or not. If he did, he would be cheating on both his new lover and me, in which case he was a pure cad. What am I thinking? He was an asshole, pure and simple.

Kate called to inform me she would be up on the weekend and would stop by Monday after everyone had departed—meaning Dan. I explained the reason I sent the photo of my daughter when I had broken curfew. I was making sure that I had done a good deed and had not violated a court order. "You know how picture evidence can go missing?" I inquired how she was. Kate said that she was conducting research on a few subjects, and I might like to hear what she had learned.

I thanked her. Prior to hanging up, I remembered Dan said Dolly was returning to South Australia this weekend. I told her what Dan relayed. Kate was delighted to hear about this and looked forward to seeing "Aunt Dolly." She expressed it in the exaggerated tone of a high society Australian socialite.

Jedda dropped off the girls after school and headed to her own home. I suggested she bring Banjo next week. She agreed. The girls were excited about it, too. Dan called to say he was delayed and wouldn't be home until well after the girls were asleep. Of course, they were upset.

The girls were exhausted after a long week at school. They were asleep shortly after dinner. Casey had been invited to a birthday party. This celebration would probably be the beginning of hundreds of invitations over the years. The party was scheduled for the following weekend, and the theme was ponies. Sweet.

I'd been worried about how well she would be accepted in school. It's hard enough when your mother isn't a jailbird, let alone when she is one. Casey asked me to print out the picture of her helping with the surgery. She was pleased to be included in the social aspect of the school. I didn't know the family, but I would call them the next week to obtain further details. I was still reliving my escape back into my old life. It was so enjoyable to be doing real work and saving lives.

The ketamine disparity was weighing on my mind. I'd kill for the original I had written. I wondered if Mrs. T had ever noticed any discrepancies. I'd never heard about any agency checking at a vet clinic regarding its controlled-substance logs. We all lived in fear, but there probably wasn't any government money for hiring individuals to check inventory and logbooks.

Sometime after eleven o'clock, Dan came into the house. I was in bed, and I pretended to be asleep. He stripped down to his jocks and got in bed with me. He reached over, kissed the back of my neck, moved away, and fell asleep. That was easy.

The girls came in early the next day. I got up and made coffee, and they got in bed with their father. Casey brought up the pictures of Tigger and his surgery, which Kendall had sent. She was extremely proud of her adventure. Dan was quite complimentary. Casey announced that Dr. Hamilton said she could go on calls with him. Dan pretended to be happy, but I detected signs of jealousy in his questions about the morning.

Dan kissed me and ate a quick breakfast. I wanted to know where the files were, and he said they were with Dolly at Nigel's house. He asked if I wanted to go with him to get them. I pointed to my ankle with the security bracelet and to the other with the moon boot and shook my head. I believe we were both relieved. I didn't want to see Dolly, and it would be awkward to see Kate there, as well. I realized Dan must know that we met, but there was no point in having a big confrontation with everyone. The one innocent person was Nigel. Since he had provided the money for my bail, I didn't want any dramas in front of him. I don't think Dan was aware of Nigel's role in springing me.

The girls wanted to accompany Dan. I was torn between letting them go with their father and protecting them. He said he would retrieve the files and return within the hour, and Dan was spending the entire day with them when he got back. The day promised to be hot, so he thought the swimming pool would be good to start with before lunch. This could be the beginning of what divorce and custody would be like. The children would be transported back and forth between parents, but never together.

Dan returned with two files, which were a compilation of scratched notes and a few actual documents that appeared as if they were from the department of prosecution. They were not organized, and there were no papers relating to any surveillance by her private investigator. Even Dan was sheepish, as well he should be.

"You were the one who hired her, if you recall. I simply agreed." Dan was smug.

244

"Unlike you, I had no previous experience with her." I stared squarely at him. "Make sure the girls have their sunscreen on." My big mouth spilled the first few beans. He didn't say anything or acknowledge he even knew what I meant. He received the message, and that was the first shot fired. There would be more.

Later in the afternoon, they returned hot, red, and exhausted. The girls had sausages and icy poles for lunch. They were so happy. Damn, why couldn't he be a bad father? It would be so easy. They played chutes and ladders, and then both fell asleep in their father's arms. I grabbed Dan's phone to take a picture as all three were now sleeping on the couch. I typed in his security code. It didn't work. At least I hadn't changed mine. Well, that would change too.

I took several photos of them with my old digital camera, which I would download and send via the computer. I saw a message notification on Dan's phone from someone named Heather. Then two more arrived in succession. *Who was Heather?* The phone was on silent, and I could see the notifications but not view the actual message.

I started dinner as the girls woke up. Dan remained asleep. They heard his phone vibrate and went to it. Since Dan let them play games on his phone, they knew the security code. They saw the message notifications and recognized the name.

I heard Casey whisper to Faythe, "Should we wake him up? Daddy will want to know."

Casey could read many words. She would be able to relate the messages if I asked, but I didn't. When Dan finally woke up, Casey called to her dad, "Heather wants you to call her again, Dad. Can't you tell her to stop bothering you?"

"Casey, get off my phone, and mind your own business." This hurt her feelings, and her lower lip came out while the tears started. Faythe watched this and said nothing. Dan came around

245

the corner and explained he needed to make a call. "It's as if they can't do anything at this hospital without asking me." I smiled and pretended I believed him.

After dinner, Dan took Casey and Faythe bike riding because there was still plenty of daylight and the temperatures had dropped. Dan said they would ride up to the school, look in the windows, and come back. I'd already begun to peruse and organize the case files that had been returned. I received an email with a picture from Rich, saying that Tigger was doing well, and he would discharge him on Monday. He noted the investigations into the cause of Tigger's problem were ongoing. I recognized the meaning, but no one reading it would be suspicious.

When Dan and the girls returned, I showed the picture to Casey, who also wanted it printed. She told Dan she was going to be a veterinarian. He replied, "Next to becoming a doctor, that's a great idea, but the future is in the trades. You might want to be a plumber or an electrician." A discussion about what Casey had to do to become a doctor or veterinarian versus a plumber ensued. Dan did the bath and bed rituals, and I retired to our room. I wondered if Dan was going to bring up my mention of his prior dealings with Dolly.

He didn't. I think Dan knew I was onto him. He commented that he met Nigel's mistress. "I think Dolly was less than impressed with her being there at the same time."

"It's not what you think, Dan."

"Well, you obviously know since you two are friends. Was she the one who told you not to use Dolly anymore?"

"It's no secret, and you should know. Kate Kilroy is Nigel's daughter. And no, I don't know if she even realizes I fired Dolly."

He did look surprised. "You're making a huge mistake, you know. You're going to end up in prison. I will have to care for four children and make a living trying to support your mistakes."

"Kate Kilroy wants to help us. She's on our side, Dan. Did you look at these files? A dog's breakfast would be more ordered. Dolly doesn't even have a copy of my bail agreement. I can't risk this anymore. You might have to raise four children, but I will be doing hard time for at least fifteen years. Whose shoes do you want to be in then?" I didn't bring up his past connection to Dolly, and he didn't, either. I think he was hoping I meant something other than his love child and the abrogation of his responsibilities. We sat staring at each other, and nothing more was said.

"I'm sorry. You're right. What has this Kilroy lady discovered? Does she know a solicitor who can defend you? Why are you wasting time with her?"

"No, nothing. Kate Kilroy only said she wants to help." No sense in mentioning any financial help until I see the green stuff. We had a bit of a standoff.

"Carls, I'm bushed. Those kids wore me out. Do you mind if I have an early night?"

I bet. "No, with two in the oven, I'm not really in the mood for anything, either. Be my guest. I will do a bit more on these files and be in soon. Sweet dreams." He sealed the end to our marriage by turning and heading to bed without a kiss. I wasn't sure how I felt. It would have killed me a month ago before I knew what I knew now. I was in flight or fight mode. I needed to be strong. When everything was done and dusted, I guessed I would fall in a heap.

Dan told me he had gone from part-time work to permanent full-time work within a week of starting. The new hospital was desperate for trained doctors. He described supervising the nurses, and he always had to talk with them. He received text messages on an hourly basis. Surely, he realized I was aware this approach is not the way hospitals manage the nursing staff. I shook my head, and I could see he was embarrassed. Finally, he turned his phone off. *Smile and nod, smile and nod.*

We tiptoed around each other and avoided any confrontation in front of the girls. I could see they were stressed and did their best to avoid choosing sides. That part was heartbreaking. Both girls were teary when they saw their father packing his bag. They would have done anything to prevent Dan from leaving them. I wondered if he was ever going to come back.

This situation reminded me that deaths and traumas in families could be the wedge that broke families apart. I couldn't see how it could be reconciled. I was alone on a large island that I could not escape. I wanted my family and a few close friends to console me. I couldn't tell anyone what was happening for fear the telephone tap would be used against me. I was so alone. The only emotion that drove me out of my sadness was anger toward whoever did murder Mrs. Miller and toward Dan and Dolly.

Chapter 39

Mrs. Tankard called to say she and Connie were canceling the dinner, but she and Rich Hamilton wanted to come by that evening. Mrs. T said she would explain later. Around midmorning, Kate pulled up in her Lexus. Kate was alone and brought a stack of papers and flowers. Dan used to bring me flowers all the time. Life moves on.

"Coffee or tea?"

"Tea, and I'll get it. Just sit and rest your leg—I have lots to discuss. My boss is excited about your story, and the network wants to go national with the story. We believe you. Oh, have you received any bills yet from Dolly?"

"No. Do you know how much money your network will give me? I asked your boss to hold off. My account is a joint one with my husband, and he's opposed to any involvement with the media. I figure we need to talk about Dan too."

Kate set a cup of coffee on the table for me and opened one of the files. She sipped her tea, and the first thing she did was hand me a bank statement with my name and the network's name on it. Fifty thousand dollars had been placed in the account.

"Happy?" Kate smiled and peered into my open pantry. "I'm starving."

"Eggs, bacon, caviar?"

"Toast?"

I started to get up, but she spied a loaf of bread and made toast for herself.

"I spent an interesting weekend with my father and Dolly. I met Dan. He and Dolly had a powwow outside. He sure is a stud muffin, isn't he?"

"Yep. I guess you need to know if you didn't already, I'm preggers. The good or bad news, depending on your perspective, is it might be twins."

She didn't look surprised. "How do you feel about it?"

"Before my dramas, I would have been thrilled. You know, though, it's kind of inconvenient right now. Well, it definitely helped me get home detention."

"Some good and some bad?"

"Yeah, I guess. I had terrible morning sickness at first, but even that's settled down. Now I crave food and sleep. I have my first obstetrical consult this week and will receive confirmation."

"Dolly left this morning, and I doubt she'll be back anytime soon. She and Nigel had a row, and he told her to pack her things and leave. He is the most placid, quiet man, so this was a big deal."

"Do you know what it was about?"

"I figure it was about you and me. Among other things, Dolly was ranting about how my involvement ruined her association with you and the case. She said she was going to lose hundreds of thousands of dollars in fees."

I handed over the files that she had produced. "This is now in order. It is simply papers and notes and was in no order when I received them. I realize lots of important documents are missing. Kate, I need a solicitor. No one wants to take my case. I'm no fool. I need help."

"Carly, I have someone in mind, but let me do a bit of sleuthing. Do you want to tell me what you know, or should I go first?"

"It's probably easier for me to tell you. I don't know if it's related to Mrs. Miller's death, but my clinic seems to be doing something strange with drugs. I'm certain it must be distributing drugs that it shouldn't be. The locum who replaced me mentioned

250

drug dosages he found on the medical records and in a logbook for ketamine. The amounts have been changed in both places. He asked me about it because the dosages were not standard. The clinic hadn't bothered to even attempt to use my correct signature. The ketamine doses were far more than I actually used."

"Oh, really. Give me an idea of how it might be related?" Kate continued to write as I talked.

"I can't really. I will say that my bosses deliberately threw me under the bus with the tooth-extraction case. They altered the time, the bill, and deleted my pictures. Why would they do that, and what did they expect to gain?"

Kate glanced up at me. "What is the client's name?"

"Tracey Galt. She's a former employee. She called the clinic after I left to claim she was overcharged since I was there for only a short amount of time. They refunded her most of the bill and never even consulted with me. It isn't the first time they've done something like this, but they usually asked if I minded and had a reason for doing it. I never complained or argued. I still was paid. They lost the money."

"How did she pay?"

"Credit card. I asked Rich to search for the original receipt. He hasn't been able to come up with it yet, though. The business side of the practice is pretty locked up. The office receptionist is coming here tonight with the locum. Maybe they'll have some information to aid my case. The obvious explanation would be that Tracey Galt realized what was going on and used that to bribe my bosses. Is it true? I don't know. Tell me something that I don't know."

"Your husband and Dolly met in Adelaide before either came up. I'm sorry to tell you this, but they are up to something. The reason that Dolly didn't send the files was that they were left up here. Dolly and Nigel had a big fight when she found out that

Nigel had provided the security for your bail. Dolly stormed out and left them by accident." Kate was turning the pages in the file and shaking her head. "There isn't much here, is there?"

"Nope, and I put it in order yesterday. Only papers and scribbling were thrown in the folder. At least, it seems it's in chronological order now. You can thank me, and not Dolly, for that. Want more tea?"

"No, it's getting hot. I have a long way to travel back home, and there's no place to stop in between. As I was saying, when your husband arrived for the files, he didn't come into the house. He waited outside, and Dolly went out to see him."

"You didn't meet him and talk to him?"

"No. I went to my car, purely by accident. He and Dolly were talking, and I wasn't introduced. So good-looking."

"You already said that."

"I did? Hmm. How are things between you and him?"

"Rocky. I think he feels I actually did it." I didn't want to say too much at this stage. "Did she add anything? You know, Dan thought you were Nigel's mistress. I feel most people think that. I told him about your relationship with Nigel. I don't think he believed me."

Kate laughed, "He and the rest of the world. I don't care. Frankly, it is somewhat easier knowing they believe that. Dolly knows for sure, but she doesn't say anything. After all, the town feels she's his cousin."

"All right, what else are you aware of?"

I could tell she was trying to decide what to divulge next. I guessed the topic.

"My husband is probably having an affair. Is that what you know?" I read the relief on her face.

"Yeah, I think you can drop the probably, though."

Despite the evidence, it still hit me like a kick in the guts to hear it come from anyone else. I turned away to compose myself for a minute. "Is that connected with Mrs. Miller's death?"

"Would Mrs. Miller have been aware of the affair? Would he have wanted to silence her? How long do you think it's been going on?" Kate sounded sympathetic.

I told her I didn't know. I also told her about how Dolly had worked for him, or his parents, several years ago in a paternity case, for which there was a large settlement. I informed her about Dan living in Adelaide with a woman who had a son that might be Dan's.

Kate shook her head. "The son lives in Sydney. The woman Dan is seeing is a single woman with no children. Heather Smart is a respiratory therapist at the hospital. I have more information which you likely should know. Do you want me to proceed?"

"Don't tell me she's pregnant too?"

Kate looked away. "I'm really sorry. How long have you known?"

"A couple of days. How sure are you?"

"Want to see pictures?"

"No, not really."

"She seems fairly far along."

"Are we sure it's Dan's?"

"No."

"My husband is quite a caring person. Could he simply be helping her?"

"Yes, it might be that."

"It's not, though. Dan lied to me and explained it was a nurse who texted him continuously this weekend." *I thought I'd hit bottom when I went to jail. This was bottom, and it was a pit that I wasn't sure I could crawl out of.* The tears came, and Kate put her hand on my back and said she was sorry. All I could think about were the girls and whoever was growing inside me.

"Carly, I'm so sorry. You love him, don't you?"

"I did, and I probably still do, but I've had my suspicions for a week or two. My biggest concern now is who will raise my daughters if I go to jail?"

"You won't be going to prison. We need to put all of this into one box. It must all fit together. I'm sorry to change the subject, but do all of these things concern one another?"

"I guess that's the question we need to figure out." I was still crying.

"Do you want me to come back in a few days?"

"Yes—no. I don't know. I might have a few answers later tonight." I dreaded the possible conversation that I would have with the girls about a change in our lives. There was no doubt I was headed for divorce. The money in the account would cover the current bills, but I would have to pay for a divorce, as well. I was in emotional and financial ruin, and, despite what Kate said, I might still go to jail.

"I'll head out to scout for a solicitor who might be helpful to you." Kate returned the cups back to the sink. "Let me ask you, are you in fear of anything?"

"Other than jail, financial ruin, a looming divorce, and losing custody of my girls? No, not at all." I remembered the basement. "Do you mind waiting here for half a minute? I should go down and do something."

She waited in the living room while I slowly made my way downstairs. I inspected the threads I had placed under the boxes. Nothing had been moved. I climbed the stairs on my knees as I had done in the past. I wanted to go to bed and roll up in a ball, but I hugged Kate and thanked her for coming. She said she would be back on the weekend to talk. She would either email or call me if I had anything pressing. Kate thought she would have a solicitor's name later that afternoon.

I assumed the fetal position in bed. I don't know how long that lasted, but an urgent knock sounded at the door. When I opened it, there stood Nigel Thompson.

Chapter 40

"Is this a bad time?" I was a mess. My face was swollen and red from crying. After Kate left, the enormity of how bad things were and the realization that they would only get worse hit me.

"No, please come in. I'm sorry. I'm a bit of a mess." I wanted to hug him, but I did not know whether he was a hugger. His dog, Sheba, was by his side. He appeared embarrassed, stared away, and he started to apologize.

"I can tell I've come at a bad time."

"Please, Mr. Thompson, I genuinely want to talk to you. I owe you so much."

"Can I help? May Sheba come in, too?"

"Sheba's always welcome. Do you want anything to eat or drink?"

"Ice water. If you don't mind, how about some water for Sheba?"

"Coming right up. Have a seat." He noticed my leg when I hopped into the kitchen.

"Oh, what's happened? I should be waiting on you."

"It's really not that bad. I cracked my tibia. I'm almost ready to dance."

Nigel entered the kitchen and took a tray with the water and a few cookies. He gazed at the kitchen table where his daughter and I had sat in the morning. I placed a pan of water on the floor for Sheba. I petted her and smiled at Nigel. "I hear she's a new dog. The medicine is quite a miracle, isn't it?"

"It definitely is Carly. How can I ever thank you?"

"I'm not the one who needs a thank-you. If it wasn't for you, I'd be down in prison right now." I didn't think I could express my gratitude to this kind, generous man. Sheba then rested her head on my lap.

"I think the risk was small. I'm an exceptional judge of character, one ex-wife aside. Sheba knows a trustworthy person when she sees one."

Instinctively, I patted Sheba's head as we talked. "How is her arthritis? Does she require another injection?"

"That's partially why I'm here. Can you obtain more?"

"I'm certain I can. Two of the people who work at the clinic are coming over tonight, and I'm sure they could bring some. Can you bring Sheba back tomorrow?"

"That would be wonderful. How can I repay you?" He clasped his gnarly hand on mine and held it. We stayed like that for several seconds. I could tell he was emotional. "You know, you probably think I'm a crazy old bugger, but I realize Sheba does not have long to live. It's not longevity I'm after. It's quality-of-life that matters. If she lives another year, can climb up and down the stairs, and wants to chase a b-a-l-l, her life is worth living." I laughed as he spelled out the word "ball."

"If I call a spherical object by its common name, she will go crazy?"

He nodded. "That which cannot be spoken."

"More water? I'm sorry I don't have air-conditioning in my house."

Nigel gazed around. "It's an old house, isn't it?"

"It's suited its purpose. It's quite livable unless it gets hot. We must move soon." I glanced at my abdomen. He already knew.

"I suspect your life will change in many ways during the next few months. That's another reason I'm here." He paused to take another sip of his water. "I need to tell you a few things that might influence what you do when you are acquitted, or the charges are dropped. I'm hoping for the latter."

"I think you probably know I can't stay here either way."

"Yes, I understand. This town will miss you."

I laughed. "Only a few people, it seems."

"Now that I know you, I'll miss you. It appears that people in a small town can be your best friend until they suspect you of something. Despite your innocence, they will then turn on you, and you are condemned for eternity." He sipped his water and fanned himself.

"Merely eternity? I thought it was longer."

He laughed, recognizing my pathetic joke. "Carly, I should tell you what I know. I'm sure you consider me a hermit, and I am, to some extent. I do, or did, have friends. I try to keep my life simple, but I enjoy company. One of my good friends was Millie Miller. My, could she bake a cream cake." He shook his head. "Anyway, we had a standing dinner once a week. She brought dinner to my house, and we would play billiards. She was a wicked player, you know."

"Mrs. Miller had a secret life besides caring for my girls. I had no idea. I thought she was baking for Meals-on-Wheels."

He laughed. "Yes, exactly. Anyway, Millie was an extremely astute woman. She was knowledgeable about the things that most people in the town were not." Nigel paused and stared at me. I sensed he had information that I would want, or not want, to know. I quietly observed him while he studied me. "I am not a gossipmonger, but you need to know that Millie had some information about your husband, of which I don't believe you were aware. He's been having affairs for years. She didn't tell me for a long time, but one night she brought over her will, which had been changed to make you the beneficiary. She wanted to protect you and ensure you, and especially the girls were protected. She asked me to have Dolly look it over before she signed it. In the original, you weren't the executor, and you would have no reason to suspect you were the primary beneficiary. When Dolly saw it several months ago, she blew a gasket and couldn't believe she wasn't the beneficiary. She had known Millie for many years and was confident she was in line for Millie's estate."

"How was the executor changed? Do you know the way my signature was put on the will?"

"That was when your husband and Dolly, shall we say, became reacquainted. I'm so sorry to tell you this. I can stop if you don't want to hear it. I've suspected they colluded, but I've never said anything until now. I haven't even told my daughter, Kate. I know you are collaborating. Isn't she a wonderful woman?"

"Yes, and I feel she will help me turn the tide of public opinion, as well as assist me to have these charges removed. I didn't know my husband was having an affair until recently, but I had no idea it went beyond the current woman. I'm in a bit of shock, you know."

"Dolly is not a nice person. I didn't know she would go to this extent, and I'm sorry this has happened to you. You are an innocent casualty. Your husband met with Dolly several months ago. She had represented his parents and your husband several years ago. I don't know for certain, but I think Dolly blackmailed him."

"You think Dolly got her to change the executor to me, and Dan acquired a copy of my signature and signed the document? It all seems a bit far-fetched, doesn't it? Why would Dan do that? We're married. I would have shared anything I received as an inheritance."

"If you knew your husband was cheating on you, would you have?"

Nigel was right. "I understand your point. Dolly was blackmailing Dan to do what he did."

"I think it's even more sinister than that."

"Could it be any worse? Were they going to frame me? And have me charged for the murder, and then the fallback would be Dolly or Dan. Then they would share the inheritance?"

"I can't be certain, but I don't believe so. Dolly felt you would still inherit the money. They never suspected you would be charged with the murder."

"Can you explain this? I don't understand this."

"Your husband had very little money to pay for Dolly's hush money. I think the idea was for you two to receive the money sooner, and Dan would make a large payment to Dolly, after which they would go their separate ways."

"Why are you telling me this now?"

"I didn't know for sure. And I still don't. I know that Dolly took Sheba to your clinic before Christmas when I was down in Adelaide, helping Kate, and she said Sheba was having seizures. I know she received medication for Sheba, and I suspect that killed Millie. The stupid woman didn't pay the vet bill, and it was sent to me. I told them I wouldn't pay it, and they might be sued if they either persisted with the bill or ever treated Sheba again without my consent."

"But why would the clinic prescribe her medication without a proper diagnostic workup?"

"Dolly's been going there for years. I don't know the reason, but she frequently visits them. I think they're friends. I suspect they give her drugs that aren't intended for animal consumption."

260

I shook my head. "You think Dolly intended to expedite Mrs. Miller's death to extort money from Dan? And the timing was supposed to be that I would be at work and have an alibi?" I remembered Dolly saying that "it wasn't supposed to be like this," or something to that effect. "Are you going to the police?"

"Should I?"

"Do you have any evidence to back it up?"

"I have the bill from the clinic, and only what I overheard at the house."

"Do you mind waiting for a day or two? I believe we need more evidence for the police to even consider this. If I can identify some evidence that my clinic has been dealing in drugs with others, it might tie up the entire situation. If it can be aired in public, then the police can't bury it. I don't want the dingo-baby fate hanging around my neck for the rest of my life. I must protect my children, as well. Can we sit on it for a few days?"

"I see what you mean. Yes, but you need to be careful. Dolly's been sent packing, but her son, who has been up here for a few weeks, is still around. He could be in on it, too. Dolly may be funneling the drugs to him, so he can sell them to other people."

"Mr. Thompson, this has been quite an informative chat." When I petted Sheba, she put her paw on my thigh. He walked toward the front door. He turned and hugged me. "Next to my daughter, I think you might be one of the nicest women I know. I wish my first wife could have met you. Oh, and call me Nigel, please."

"Because I can't phone you, please come by tomorrow or the next day with Sheba, and I'll have the miracle drug ready."

"I can't wait. Please be careful." With that, he left.

The girls would not be home for another hour. It all made sense. Getting this information into the right hands was going to be tricky. I called Rich, and thankfully he answered. I asked him to bring the arthritis drug, and I would buy a bottle. Sheba was going to receive the best care I could provide until she died. I now anticipated Rich's visit with the not-so-terrible Mrs. T. I had friends who constituted a small bright light in a sea of darkness. I realized I would survive, and I would experience joy. I had to endure hell first, but my children and I would endure.

Chapter 41

The girls arrived home with Jedda. She had her car and had stopped by home to pick up her dog, Banjo. This was not a good day for the girls. Faythe was confused and was expecting her father to be home when she arrived. Casey knew he was gone again, and both girls were teary and exhausted from the weekend and school.

I hoped never to tell them that their father was a cheat and a philanderer. They were far too young to hear anything like that. I would be happy if they could grow up without knowing anything about this time, but I knew Casey would have issues with her father in the future. My dad was a typical father. He was rarely around and hardly ever came to watch me show jumping or playing any of my softball games or tennis matches. Still, he came home at night, and he was loyal to my mother. I wished he could be around now to help me.

Since Jedda said she was overwhelmed with homework and an assignment with a classmate, she went to her friend's house right after dinner. I bathed and dressed the girls for bed. We didn't finish reading the first book before they were dead to the world. It killed me to watch them struggle with the new family life. I imagined it might be their dad who might be jailed, instead of me.

Thirty minutes later, Rich and Tanya Tankard arrived with takeaway chicken and vegetables. I'd had a bite of the girls' dinner of fish sticks and tater tots. However, in two days, I would find out that I was eating for either two or three. My guess was the latter. I was scared shitless, and I could tell how my life was evolving. My bills would be paid by the network. I would have to sell this house and relocate, with no income for several months. How was I going to survive?

We ate dinner without anything more than idle gossip. The Gilberts were due back on Friday from Bali. George and Ronny were regulars with calving issues. Tigger had gone home, and the owners were grateful and had brought a chocolate cake.

"Where's my piece?" I stared at them and tapped my finger on the table.

Tanya and Rich looked at each other and shrugged. "None left, Doc."

I shook my head and told them not to call me again. I had already safely secured the arthritis drug in the fridge for Sheba. "Anything else?" They smiled at each other as Tanya opened her purse. She pulled out an envelope with several papers. She and Rich searched around as if the dining room was bugged, or we were on a hidden camera.

Tanya began. "Carly, I've worked for the Gilberts for fifteen years. In a million years, I would never have suspected anything was going on. I feel like such a fool."

I waited as she removed a paper with a picture of the credit card transaction that I initially processed for the Galt woman when I extracted her horse's tooth. It was done at 11:36 AM on the day Mrs. Miller died. "I think this is your alibi."

"If you recall, I called you right afterward, to see whether I should do anything else while I was still on that side of town. Do you remember?"

Tanya pulled another sheet out of the envelope, which listed calls from my cell phone to the office. "I do now. I'm sorry, Carly. It was a hectic day with the storm and all."

"How did you break into the inner sanctum?"

"I'll get to that. But wait, there's even more."

Tanya recounted her morning. "I received a call from our veterinary drug distribution company this morning. A backorder was pending, and they wanted to replace one of the drugs with a different brand. I asked which one. It was fentanyl, which wasn't even on our computer. The caller suggested the oxycodone and fentanyl could be replaced by using a generic brand. At first, I thought she had confused the pharmacy with our clinic, but she confirmed we had ordered it. She usually talked to either Henry or Jill, but both of their messages read they were out of the country. That is the reason she called the clinic directly."

"Holy moley! They're big-time drug dealers, aren't they?" I believed they might sell a few things that weren't quite kosher, but I had no idea they were involved in this level of activity."

Rich had not commented until now. "You could say." An understatement. He appeared to be thinking. I knew how I would feel if I were him.

"Rich, you need to move on ASAP."

"Yeah, I think we all need to move on. Carly, I am afraid they will try to pin all of the blame on you."

"Not if I get in first. It's Monday, and they won't be back until Friday. I'll deliver this to my new favorite television star tomorrow."

Tanya opened her purse again to produce a computer-generated list of all the medication sold in the last financial year. I perused the list. "No drugs are listed that could be considered a narcotic. There must be two sets of books."

Tanya leaned forward and smiled. Rich was watching her and leaned in, too. "I called their daughter, Katie. I knew she didn't accompany the rest of the family to Bali because she's doing year twelve and couldn't afford to miss any school. I told her the entire system was down, and I required a password to enter the system. She offered me the password that I knew, but it didn't work, and I asked if she was aware of another one. She explained that most of their passwords were from the children's birthdays with initials, and she furnished me with hers and those of the boys. Bingo. Another whole world opened to me.

"There were duplicate names and dates for about fifty clients and entries into a second journal that was password protected. With a second password, a new set of entries, under the word 'services' popped up. Another password-protected area had the drug invoices with and without the narcotics." Tanya handed them over to me and turned to Rich. "This is too dangerous for all of us. Rich, you should leave now. The Gilberts will return on Friday, so Thursday's a good day to finish up. If there aren't any hospitalized animals, we can put a sign on the door that reads, due to an emergency, the office is closed."

We stared at one another and didn't say anything for several seconds. Rich placed his flattened hands down on the table. "Yeah, I think I need a vacation."

"Where will you go?" I liked this man and would love to work with him or help him find another placement. "I can ask around for you."

"Not the best time to get hired back home with the winter. Since I don't know anyone else around here, I might head to Sydney or Melbourne. I'll call the locum agency tomorrow or look online."

"I think I'll call my new bestie, Kate Kilroy. I kind of feel we'd better strike tomorrow morning. Anyone want to be on television?"

Was tomorrow going to be Emancipation Day? Was I in physical danger? Who was going to stand up for and with me tomorrow? Neither Rich nor Tanya would commit. I told them I would call and notify them when there might be a taping of the story. I left a message with Kate to contact me.

"Anyone want some crack?" I passed around the plate with the brownies.

Chapter 42

Jedda returned at about ten o'clock. She had taken Banjo with her, and the two of them went straight to bed. I decided not to discuss the upcoming day until tomorrow. I didn't want her to worry. I hadn't heard back from Kate, and it might be postponed until another day. Banjo woke up that night and began whining and growling. I shot up and immediately checked on the girls, who were sleeping through it. Jedda wasn't. She was up in a flash with her cell phone in hand.

"Is this normal for Banjo?" I asked as we switched on lights.

"No way. He seems interested in the basement. Do you smell smoke?"

"I don't think so." When I opened the door to the basement, though, an acrid smell of smoke hit me. "Something's on fire downstairs. Jedda, call triple zero. I can't get down there on this leg. We will wait for the firemen. Wake up the girls. We need to get out."

Jedda alerted the emergency call-center, which directed her to the local volunteer fire station. The firefighters were already on their way to another fire, but it was an abandoned barn. They diverted to our house and were present in a flash. Jedda, Banjo, and the girls huddled across the street in their pajamas. It was a hot night. Even without bathrobes or jackets, none of us was cold. The firemen quickly put out the small blaze centered in the area near the washing machine.

Tigger's owner, Randy, was one of the volunteer firemen. Despite having a well-populated area, we weren't big enough to support a fire station. Consequently, as many rural towns did, our community relied on the Country Fire Service, or the CFS, to fight fires and attend emergencies.

While the firemen finished mopping up the mess downstairs, I returned the children to their beds. They were scared and wanted to sleep with me.

"Of course, you two lie down in my bed, and I'll be right there." I was surprised they went so fast. Kendall showed up a few minutes later. She talked to the firemen, who were convinced it was an electrical fault.

Tigger's owner told me I was lucky. "Carly, while an unlocked basement door makes it easy to get in to extinguish a fire, I don't recommend that you leave it unlocked." He hugged me and said he would come by in the morning. He was an electrician by trade.

"How's the boy?" I was shocked but tried not to show it. I knew I had locked the door.

"Tigger's ready for a birthday party, Doc. The stitches in his flank might be a bit off-putting, though. See you bright and early. Because I was able to isolate the power, you still have it upstairs."

"I can't thank you guys enough." He waved as he climbed into the fire truck and drove off. I turned to Kendall. "When I was down there this morning, the door was locked."

Kendall raised her eyebrows and let out a slow whistle. "Are you sure? Could one of the kids have gone down there?" She turned to Jedda, who had come back outside. "Jedda, were you down in the basement today?"

"No, ma'am. I haven't been down there since last week." She watched me as I shook my head.

"Well, someone's been down there. I certainly am glad we have Banjo," who wagged his tail and came up for a pat. He immediately returned to Jedda, and they started back into the house.

"I doubt I'll sleep, but I have school tomorrow." I wished her pleasant dreams.

I turned to Kendall and, without saying anything, I hugged her. I still wasn't certain if she was in the good-guy camp, but I had no reason to believe otherwise. "I see you're on duty. Want some coffee?"

"I get off in an hour and want to go straight to bed, but I would kill for some hot chocolate." She glanced at me and grinned. "Maybe not kill."

"Yeah, that's my role. Come on in. I doubt I'll sleep anyway."

We sat without talking for a minute before Kendall offered, "I'll stop by with a dead bolt in the afternoon. Do you have any tools?"

"I believe there are tools in the garden shed. Not sure that I have a power driver, though. We had one, but the battery died, and I'm not sure if Dan got another."

"I'll bring my own. This is serious, Carly. I'm pretty certain you lock your doors, don't you?"

"When I checked the door this morning, it was locked. I think someone has a key. The door has been left unlocked several times, and I know I always lock it. Do you feel I should have a security camera for the backyard?" I didn't want to tell her that I might be featured on television the next night until I definitely knew. "Kendall, if I had evidence that exonerated me, how long before I could be set free?"

"Do you?"

"No," I lied. "If I did, however, would I be set free the day I showed it to the police, or would a judge be required to see it?"

"No, the public prosecutor could say they were dropping the charges. It still might take a week or two while they checked it out."

"If I took the evidence to Reggie tomorrow, how long would it take until I could be free?"

"At least a week. Seriously, do you have evidence? You'd tell me, wouldn't you?"

"Remember when this first came down, you wanted to still be friends, and we agreed not to talk about it?"

"Yeah, but," she started. I put my hand on her arm.

"Talk to the hand." When I held out my other hand, she laughed.

"Oh, for a moment, I thought you really had something. Despite what it seems, I know everyone would be happy if this all went away, and we could get back to normal. Are you still consorting with the enemy?" I realized she meant Kate Kilroy.

"I thought I was the enemy."

"Yeah, well, about half the town believes you are. The other half of the people call the police daily, complaining that they have the wrong person, and you should be let go."

"Wait a second. Are you kidding me? Should I make 'Free Carly Langley' T-shirts?"

"Yeah, it would nearly pay for your defense. I'll bet you could sell ten, at least."

"I must get together with my people. I thought everyone considered me guilty."

"Nope, you have a hard-core fan club."

"Interesting."

"To say the least, given all the negative press. Be careful about your reporter-friend and her station. The press would sell your soul to get a story about you."

"I'm definitely for sale."

"Later, dudette." Kendall returned the cups to the sink, hugged me, and left.

Not sure how, but I returned to bed and fell asleep. We overslept. Thankfully, Jedda woke us up and readied the girls for school, so she would be on time. God, I loved that woman. The girls were excited about going to school to tell their teachers about their night. Despite their bravado, I could tell they were distressed. I promised them we would call their father, and they could talk to him later in the day.

After they went to school, I left Dan a message about the fire. I didn't refer to the unlocked door. Dan called back an hour later and wanted to know if everything was all right. I told him it was an electrical fault that would be repaired that day. He said he would come up the following day as he had the afternoon off. I declined the offer. "You have too much going on, and I have my first obstetrical exam, anyway."

"I'd be happy to come. It's my baby, too."

"Nope. I've got this. I know you have commitments down there. I'll call you after the appointment but be sure you're available to talk to the girls tonight."

He hung up, and I hoped my mention of his "commitments" spawned a bit of fear. This story was not going to end well for my two precious girls. No way. I dreaded what was going to happen during the next few days.

The doorbell rang. It was Randy. "Town and Country Electrical Services are here to send a shock through your system." He laughed as I opened the door.

"No, I think last night was shocking enough. Can I bring you anything? Do you need a flashlight?"

"Carly, how long have you been in this country?"

"I forget. About six years. Why?"

"When are you going to learn the language? It's called a torch."

"Okay, coffee or anything?"

He carried a big tray of items and a large torch. "No, I have a full day, but I wanted to fit you in. Our family is quite indebted to you for saving Tigger."

"Just remember that when you fill out the bill."

He laughed as he descended the stairs. He was back in thirty minutes, said the damaged lines had been replaced, and even fixed the latch on the washing machine.

"Oh, thanks, and what do I owe you?"

"You owe me the courtesy of being more careful by locking your doors and having these ridiculous charges dropped. I didn't want to scare you last night, and I don't think anyone realizes it, but that was arson. I talked to Reggie this morning on the way to your place. Someone is out to get you. For God's sake, be careful. Tigger needs you. Oh, I put a deadbolt on the door." I hugged him. Despite my bravado, I was about to cry.

Chapter 43

Kate called my cell phone shortly after Randy left. She mentioned the network was somewhat nervous. I couldn't discuss any of the information I had received the previous evening. I informed her about the small electrical fire in my house. I mentioned that perhaps the police might be looking into it.

A meeting was scheduled with her producer and the legal team at four o'clock in the afternoon. I was convinced nothing would happen that day. I was disappointed, but what was another day compared with the last few weeks? My increasing concern was for our safety. *Who was getting into my basement?* They must either have a key or know a way to break in without a proper key. The deadbolt would stop any of that. The small window, which was barely above ground level, would be too small for anyone larger than me. I couldn't risk the lives of my children.

My prime suspect was Dolly's private investigator or son. I planned to ask Nigel about him when he arrived later in the morning. *It could be Dan or a jealous lover. Is it someone in the drug trade involved with the Gilberts aware I was on to them?* I really didn't know.

Nigel and Sheba showed up after lunch. Ever the gentleman, Nigel, declined a late meal. He wanted to make sure I was all right and wished to chat for a minute. He was concerned that I might be the target of Dolly's retribution. He admitted he had talked to his daughter. She expressed her frustration with her network's delay of a story about the evidence that would clear me. "Kate has proven herself to me as an honest and reliable person. I wish I could take some credit for raising her, but I didn't. All credit belongs to her mother."

"At least you found each other before it was too late."

"Yes, and I would move heaven and earth to compensate for my sorry lack of parental responsibility."

"I don't believe she resents you. In the short time since we met, she hasn't said one bad word about you."

"She's extremely independent, you know. I've offered her help over the years, and she has taken nothing more than a few hours of my time every month."

"She's persistent. Did you know she sat outside my house for weeks, waiting to talk to me?"

"That's from my side of the family." He sheepishly smiled.

"Yeah, I get mine from my dad, too. You have a grandson, as well. Have you met him?"

"Yes, he's a fine young man. I see him every now and then when I return to Sydney. Carly, are your parents still alive?" He seemed concerned as he inquired.

"My mother is. My father died a while ago."

"Is your mother okay? Does she know about all of this?" Nigel waved his hand.

"As little as I can get by with. Mom's not able to come over, and she can't help, anyway. I try not to upset her."

"I'm sorry." He placed his gnarly hand over mine. I'm not a touchy-feely person, but I felt kindness, security, and strength in his hand.

"If I can help in any way, please let me know."

"I will." I realized I couldn't and wouldn't. This man had gone to great lengths to assist me. I understood he was out of his comfort zone—even coming away from his house. The love of his dog was his driving force for coming to visit me. Now that Sheba received her weekly fix, I doubted I would see him again for another week. Kate was a fortunate woman to have such a caring father.

I thought about all the implications of the next few days and weeks. I was confident I would be exonerated. With the aid of Kate and her television program, I would receive a pass with the public. Such an outcome would allow my daughters to be safe and, hopefully, free from bullying.

Kate called back and quickly gave me the name of a solicitor who might handle my case. When I requested his credentials, she laughed. "You haven't heard of Luke Sullivan?"

"No, should I?"

"Yes, you should have. Are you living under a rock?"

"Apparently. So why should I know the man?"

"He's a major thorn in the side of the government. He takes cases of wrongdoing in all kinds of areas. He took several ICAC cases, in which the government tried to sell land at reduced prices to friends, shall we say?"

"Remind me about what ICAC stands for?"

"Independent Commission against Corruption. It's a watchdog for the state."

"Don't I just need a divorce solicitor now?"

"Carly, you require the entire Australian legal team, but this guy's your first stop."

"How do you know him? Can we trust him?"

"He's my partner. I didn't want to say anything until I talked to him. He's rather busy, and he charges like a wounded bull."

"Ouch. I don't think I'm his type of client."

"Yes, you are. Luke assumes tons of pro bono work. He's been interstate on a case regarding the sale of a cattle and cotton station that's stealing water from the Murry River Authority. It's completed, and the sale is sorted. I don't know much about it because it was confidential."

"How do I contact him?"

"You don't. Luke will contact you if you're happy to use his services."

"I'm guessing you recommend him?"

"You'd be a fool not to use him."

"All right, what have I got to lose besides several thousand dollars? Would you please tell your partner that I am happy to use his services?"

"Done. He's excited. He doesn't know what it's all about. You will have to tell him."

"Haven't you told him?"

"Nope. There is a confidentiality contract between you and me, my network bosses aside."

"I'm impressed, Kate. When should I expect him to contact me?"

"Anytime. Got to go. We're meeting again today about a promo for your story."

When we hung up, I conducted an internet search on Luke Sullivan. He did not have any webpage or social media, as far as I could tell. Several news articles referred to him as a legal eagle. Neither federal nor state judicial authorities liked him very much. He appeared to be a thorn in the side of his opponents in many legal jurisdictions. I needed his expertise.

I prepared lunch and opened the curtains to my front room. A police car pulled into the driveway, and an officer I didn't recognize walked up to the door. I was starting to bear more weight on my foot, and I limped to the door as she knocked.

"Carly Langley?"

"Yes?"

"I'm Officer Turner. I'm here to ensure you are all right and that you are at home per your bail requirements."

"Yep. I'm here, as you can see."

"May I come in?"

"I guess. Do you mind if I quickly check your credentials?"

"Of course. Good idea. You can't be too careful. Do you want to call the station, or will Kendall do? I think she should be waking up about now."

"Oh, you know Kendall?"

"Certainly do. Kendall and I went through the academy together. I've recently been assigned up here. The city boys like to move us around a bit."

"Oh, I didn't know. Do you want some coffee or alcohol?"

"Coffee would be great, and I was told you would squeal like a pig if I gave you some of this." She held up a bag from Angel's.

"If that's what I think it is, then oink." I held out my hand.

"My name's Mary. Mary Turner. I'm up here for a special reason, and you should know I have a horse."

"Nice. What's your reason, and how do you take your coffee?"

"White with two and you."

"Pardon?"

"You. You are the reason I've been assigned here."

"What have I done now?"

"Let's simply say you have friends, or should I say, interested parties, in high places."

"Do you wish to enlighten me?"

"Nope." I offered her some carrot cake. "This is good. I can see why you might kill for it."

"Just so we're clear, I didn't kill anyone."

"Well, that's for a court of law to decide. My job is to guarantee you get your day in court."

I didn't know if this was good or bad. "I'm a bit clueless here. Are you on my side or on the prosecutor's side?"

"I don't take sides, Carly. I have no sides other than the law. I'm here to ensure you don't end up in the wrong hands."

"Meaning?"

"Meaning dead."

"Oh, then you're definitely on my side. I don't do dead. I look terrible in formalin."

She laughed, and then her walkie-talkie went off. She stood up and took one more sip of coffee. Mary pushed a button on her walkie-talkie. "Officer Turner, reporting back from a coffee break. Situation in hand, and we need to preserve this life until we can figure out how the perp makes this delicious coffee."

I laughed, and she winked and walked to the door. "Lock your doors at all times. Am I clear?"

"Crystal."

"*Parent Trap?*"

"None other. Do you want the 4-1-1?" I loved that movie. I would get it for the girls. They were old enough now.

"I'm serious." She shut the door.

As she began to leave, a red Porsche pulled into my driveway. I could see Mary Turner smile and wave at the driver. They must know each other. With that make of car, I was convinced it wasn't another cop. I ran to the bathroom to relieve my pregnancy bladder. I returned to the front room to wait. Finally, there was a knock on the door, which I opened.

"May I help you?" I thought it must be another reporter. Whoever it was seemed to know the last visitor. The place was incestuous.

The man held out his hand. "Luke Sullivan, and I think it's you who needs assistance."

Chapter 44

"It must be the red car." I immediately realized that Kate counted on my acceptance of her offer. He must have driven up early this morning.

"Huh?"

"I just got off the phone with your partner. No regular Porsche could get here from Adelaide that fast. It must be a red car. Come in. Coffee or tea?" I felt like a broken record.

"Yes, the red ones are fast. Just cold water. It's getting hot." Luke Sullivan must be in his early fifties. He was tan, tall, and fit. Luke, who had curly salt-and-pepper hair, wore clothes that came out of "Gentlemen's Quarterly." He was hot for an old guy. For my taste, however, he needed to lose the bling, which was the thick, heavy, overdone stuff of movie stars. Money did not appear to be the object. He pulled out a yellow notepad and ask if we could sit someplace where he could make notes.

He asked me to retell the entire story. He wanted to know everything from the time I met my husband to when I migrated and started my job. He inquired about all that had happened in the last few months, including a few weeks before Mrs. Miller's death and the timeline for everything since then. He questioned me about my children and birth dates, gazed at me sharply, and asked, "And when is the next one due?"

He was meticulous. He inquired about my family and friends, if I were a naturalized citizen and whether the children were dual citizens, as well. I don't think I have ever experienced such a grilling in my life. I was getting nervous, though.

"Mr. Sullivan, I think we need to discuss a topic that is probably near and dear to you."

"Yes, I go for the Crows. I'm a member. If you're a Port supporter, I will still respect you in the morning. You may call me Luke if I can call you Carly. I believe that will answer your questions." The Crows and Port Power were the two footy teams based in South Australia. Most people barracked for one side or another. Barracking is the Australian term for rooting, which is considered rude and a variation of the horizontal hokey pokey.

"Your footy allegiance is a naturally important consideration, but I was thinking along the lines of fees and payment."

"Crows or Port?"

"Crows, naturally. Is that the right answer?"

"Your fees have been paid. You have friends in all the right places. Close call, since I thought I detected some wavering about your choice."

"Excuse me for a second." I limped into the bedroom, from where I brought out my Adelaide Crows scarf.

"Nice. Now let's do a summary. One, you didn't kill your neighbor. Two, you didn't sign any will, and you had no idea about the inheritance. Three, according to your employer, you were not working on a horse's tooth during the time Mrs. Miller was supposedly given the medication that killed her. Is there anything else?"

"Should we talk about Dan?"

"Should we?"

To her credit, Kate hadn't told him anything. I discussed my suspicions and the papers I found relating to Dolly's interactions with Dan years ago. I mentioned his failure to tell me he had a child, his lack of surprise when coming into Nigel's house for the first time, and Dan's supposedly knocked-up paramour. I told him that Dan claimed the hospital had let him go, and the way I discovered my husband had quit, so he could move to Adelaide.

I explained how he never once visited me when I was in jail, yet I realized he had been down in the city while I was in prison, awaiting a bail hearing.

"I'm surprised you can get up in the morning. Anything else?"

"My bosses, or my ex-bosses, who were probably dealing in drugs, changed all my ketamine logs to make it appear I had administered three times the amount that I had actually given. They order unbelievable amounts of oxycontin and fentanyl. Neither the receptionist nor the locum, who is subbing for me, was aware of the existence of their second set of books until two days ago."

I couldn't remember anything else, but I offered to show him the pictures from my company phone that had mysteriously disappeared. He was eager, studied them, and grimaced. "You make a living doing this?"

"Yep. I do, and that's the lady who owns the horse. It's her tattoo, and it's her ring."

"You know, you can modify the dates and times on photographs. Do you have anything else to corroborate your version of the timeline?"

I brought out the credit-card receipt with the recorded time. "Can this be changed?"

I produced the phone bill that showed where she complained about her account. It was well after lunch.

"And the police didn't find it?"

"The police said they didn't. They claimed no photos were on the telephone. I had submitted it to my bosses, who turned it over to the police. I had that phone with me all day, and I never came close to the house all afternoon. Couldn't the police tell from the pings, or whatever, off the towers that I wasn't near here?"

"Is it such a small area that there's only one tower?"

"The client lives fifteen kilometers on the other side of town."

He paused, reexamined his notes, and looked at me. It was approaching the time the girls were due home.

"You're being set up. You realize that, don't you?"

"Without a doubt, but who is covering for whom?" I refilled his water. "And who really killed Mrs. Miller?"

"May I see the files that were returned from Ms. Myler?"

He picked up the two files I had put in order and perused both.

"Where's the toxicology report?"

"Where's anything? There isn't even a copy of my bail conditions."

Luke shook his head. "Don't worry about one thing. If she attempts to bill you for anything, she will have the Law Council and me to answer to. Carly, I think we can wrap this up quickly. Kate's right. While I can free you and have the charges removed, it won't help if we can't place the blame on whoever should be charged with the murder. Until then, you're still guilty in the court of public opinion. When did you say your bosses are returning?"

"Friday. Luke, I'm worried about the safety of my kids, the receptionist, and the locum. I'm not even certain it is all tied together, but I can't wait much longer. If I send the girls down to their father, he will put them with strangers. Even then, I don't know for sure that he didn't do it. I was hoping to get the evidence out today. Waiting two days is a risk I'm not convinced I want to take."

I could hear the girls coming up the driveway. Luke stared out the front window. "Gingers. Can you send them somewhere for the next two days? I'm not happy about you being alone, either."

I showed him my leg jewelry. "I'm not going anywhere right now. Let me see what I can do about the rest of the clan."

"I'm headed back to Adelaide to talk to a friend. I'll call you by eight tonight."

The phone rang. Dan's voice sounded perturbed. "Who owns the Porsche?"

"My new solicitor. The girls are walking in the door. Would you like to talk to them?"

Both girls hugged me. "Hey, Daddy's on the phone. Do you want to talk to him?" They fought over the phone, and I shook my head. I introduced Jedda to Luke, who exchanged greetings. "Luke, she's my savior."

"Looks and brains. Can't beat that combination. All right, you two, be careful. The Crows need all the supporters they can get." Jedda rolled her eyes. Luke shook his head in mock disdain. "What? You don't go for Port, do you?"

"No, Collingwood."

"Now, there's the danger."

That was a revelation. "And I am telling everyone you are the second coming." I lowered my head and shook it. "So disappointed."

Luke nodded and smiled. After we shook hands, he left the house. I walked out on the porch and whispered that Dan knew a Porsche was parked in the driveway. We didn't see anyone when we glanced around.

He pointed his index finger at me like a scolding father. "Be careful. We'll talk. Eight o'clock tonight. Try to send the girls to a friend."

Chapter 45

While the girls were talking to their father, I requested that Jedda step into my bedroom. "I need a favor. I need a place for you and the girls to bunk tonight. What's happening at your house tonight? Is your father home?"

"Did something happen? Yes, he is. Do you want me to call him?"

"I can do it. I wonder whether you and your parents would mind if you and the girls slept over at your house tonight?"

When the girls had finished talking to their father, Casey handed the phone to me. I tried to sound casual. "Hi. How's work?"

The girls could not hear his reply. "What the hell are you doing?"

"I don't understand. Everything's great. I have it all in hand." I wanted to tell him I would be free soon, and he was going to get what he deserved. Oh, it killed me not to say something. "Dan, I know you have a lot on your plate. You're juggling your life right now, but don't worry about us. We'll be fine." *Yep, fine and dandy, you bastard.* "I've got to go and get the kids out of their uniforms. They are always thrilled to talk to you, so please call as often as you can. I know you're busy and probably overwhelmed, but don't stress about us."

The girls had gone across the street to the park. I could see them from a distance, playing on the monkey bars while Jedda read. I called Jimmy Medika first. When he didn't answer, I called the house. Jedda's mother was usually at work, but I knew they had a message machine. I left a message to call me without any explanation. Two minutes later, Jimmy showed up at the house.

I explained about the electrical fire the previous evening and that I wanted to ensure the safety of all three girls. I had no visible evidence of arson, but I would be remiss not to consider it. I wanted to protect the girls. I wondered if he and his wife would mind having my two girls overnight for the next two nights.

"Yes, ma'am. We would be delighted to help you out. Do you want to come, too?"

I pointed to my leg and shook my head. "Not unless I want to go to jail again. I'm certain everything's all right, but who knows if someone is trying to get revenge for Mrs. Miller's death. Have you seen Dolly's son lately?"

"No, but I've just returned from up north. I'll check around."

"Jedda can bring the girls over after I feed everyone."

"I was on my way to drop Banjo off to her. How about he stays here tonight with you?"

"Definitely. I would love for Banjo to stay with me." I wasn't kidding. I would kill to have Banjo stay with me at night.

"You might regret it because he is rather restless at night."

"Oh, I'll get used to it." With any luck, he would keep me up all night. I'm not much of a gun person. Australia had a mass murder before I arrived. The government decided that regular citizens would not be allowed to keep guns at home. I'm a second amendment kind of person, but I chose not to own a firearm.

The clinic had a rifle for euthanizing animals that were too dangerous to approach. I preferred injectable euthanasia, though, rather than shooting the animals. Tonight, a gun would have been handy. Plenty of murders were still committed in Australia, and numerous people still had guns. I never thought about it until now.

When the girls returned from the park, I gave them the good news that they had a special school-night sleepover at Jedda's house. You would have thought it was Christmas. The story was that Jimmy had left Banjo because I would be lonely, and the girls would all sleep in the same bed. We had dinner, bathed the girls, and dressed them in their pajamas. They each took a book and their current sleeping cuddle toy. Faythe changed her sleeping cuddle toy several times. The first one was too small. The next one was too hard. At last, she suggested that since I was going to be alone, I might want the big doll, so I could pretend it was Daddy. Both Jedda and I killed ourselves, trying not to laugh.

They took their uniforms so they could go straight to school in the morning and would be back tomorrow after school. If all went well, we might even do it again. I thought Faythe might cry, but all Faythe could talk about was sleeping next to Jedda.

Banjo was restless after Jedda left. He walked past the hallway, from the kitchen to the bedroom, and back again. He finally settled next to the couch, where I was fanning myself. The afternoon had been a scorcher. I usually open the windows for some fresh air, but I had shut and locked them after Jimmy Medika had left. A ceiling fan moved some air, but it was sweltering, nevertheless.

Julie called. She'd heard about the fire. "You okay? I'll bet that was a bit of a scare?"

"And then some. Are you still available for my appointment and drug check?"

"That's what I'm calling about. I have a bit of a conflict. Can you get someone else tomorrow? It seems I double-booked myself. I'm really sorry."

"Of course. I'll sort it out or maybe even get an Uber." There were no Ubers up here yet.

"Oh, great. Hey, gotta go. Sorry to run. Take care and be careful."

"Yeah. You, too." *That was a strange conversation. Somebody has her ear. Was she talking to Dan? Was she the one who reported the Porsche parked in our driveway? Which column did she belong in? Was she a force for good or a force for evil?*

I heard the clinic truck pull into our driveway. Rich came up to the door, which I opened for him before he knocked. "Can you do me a favor?"

"That depends."

"Will you let me knock, request who it is, and ask what that person wants before you open the door? I heard about your fire last night. I came by to tell you I'm available to do a bit of guard duty if you need someone."

No question where this guy belonged on the prospective good-guy list—he was a card-carrying member. "I recognized the engine. I knew it was you."

"Electrical fault?"

"It certainly was.

"I talked to Randy yesterday. There may be another explanation."

It was approaching eight o'clock, and I was expecting a call from my new solicitor. I hated to brush Rich off. "Got anything new to tell me?"

"Yeah. If you need someone to vouch for you, I'm in. Are they going to film tomorrow?"

I almost got teary. "I don't think so. It may be Friday or even next week."

"The Gilberts have gone quiet. We're wondering if their daughter tipped them off that Mrs. T might have entered the inner sanctum."

"Then I'm not the one who should be careful. It's you two. Do any of the nurses realize anything?"

"No. We are keeping the staff out of the loop to safeguard them from any retribution. We don't know if any of the staff members are involved in the scam. It is just us three. Tanya and I are submitting our resignations Thursday evening."

"Where are you going?"

"That equine practice down near Adelaide. The owner is leaving for a month, and I offered to perform a stint at the clinic. The practice treats a number of colics during the summer, but her home is air-conditioned."

"Half your luck. I can't thank you enough for what you've done."

"Hey, like I said, we Yanks must stick together."

"I guess there's nothing up here to keep you?"

We both knew I meant Kendall. "Sadly, no."

I didn't question him about it. I had enough on my plate regarding the breakdown of my own relationship. "At least you had the pleasure of Angel's carrot cake."

"That was worth the stress and agony. And I met you, too. Oh, by the way, a few of us are watching you. Don't do anything crazy like leaving your doors open at night."

"Thanks. That was stupid of me, wasn't it?" I didn't want to tell Rich or anyone that the door was locked. Whoever came in, if they did, had a key or could pick locks. I assumed Randy told Rich that he not only fixed the electrical fault, but he installed a deadbolt, as well.

At precisely eight o'clock sharp, my cell phone rang. Luke Sullivan stated he had conducted a small amount of research and had the situation under control. He wanted to ensure my safety and expected his involvement would be wrapped up in a day or two at most. I had been granted his full permission to continue with my endeavors if they didn't violate my bail. He had copies of the toxicology report and the conditions of bail, along with other items of interest.

"No promises, but this should be over in a few days." He remarked he would be back up Thursday to offer me additional support. He suggested that anyone listening in should be aware that our conversation is privileged and not for public or police consumption.

I had to survive for two more nights. All good. That should be doable. Someone else knocked on the door. I was more cautious this time. "Who is it?"

"It's Lois, Jedda's aunt." After last night's drama, I was dead. I'd entertained people all day. Despite my desperation for some sleep, I opened the door. She walked in with a small travel bag. "I need a place to sleep."

"Huh?"

"Carly, Jimmy said you're alone. We wanted to be certain you are all right. I was hoping to be the day caretaker, but it seems that it isn't necessary anymore. I will make sure you get some sleep tonight, with no intruders. Clean yourself up and go to bed. Banjo and I are on duty."

"Yes, ma'am." I saluted her and went to bed. I closed my eyes, and that was it. The next sensation was the sunlight hitting my face. Oh, did I need that? Lois was up, she had made coffee, and some breakfast was warming in the oven.

Lois smiled. "You snore a lot. Is any company coming today?"

Because I was so groggy from the full night of sleep, I almost forgot my doctor's appointment. "No, but is there any chance you could take me to the police station and the hospital for an appointment?"

"There's every chance. Such activity is what old people like me look forward to. When do we go?"

I glanced at the clock. "Actually, I'm supposed to be at the hospital in fifteen minutes."

I ran while limping to the bathroom to brush my teeth, and we jumped in the car. I take back anything I ever said about the elderly and their driving skills. This woman was Mario Andretti on steroids. I was at the hospital with two minutes to spare. Lois sat in the waiting room while I went into an examination room.

Dr. Loomis was an older, petite, no-nonsense person, who greeted me with a handshake and pointed to a gown and table. A curtain could be pulled around the table if necessary. "Get your gear off, Dr. Langley. I charge by the minute." I did as I was told. "Is your partner here? Do we need to wait for him?"

"No, ma'am. He's down in the city. He used to work here, but he transferred to the new hospital a week ago."

"I see. What kind of work does your husband do?" She did not waste time. She palpated my abdomen and took my blood pressure as we conversed.

"He's an ER doc." I was surprised she didn't know him. It seemed most physicians knew one another.

"I'm straight off the boat. Kiwi, if you didn't pick up the accent."

"No, I didn't. I'm sorry."

"Let's not jibber jab. I hear you might have more than one bun in the oven."

"That's the reason I'm here. This will be my third or third and fourth. I already started my vitamins and diet changes."

She rolled over a cart with the same portable ultrasound that Roger and I had used when I fell down the stairs and cracked my tibia.

The gel was cold, and I involuntarily cramped and tightened my abdomen. "Steady on, girl. Don't make this any worse than it is. I heard you might be a bit of an expert in this field."

"Just in horses and a few dogs and cats." I didn't tell Dr. Loomis that I regularly scanned myself throughout my two previous pregnancies. I figured she could guess.

"Oh, there's one. You're definitely pregnant. Let me look around a bit." I saw the single embryo and sighed in relief. One was plenty. I knew this would be much easier considering what lay ahead. I was beginning to relax and even closed my eyes. My bladder was full as I knew my next mission was taking a urine test at the police station. I was starting to feel uncomfortable as she pressed the probe deeper into my abdomen. "Yep, looks like twins to me." I shot up, and she looked at me and said, "Are you surprised? I thought you saw twins before?"

"I— I mean. Yes. Are you certain?" She had saved several images, went back through them, and requested if I wanted any copies.

As she printed two images, she inquired whether twins were in my family. "Not to my knowledge. I guess it's for sure?"

"You don't sound happy. Do you wish to discuss anything?" The doctor could see my ankle bracelet, and I was convinced she knew about my problems. She observed me and sighed. "I'm always available to chat, and I'm not leaving the state. I'm based in Adelaide, and even if you are down in town, I can deliver your children."

"No. No, thanks. I have another appointment. When do you want to see me again?"

"Did you know the sex of your other babies before?"

"Yes, I don't do surprises unless it's necessary. I know it's way too early for that."

292

"Why don't we have a visit in the month? Unless your blood results are abnormal, we won't see each other until then." She handed me a card with her personal number in case I needed anything.

"Oh, wow. Thanks."

"She patted my arm. I give my number to everyone, so don't feel special."

"No problem there." I would love nothing better than to feel anything but exceptional right now. I left the room and had to step back. Coming down the hall was a gurney with a woman with a surgical hat and several attendants holding various equipment pieces. I did a double-take as it went by. It was Julie. I was confused and shocked. She was waking up from anesthesia. Her husband, Mick, was coming down the hall a few steps behind her. He saw me, stopped, and looked at me with hunched shoulders. He was crying, and I stepped toward him and hugged him. I didn't say a word.

"Oh, Carly. She felt so bad standing you up today. She simply couldn't bring herself to tell you. She felt your problems were worse than hers."

I didn't ask if she was going to be all right. It was apparent she was not.

He hugged me again. "I don't know what I'm going to do."

"Oh, Mick, please tell me this isn't true."

"I need to go. Julie will be transferred down to Adelaide as soon as she's stable. I want her to try some chemo, but she is on the fence."

"What about the kids? Can I help at all?"

He shook his head. "We're all good, Carly. Take care of yourself and those beautiful girls." As he walked off, I saw Roger coming down the hallway. He had tears in his eyes, as well. He hugged me.

"God damn, Carly. If you ever feel something isn't right, get your bloody self to a doctor as soon as you can." I nodded, which was all I could do. He turned and went in the direction that Julie and Mick had gone. I felt awful. I was so shocked and disappointed in myself for my stupid list of good and bad people.

I barely made it to the police station without wetting my pants. I had an interview with Reggie, during which he observed me and inquired whether everything was okay. He kept asking if I wanted to tell him something, but I shook my head. I couldn't talk about my problems. If I started, I might break down, not for my dramas, but for my friend and her journey. I was so, so sad.

Chapter 46

Lois dropped me and said she would be back that evening. Jimmy and his wife were going to keep the girls again. They would all come here after school and would go to the Medikas to stay after dinner. Jimmy called to say that all had gone well, and the girls had slept without a fuss. Casey was up early and helped Jimmy feed the stock. She even held his tools when he replaced a shoe for one of his horses.

"They were no problem, miss. Your oldest is going to make a fine horsewoman. I told her she could ride with me on the weekend. How are you? According to Lois, there were no problems last night."

"No. It was great. How can I thank you, Mr. Medika?"

"Stay safe, miss. Just stay safe. Oh, and get back to work."

"I will."

I spent a quiet afternoon. I was disturbed only by two hang-up phone calls with no caller identification. I sent a digital copy of the sonogram of the twins to Dan and added, "Congratulations 2X" to the message. He didn't reply. When the girls arrived home, he called to talk with them. They told him about their stay at Jedda's house and how much fun they had. After several minutes of talking to them, he wanted to speak to me.

"I guess our course is set, Carls. Are you convinced you want to go through with this?"

"And your suggestion for an alternative?"

"You know."

"No, Dan, I don't. Do you want to spell it out in case someone is listening?"

"Okay. It's your body and your time off this time around. I can't do it again as we did with the first two."

"Not asking you to." One more day, one more day. Do not blow it yet. "It will be great."

Dan smartened up, realizing that, indeed, someone might be listening to this conversation. "I'm ready if you are. Can't wait."

Yeah, I bet. "We'll be fine. Oh, bad news. Julie has terminal cancer."

"I know. She's been admitted to the oncology ward. I saw Mick. She's too out of it for a visit. Why did the girls stay at Jedda's?"

Think fast. "Randy explained we needed to upgrade several electrical points, and he said he would come by on Friday to do it. I didn't want to take a chance." I paused and held my breath. "Obviously, Julie wasn't available, and the girls are so bonded to Jedda. It will only be for one or two more nights. Did you have someone else in mind?"

"No, that's probably for the best. How about you?"

"I talked to Reggie, and my only other option was a night in the town jail. I checked all the smoke alarms and decided burning in hell was the better choice."

"I guess. Okay. I'll call tomorrow. You got anything on?"

"Nope, just incubating."

"I know who owns that Porsche. I'm not working to pay that lowlife and all his fees."

"Got it." I hung up. There's a mole somewhere.

"Mom, can we go down to stay with Dad sometime?" Casey asked.

"Anytime, darling. As soon as your dad gets his own place."

"When will that be?"

"I don't know, but soon."

"Are we moving down with Daddy?"

"We don't know for certain. It will be a while. Would you like to live down in Adelaide? You know, they have all kinds of things to see and do."

"Will Jedda come with us?"

"Jedda will move down to Adelaide next year when she starts university, but she'll be busy with school. I'm sure we can see her plenty, though."

"Are we still having a baby?"

"Hey, Faythe and Jedda, come here." I'd printed out two sets of pictures of the babies. "Yes, so far, it looks like we are having twins. One for each of you."

Casey and Jedda hugged me immediately, while Faythe hung back. Her lip came out, and the tears started. I picked her up and told her she was still my special little girl, and nothing would change that. *Oh my God, does she exhibit middle child syndrome already? Sheesh.*

After some time, Faythe wanted to know whether she could share a room with only one of the babies. I said at some time she could. When babies are little, they wake up in the middle of the night, however, and no one wants to sleep in the same room with them. Faythe asked if she could name one. "You can suggest a name, but that's a family decision, and we all must agree." I wondered what part of the family would be around at their birth.

Once dinner and baths were completed, it was time to ship the kids off to Camp Medika. No tears about that. Jimmy called when they arrived and mentioned that Lois would be over soon. I thanked him again and finished the dishes. My leg was healing, and I was now limping, but didn't need the crutches to get around for short distances.

I called Kendall, and she'd heard the news about Julie. She was off duty and came over. We hugged each other and had a good cry. I would have given anything to be free to go visit Julie. Kendall had heard they were moving her to a hospice unit. It was so quick. It was the old ovarian cancer, which had metastasized to most of her organs. I told her that Julie was already down in Adelaide.

"Surely, she must have known something was wrong. She's a nurse, for God's sake." I reached for the tissues.

"I don't know. I think Julie thought it was indigestion. How old is she?" Kendall brought some carrot cake, but neither of us ate any of it.

"Immature, whatever age. Was she fifty-two? Those poor kids. Poor Mick. He looked awful."

"Yeah, I think that's about right. Do you feel that the world we know is ending? Got any grog?"

"Above the fridge. Help yourself."

Kendall hugged me. "You won't go down for one drink. I'll vouch for you."

I pointed to my lower abdomen. "Naw, it turns out I've got two in the oven."

"Bloody hell, Carly. How's this going to work?"

"Not a clue." *Oh, I had a clue and a good clue. It killed me not to share it.*

Kendall and I were still commiserating when Lois knocked on the door. She was also remotely related to Kendall, and they greeted each other warmly.

Lois declined a drink, too. "I'm on guard duty." She pointed to me.

"I'm not stopping you." I laughed, but Lois saw that we both had been crying. When we told her about Julie, Lois gave us her condolences. She didn't know Julie that well.

Lois had a book. She went into the office bedroom, where Jedda slept and left us to our misery. Eventually, Kendall wanted to sleep off her alcohol. She climbed into Casey's bed. Banjo and I slept in my bed. I felt safe and protected for the second consecutive night. Banjo woke me up growling and went to the window twice. My light was off, but I didn't dare look outside for fear of someone looking back at me. My heart was pounding. At last, I heard the distinctive growling of a koala bear. The rest of the night was uneventful.

We all woke up early the next morning. We drank coffee, and I made breakfast for us all. Kendall was on duty at eleven. Lois had a quilting guild, while I was scheduled for the interview of my life. They left, and I showered and applied makeup. I doubted they had a makeup person for remote events like this one.

Kate Kilroy was dressed to the nines. I was instructed to look like a horse vet—neat and clean, but slightly wholesome. Luke arrived a few minutes before the interview and advised me about what I could and couldn't say. I was supposed to address the questions that Kate and Luke had prepared and not stray from the script. I was to cover my relationship with Mrs. Miller and how I learned about her death. I was expected to speak about my timeline that day and present the evidence that corroborated what I said about the appointment. The network would insert the pictures of the tooth and the receipt from the credit card transaction. I was directed to not speak about the Gilberts and the reason they might want to modify my timeline. Luke said Tracey Galt most likely knew about the Gilberts' side business, wanted a discount, and was probably blackmailing them.

Luke said it was pure coincidence that the Gilberts' timeline adjustment conflicted with my alibi. It was one gigantic error, and they paid me a two-week salary to compensate for the drama it created for me. The sticky issue was that someone with a name suspiciously close to Dolly's name bought phenobarbital. This would be aired in the first night's episode.

The second part would introduce Dolly's relationship with Mrs. Miller and her relationship with Dan. Luke was working with the drug squad on the Gilberts' little enterprise that wouldn't be in the program. Luke had negotiated to keep that fact quiet, and the veterinary clinic would be raided the following day.

Luke had met with the members of the prosecution team. They were going to drop the charges, pending verification that the pictures were real, and the credit card receipt was authentic, as well. "If things go according to my timeline, you'll be free this weekend. There will possibly be a raid on the veterinary clinic tomorrow. The Gilberts need to be back in the country before they swoop. International extradition is an expensive, drawn-out affair, and they will be arrested when they hit the tarmac in Sydney."

Kate was a pro. She made me seem like a long-suffering hero. I was, wasn't I? Thoughts of a pending divorce and Julie's imminent death tempered my excitement and joy. I would be so happy when this was finally over. However, I felt guilt and dread about the next few days. I wondered if I could keep the divorce a secret from the children for a few days more.

The police were already checking Dan's role in this entire saga. *Was he cognizant of the drug trade up this way? Did he send patients to the Gilberts? Did he supply the phenobarbital to Mrs. Miller, explain to her they were antibiotics, and instruct her to take them at a particular time? Did he know about the will?*

Where was Dolly, and what was her role in all of this? Why did Dolly continually come back to our town every year? Did she have a hand in the Gilberts' drug trade? How many people in town were aware of this little enterprise?

We taped my part all in one session. Kate and her crew of two were packed and ready to go by lunchtime. They did not interview Tanya Tankard or Rich. That might come in a follow-up interview. Luke stayed to discuss a few more aspects. The major crimes squad was handling the case. The local police did not know what was going on. They would not be told about anything until the following day. The major-crimes unit didn't want to alert them in case one of the local cops was involved. Dan would be taken in for questioning either later today or tomorrow.

Luke had divorce papers ready for filing and suggested that we present the documents the next day. He would not be the solicitor to handle my case. Luke would pass that portion of my legal issues over to his friend, who would ensure that I was taken care of. If Dan had not broken any laws, he would be free to work and support me until I could care for the children and financially support them on my own.

"What can I do? Will I be able to leave the country? I know there are international-custody laws. This is going to be awful for the girls."

"We won't know until Dan is investigated, but my gut feeling is he will spend some time in jail, and you will be free to leave. Are you certain that's what you want to do? You have a free ride with the twins' birth over here with our health system."

"I really don't know. I guess I'll make that decision when things settle. I wonder what will happen to the veterinary clinic. Illicit-drug sales aside, it was a nice practice."

"It's not really your concern. You should focus on your children, your safety, and your health. You have a generous windfall from the network. I made sure they topped it up. I also convinced the network not to give any of it to you until the divorce papers are filed. It will be yours alone. I figure it's time we discussed the reason for all of this now, too."

"The reason?"

"Mildred Miller left you a small fortune. Did you forget?"

"I hadn't thought about it. I hadn't. I assumed it would go to probate and be given to someone else or to Mrs. Miller's parish. I never wanted it, and I really didn't have any idea about the money until the day after her death."

"Kate and I think she knew about your husband's dalliances, and she wanted to ensure you and the girls were taken care of. Once you are cleared of her murder, the funds will be yours. We think you'll be set for many years. In short, you've won the lottery."

I stared at him, and tears came to my eyes. I would have relinquished it all if I could return to the way it was before Mrs. Miller died—every cent. But I could not. Our lives were going to change, and I would have some extremely agonizing times with Casey and Faythe. *Were they even going to be able to see their father, and would he go to jail? Would we stay in this town or move? Move to where?*

Luke assembled his scattered papers and left. I had a few days until all hell would break loose. Since the program was going to air at the end of the week, the chance of me being free from home detention was unlikely to occur before Monday. Luke was a master, but he was coping with a legal system that moved at a much more cautious and slower pace.

So, I waited.

Chapter 47

I was in agony because I had to sit on all this information without confiding in a soul. I couldn't call my mother or tell anyone, including Tanya Tankard, whom I now regarded as a saint. The poor locum, Rich, was additionally in the dark. I realized they were waiting for a bomb to drop and were probably collecting their personal items and signing their resignation papers. The nursing staff would be completely unaware of any of these circumstances. All their lives would change, beginning tomorrow. *Were any of them complicit in the drug dealing?* I didn't know when a raid would be conducted on the clinic. I presumed it would be the following day.

The Gilberts were going to be arrested at the airport. Then, the poor boys would go through hell, as would their sister, down in Adelaide. I hoped Mrs. Tankard was going to be feted as the hero she was. Rich would move on, and it sounded as if he would practice an hour away for at least a month. I suspected Rich would head over the pond to home after this locum position ended. Oh, what a story he would be able to tell his family. I hoped Rich would find love. He was such a nice guy. I was so disappointed that he and Kendall didn't experience the joy and excitement I'd had in my marriage. It didn't work out, but what a ride, and I didn't regret anything that brought me my two beautiful daughters and those growing inside me.

You would never know that my life was going to be turned upside down very soon. If I ended up living close to Adelaide, God forbid, I knew Jedda would play a long, significant role in the girls' lives. How lucky was I to find such a fun, savvy woman?

Dan didn't call. I didn't ask the girls if they wanted to talk to their father. They needed to become accustomed to not having a father around. So, I was back to the adhesive-bandage conundrum. Rip it off and get it over, or let it fall off slowly? That would be decided in a few days. I left it in place for now. The girls were oblivious to either Dan or me, anyway.

Jedda was the flavor of the month. If they arrived at her house before dark, they would see the horses. Faythe wasn't interested, but Casey was trying to hurry the departure in anticipation of a quick ride. The previous evening, Jimmy had popped Casey on his horse, Froggy, for a walk around the paddock. She was wearing her pajamas. I heard that Casey refused to put on her nightclothes until after her next ride.

This time, Jedda took Banjo. Lois was coming at eight o'clock. I retrieved some photo albums to peruse some of the happier times in my life. Rich called to say goodbye. He was headed down to the new practice and would be there for at least a month. I thanked him for his help. He was aware that things would change soon, but he knew not to discuss it on the phone. We wished each other well. After eating dinner at Tanya Tankard's, he was leaving in the morning.

"Say hi to the terrible Mrs. T for me." I laughed at how my feelings toward that woman had changed during the last few weeks.

"Will do. Take care."

There was a knock at the door. I didn't even hear a car pull up. Was it my neighbors? I went to the door and asked who it was.

"It's Tanya. May I come in?"

Phew. "Oh, of course. I was worried." I unlocked the door and opened it. Henry Gilbert was standing behind her. He had a bag draped over his shoulder, and his arm was inside the bag. Tanya was shaking, and she had an expression of terror and sorrow. She mouthed, "I'm sorry."

Chapter 48

Henry Gilbert turned to the car and ordered, "Go, now."

"Can I get my crutches?" *Could I use them as a weapon?* I wanted to stall him.

"No, get in the car. Now," he hissed.

Jill Gilbert sat in the driver's seat. I was directed to get into the front passenger's seat, and he and Tanya climbed into the back. As we left, I glimpsed a car that appeared similar to Dan's pull into our driveway. He must be involved. My heart sank. Tanya and I were going to be killed, and the girls would be left to a murderer. I had to think.

"Henry, it's all over now. The police know everything, and your clinic will be raided tomorrow. You won't get by with this. It's too late. If you add murder to your list of charges, it will be a long time before you see the light of day. You must think about your children. You can tell the cops that it was you, not Jill, so you can serve a year or two and start again. If you kill us, both of you will go to jail. Think of your children."

"No one will know it's us. We aren't even in the country yet. It's Tanya's car, and she'll have taken you and killed you and herself. Murder-suicide—simple and neat."

I realized they didn't know that we had alerted the authorities. "It's still too late, mate. I'm telling you, there will be a drug raid at the clinic tomorrow. If you don't stop this for your own sake, think of your children." I turned to look at him. As I did, I thought I glimpsed a car way back behind us. It was dusk, and the car didn't have its lights on at this stage. In my truck, the lights would go on automatically when the sky darkened. I hoped this car's lights would come on, and they would realize they were being followed. Or did I?

305

We traveled to the countryside. We were now several kilometers away from town, and I saw we were heading past George's property. Despite my terror, I had my bearings. We continued, and I turned to ascertain if we were still being followed. Because I couldn't continue to look without raising suspicion, I tried to make small talk.

"Tanya, are you okay?"

She stared at me with wide eyes. "No, Carly, I'm not. I'm bloody, fucking not."

"I'm so sorry." That gave me a second to see that a car was following us. As we passed George's gate, he was coming out. George eyed us and waved. Of all the improbable occurrences, that was the most unlikely happening of my entire short life. *Why was he at the gate?* I didn't wave. I pretended not to notice.

We drove on for what seemed like an hour. Jill was not accustomed to driving on dirt roads, and she fishtailed several times. I turned to Jill. "George Hughes has now seen both of you. You won't get away with this. Think of your children. And if you don't slow the fuck down, we'll all be killed."

"The police are waiting for us to arrive in Sydney tomorrow, while we'll be taking off from Adelaide for Bali, and on to our other home. You'll be dead, and we will be," he hesitated, "reborn. New identities and new lives." Henry's voice was high-pitched and almost shouting.

"Shut up, Henry. Don't say any more."

"Honey, it doesn't matter. They'll be dead in ten minutes. Who cares?"

"I do. They aren't dead yet." Jill fishtailed again.

Tanya interjected, "You won't get away with this. You're crazy to think you'll even get to the airport."

I turned for yet another look. "You know, Henry, Tanya's right. This is a fool's mission. You won't even make it back to town." I was in agony, and my limbs felt like lead. My mouth was dry, and I was convinced I would die. I thought about the two little babies in my womb, and I shuddered.

Jill gazed into the rearview mirror. "Fuck. We're being followed." Henry turned back, and they both saw not one car, but two of them.

"Who the hell is that?" We all turned. When Jill turned to look, there was a roo on the road. She swerved to avoid hitting it. The car veered into the ditch and rolled over on its side. It slid for several feet before coming to a halt. Jill's head hit the steering wheel, and she was bleeding and stunned. Henry dropped the gun, which went off.

Tanya screamed, "I've been hit."

"Are you all right?" I was trying to look back, but my seat belt had locked, and I was pinned to my seat. The air bags had exploded, and I was sure my nose was broken. Dust was everywhere. Henry hadn't put on his seat belt, and he was flung over on Tanya. She used her considerable weight to push him away as he grappled for the gun. "No, No, No. Get off me, you fat bastard."

The car lay on its side. Tanya was trapped by the weight of Henry, who continuously groped for the gun. Tanya had one foot on the gun. She stomped Henry's hand with her other foot and beat him over his back with her free arm. Jill, whose head was leaning toward me, continued to bleed, splattering me as blood fell off her temple toward me. She was alive, but she was not talking or moving.

I tried to unbuckle myself as two cars pulled up. Dan was in one, and George was in the other. George had a rifle, which he aimed into the overturned car. "You okay, Carly?"

"Never better, George. How's the calving?"

"All done. That was somewhat of a misadventure, though. That bull was a disaster over those small cows. Cost me a bloody fortune in vet bills. You're all a bunch of highway robbers."

"Just some of us, George." I couldn't believe I was joking. My shoulders screamed from the seat belt, and my head felt as if I had been king-hit. I was still lying sideways and trapped by my belt, which was in a locked position. I could hear Tanya still stomping on Henry's hand and Henry's swearing with every stomp.

Tanya had to be in a fair amount of pain, but she did say, "Well, we all have to make a living, George. Dinner's going to be a bit late."

So, Tanya and Rich were having dinner with George. *Why wasn't I at least invited?*

Henry couldn't be easily pulled off Tanya. He must have realized the game was up because he eventually climbed out the door. George kept his rifle pointed toward Henry. I could hear sirens approaching as I lay in the front seat.

Two police cars arrived in a cloud of dust. Reggie and Kendall stepped out of separate vehicles with guns drawn. George lowered his rifle, and Tanya shouted, "There's a gun in here, but I've got my foot on it. No one needs to shoot anyone else. Put those damn things away. Don't make me call your mothers."

It was going to be easier for us to get out of the car once it was turned upright. George, who had a winch on his truck, was able to pull the car over while the men guided it so it wouldn't be too jarring. I heard another siren when an ambulance arrived. Jill was unconscious, and a helicopter was called to move her to Adelaide. Dan was requested to accompany Jill to the trauma center.

We gazed at each other. Dan shook his head and admitted he was sorry. I merely smiled and replied, "I know." Oh, boy, did I know. He didn't realize how sorry he was going to be in a day or two.

It appeared as though I had been in an explosion, but it was Jill's blood. I was bruised, but I was not seriously injured. At first, I thought the air bag had broken my nose, so I felt my face. Despite a bloody nose, however, I was confident nothing was fractured. Tanya was loaded into the ambulance and would go to Adelaide by conventional transport. They wanted to take me, as well, so my pregnancy could be assessed. I declined.

George came over as the ambulance was preparing to leave. I walked over to bid good-bye to Tanya and thank her. I gazed at them both. "You, George, and Rich were going to have dinner, and I wasn't invited?"

"Ronny was coming, too." Both Tanya and George were embarrassed. I pretended to be hurt, but that was the reason George was at the gate. He was headed to Tanya's for dinner.

"If I told you we planned to come over for dessert, would you believe me?" Tanya was back to her old sarcastic self.

"You are all off my guest list now." I tried to hide the smile. They saw.

When the ambulance drove off, Dan and I were standing alone. He once again apologized to me: "I drove up from Adelaide to talk to you about something, but it can wait. I'm so sorry. I saw you pull out in the Gilberts' car, and I realized something wasn't right. Since I knew you were in danger, I followed you. I tried to call triple zero for the police to come, but my phone was not charged. I simply followed you. When we went passed your client's gate, I saw George, I stopped and yelled to him that you were in danger, and he followed me. He must have called the police."

I shook my head. "I've already filed for divorce, so let's not pretend anymore. I probably know more than you think. Our number-one priority is protecting our children, born and unborn."

I turned to George, whom Reggie was interviewing. "George, thanks for coming and for calling the police."

"I didn't call them. I only followed your husband."

I turned to Kendall, who heard this, and she shrugged and pointed to my ankle bling. "Comes with a nifty GPS device. Reggie and I had a bet every night that you would break curfew. We both lost."

Chapter 49

I lost the ankle bracelet three days later. Three guesses where I went first? A small group of true believers met at Angel's. All the clinic staff came, except two nurses charged for their knowledge of the drug-dealing side business.

Because Rich was already working at the new clinic, he sent his apologies. Reggie, Kendall, and Tigger's owners stopped in. Jimmy Medika was up on the station, but Jedda arrived with her mom and aunt. Several clients stopped by, as well.

In all the drama, I had forgotten about the Walkers' mare I had inseminated on my last day of work. She had conceived and was maintaining the pregnancy. As a present, Jen Walker gave me a stainless-steel bucket. "Easier to clean than the barn floor."

"I'm over the puking phase, but thanks. I have two reasons for using it."

"Yeah, we heard." Malcolm was home, and he gave me a big hug.

"Hey, Malcolm. How are you? Are you home for a while?"

"Short as possible, Carly. The boss has me up at dawn, fixing fences and working on the foals. I need a vacation. Time to get back up to the mine, so I can get some rest."

Jen rolled her eyes. "He'll never change."

When Baz and Connie came, Faythe jumped in Connie's arms. Baz fixed our gate and performed some upkeep on the garden that Mrs. Miller had started. I hugged them both.

George and Ronny dressed in their Sunday finest. They were on their way to Adelaide to the races. George's granddaughter was riding in town. I hugged them both and told them not to bet the ranch on her. "As if I had any money left after your

311

sidekick wiped me out with vet bills." George shook his head and smiled.

"Better in our pockets than yours, gentlemen. I'll pass it on to Rich."

"Oh, he's coming up in a few weeks. His new boss is happy for him to continue doing our work."

"Excellent news. Behave yourselves in the big smoke. I'm not bailing you out, you know."

I thanked everyone for coming and for their support. The unasked question was, "What now?" I responded by telling everyone I was weighing my options. I felt they all knew I was not long for this town.

The next day, as I was driving to the school to pick up the girls, I received a phone call. "Hey, defector, pull over."

"Kendall, you can't talk me out of moving, so don't bother."

"Nope, it's bigger than that. Way bigger. Stop the car. You shouldn't be driving and talking, anyway."

I pulled into Angel's parking lot. "Okay, what's the news?"

"Reggie received a second tox report. The level of phenobarbital in Mrs. Miller wasn't a lethal amount.

"But her autopsy suggested she wasn't that sick."

"They went back to review it. Millie died of a respiratory virus. The drug didn't help, but it didn't kill her, either. Oh, and Dolly's DNA was found on a cigarette outside the back door. The sole reason that homicide was even considered is an empty, unlabeled vial on the table. That made the police search around her body, and a tablet was discovered under her chair. It was a cold tablet that wouldn't have killed a mouse."

"Does Dan know?"

312

"He will tonight. I believe it will hit the news. The charges will be reduced to attempted murder if Dolly is ever found."

"Yeah, I guess. Speaking of which, I've got to get the kiddos. Thanks, I think."

Chapter 50

Oh, how your life can change. How do I explain it all? Let's start at the beginning.

Dan and I didn't end up in this town by accident. Dolly invited him. As a regular visitor to this town, Dolly was aware of an opening in the hospital for an emergency physician. Dolly had been coming up to see Nigel in hopes of rekindling their marriage. Dolly was on the take in many directions. She knew Mrs. Miller and had endeared herself to her "good friend," Millie. She, and only a handful of others, realized the extent of Mrs. Miller's wealth.

Mrs. Miller never required any material possessions. She needed to be "needed." Caring for my daughters was apparently the joy of her life. Since she did not have any children of her own, I had, without my knowledge, become the daughter she always wanted. She allowed me to pay her to maintain the pretense. Lost in all of this were two trust funds for Casey and Faythe. Every payment I made to Mrs. Miller was funneled straight into funds for their education.

When the estate funds are released, which I am told will be months away, I will order a headstone for Mrs. Miller. I will add "adopted grandmother" of Casey and Faythe Langley" on the tombstone.

Dolly learned about the will when Mrs. Miller asked her to review it before Mrs. Miller took it to her regular solicitors. I heard that's when Dolly hatched her plan. The first step was coercing Dan to obtain a copy of my signature. He was in no position to turn Dolly down. She had been threatening and blackmailing him ever since he married me. Next, she forged my signature on the power–of–attorney section, thereby giving me probable cause to want to kill Mrs. Miller. That was the backup plan.

314

Dan admitted he had impregnated a fellow medical-school classmate and had fathered her child. Instead of a commitment, she, not he, wanted a one-off payment, and she would be free to live her life and marry another man. When the classmate's marriage broke down, she decided her one-time compensation wasn't quite enough. Dan's mother paid her off this second time.

Dan confessed he had fallen in love with someone else. Heather was due to give birth to his child in a month. I was disgusted. It was so seedy and so repulsive. Other than being complicit in my name's forgery, he wasn't involved in Mrs. Miller's death. He had to stay in the marriage to acquire his part of the inheritance. He fooled me.

Until the toxicology report revealed the phenobarbital poisoning, Dan was confident she had died of natural causes. He was partially correct. Neither Dan nor Dolly believed I would be charged in Mrs. Miller's murder. At best, Dan and I would inherit Mrs. Miller's money, and then Dolly would be able to blackmail Dan for more money than she was getting. So, when I was charged, Dolly made herself available to me to take over the case. When I was acquitted, at least some of the legal fees would be directed to her from my inheritance. If I was convicted, she thought she would be second in line for Mrs. Miller's money. She couldn't lose. It must have seemed like a perfect plan to Dolly.

At some time during the day of Mrs. Miller's death, Dolly visited her and most likely administered the phenobarbital. The rainstorm may have been the reason why no one noticed Dolly going into Mrs. Miller's house. Dolly must have thought Mrs. Miller's death would be considered due to natural causes. She obtained the phenobarbital from the Gilberts' veterinary clinic. I would have thought an individual with an intelligent legal mind, who wrote crime novels, would not have been so careless to leave a cigarette stub at the scene of the crime, but she did. Dolly's son was a go-between from the Gilberts to several clients all over Australia. Dolly was well-informed on the Gilberts' other business. Dolly's son was under arrest for his role in the drug business.

The Gilberts had been back in Australia for two days. They returned immediately after Henry and Jill learned their daughter had furnished Mrs. Tankard with the passwords.

Investigations were ongoing. So far, the charges ranged from supplying drugs without a license, kidnapping and attempted murder. I felt so sorry for the Gilbert children. I still don't know who broke into my basement, but the Gilberts did have a key. Dolly's son was the prime suspect, but numerous charges were awaiting him. Breaking and entering indictments were not going to be pursued. He was the suspected mole who was spying on me.

The veterinary practice closed and then reopened only three weeks after the Gilberts' arrest. A corporation bought the veterinary practice for a song. The bad news was it was just small animals, and I was still out of work. A neighboring practice was assuming the large-animal component.

The day after my abduction, the television program was broadcast, and all that I declared was verified. I was innocent. Even though the news reported it first, the documentary was revealing. No police corruption had occurred. My friends were true friends, for sure.

Julie only lived for another day, but they held the phone up to her, and I talked to her before she died. I told her I loved her, and I would remember her forever.

Dan was charged for his involvement in the forgery. However, he didn't know anything about the attempted poisoning or the cover-up. Dan is on bail and awaiting the birth of his next child. We don't believe he will serve time. I didn't mind that he had to sweat it out for a while. He's worth more to me out working than languishing in jail. He still has his twins' births to go. We talk regularly, and Dan calls the girls most evenings. He's even started to read to them in bed over the phone. I am furious with him. For the sake of the children, though, I bite my tongue. He has unlimited access, but he's only visited twice since the Gilberts were arrested.

The girls are still attending their classes. They are devastated by the divorce and are both receiving counseling. The separation and pending divorce are uncontested. In a year, I will be a free woman. I must remain in Australia with the children. It is a small price to pay, however, considering the upcoming birth of our twins.

My mom flew over, and she and Dan's mother formed a tag-team while helping the girls learn to accept the separation. While Faythe didn't understand, Casey was aware her father might go to jail. The school bent over backward to help Casey adjust to the new norm. The school provided counselors and grief management for us all. On the surface, one would never know the inner turmoil both girls were experiencing. Nightmares and a bit of bed-wetting ensued. Faythe is still apprehensive of the pending arrival of the twins. That is going to be an adjustment.

My mom is going home soon, but she plans to return when the babies arrive. Dan's mom and I have made amends. She has been more than helpful and accommodating. In a stroke of genius, I was able to use Mrs. Miller's house for both grandmothers. They have become friends. While I know this arrangement won't last forever, I will ensure they have access to the children whenever they want it.

Nigel and Sheba are regular visitors. The girls call him Pop, and they told me how much they love taking Sheba on walks in the park. Nigel is showing the girls how to draw. He is quite the artist. Kate comes up most weekends, and we get together for dinner. Luke comes when the Crows aren't playing footy.

Casey is riding horses at the Medikas' farm. Froggy is her admitted favorite. Faythe is spending time next door with Connie and Baz, where Connie is teaching her to bake. Lois is our primary babysitter because Jedda is studying for her exams and possible entry into medical school. We are searching for the right puppy.

As for me, the death of my marriage was as emotionally traumatic as the actual death of Mrs. Miller. My heart has been broken, and my confidence is shattered. How could I trust anyone again? I will soon be the mother of four children. Replacing my husband is unthinkable. Restoration of my faith in my ability to find a partner and love again is a long time away. My job is to care for the children. I need to work, but it will be a juggling act. I feel I'm going through the well-known phases of grief. I am moving from depression and heading to the acceptance and resolution phase. I have a long way to go.

I'm on my way down to Gawler, which is north of Adelaide. A retiring vet has an equine practice for sale. Rich has been there for several weeks. He called to say it is an ideal setup for me. There's a large house at the clinic, and the nurses and receptionists are brilliant. They describe their most important job was to keep the vets safe and wealthy. Many university students commute from Gawler because the train takes them directly into the city. Maybe Jedda could live with us when she's accepted into medical school.

The clinic is perfect. The facilities are adequate, and the house is enormous. The practice has an easygoing feel, and the staff appears to be competent and friendly. The retiring vet knows all about my dramas and pending windfall, and she's happy to lease me the practice until I can buy it outright. "We Yanks gotta stick together." I didn't realize she was an American. She certainly talks like an Aussie. Rich has offered to work at the clinic until I'm ready to practice again. I believe it's an offer I can't refuse.

I had one more stop before I left for home. A store in Tanunda had two copies of the newest version of the book about the care of ponies that the young autistic boy had lent to me when his sister's pony died. I purchased one for my family and one for him. I saw him and his mother in the grocery shop. He shyly waved to me. His mother gave me the thumbs-up when she saw this. Fingers crossed that Gawler has a good bakery with carrot cake. Angel was not sharing her recipe.

Elizabeth Woolsey DVM

Elizabeth grew up in post war California. She followed in her father's footsteps into equine veterinary practice. She subsequently migrated to Australia where she practiced veterinary medicine at Adelaide Plains Equine Clinic in Gawler, South Australia for over 25 years. She has professional publications on plant toxicity, the treatment of burns in horses and surgical procedures in horses with colic. Elizabeth began writing about her experiences as a horse vet and published under the name Elizabeth Woolsey Herbert: Horse Doctor an American Vet's Life Down Under in 2005 and Jacks' War Letters from an American WWII Navigator in 2015. While veterinary medicine has been her passion, fly fishing, horseback riding and writing occupy her leisure time.

Contact info:

Elizabeth Woolsey DVM
ewoolseydvm@gmail.com

www.elizabethwoolsey.com
www.facebook.com/elizabeth.w.herbert

320

Made in the USA
Monee, IL
15 May 2021

67488927R00184